The
Forbidden
Billionaire

THE SINCLAIRS

The Forbidden Billionaire

THE SINCLAIRS

J.S. Scott

Montlake Romance

Published by Montlake Romance, Seattle

www.apub.com

Amazon, the Amazon logo, and Montlake Romance are trademarks of Amazon.com, Inc., or its affiliates.

ISBN-13: 9781477830550
ISBN-10: 1477830553

Cover design by Laura Klynstra

Printed in the United States of America

PRELUDE

Five Years Ago, Cambridge, Massachusetts

"Where the hell am I?"

The inebriated man on the living room floor was muttering, only partially coherent, mumbling to himself as he experienced a rare moment of consciousness. Not wanting to be awake again, he groaned in protest. Getting up awkwardly, he stumbled to the bathroom, his bladder ready to explode if he *didn't* move.

Looking at himself in the bathroom mirror after awkwardly taking care of business, he squinted at the image, his vision still blurred and hazy.

Oh yeah, he recognized the face beneath the growing beard, swollen eyes, and gaunt features.

Still the face of a killer.

He promptly put his fist into the mirror with what little strength he had left in his body, the reflective image shattering on contact. "Bastard!" he rasped weakly, a cut from the shattered glass starting to bleed, blood trickling from his still-fisted hand. "Stupid, ignorant, fucked-up asshole."

The relief of not seeing his repulsive counterpart anymore was brief and hardly noticeable. He turned and left the bathroom, not bothering to clean up the glass. It hardly mattered. His entire house was a disaster, and he couldn't have cared less.

Shit! He hated these moments of lucidity. They sucked. All he wanted was some reprieve from the agony of thinking.

Anger or guilt?

Hatred or love?

Fury or remorse?

Disoriented emotions entangled inside his head until he couldn't think, couldn't breathe because of the anguish it caused. A brutal pain ripped through his chest, his gut cramping as he thought of *her*. And *him*.

Don't think about it. Don't think. Don't. Think.

He tried not to reason, not to try to make sense of anything, but his brain wouldn't allow it. So . . . fury or remorse? Christ . . . he just didn't know, but the two emotions warring inside him were tearing him apart, piece by piece.

Escape!

Did he hate *them* . . . or *himself*? Or both?

He decided he loathed himself most of all, and stumbled into the kitchen, rummaging through the liquor cabinet until he found another bottle of whiskey. He tore off the top and drank straight from the bottle, gulping a healthy portion of the contents.

Landing facedown on the living room couch as he staggered out of the kitchen, he laughed bitterly at the irony that until recently . . . he rarely drank. The harsh sound echoed through the large home that was devoid of another living soul except him.

I don't give a fuck if I don't usually drink. That person who didn't imbibe often was a different man—a guy so stupid and so naive that he actually believed in love and friendship.

Not anymore. He was done giving a shit about anything. Caring about anyone or anything hurt too damn much.

Lifting his head, he tipped the bottle again, needing oblivion before the voices in his head drove him crazy and the pain in his chest killed him off. Not that he really cared.

Coward. You screwed up. Deal with it.

Problem was, he couldn't handle any of his raveled thoughts.

Rage.

Confusion.

Despair.

Pain.

Betrayal.

Everything was bombarding him, destroying him.

Starting to feel the solace that he sought in darkness, he sighed and hit the bottle one more time.

"I'll never give a fuck about anything again," he vowed in a slurred voice.

As his vision started fading to black, a tiny, lost part of his soul started to rise inside him, a portion of his old self that wanted him to get his shit together.

If I keep this up, I'm going to die.

He had no idea how long he'd been doing this, waking and finding oblivion again. But judging by the emaciated, bearded figure he'd briefly seen reflected back at him in the mirror for that horrifying moment, it had obviously been a while.

You can't do this forever. Get up.

Taking another pull from the whiskey bottle, he squashed the small voice of reason and closed his eyes, his hand falling to the side of the couch limply, the bottle dropping from his hand to land soundlessly on the carpet.

I killed two people who betrayed me.

There was no dealing with *that* for *him*.

The grim hopelessness descended just as the dim void he was seeking swallowed him whole, obliterating all thought, cutting off the well of agony he was wallowing in. Welcoming the darkness he sought, the man suspended consciousness and let the black shadows take him.

CHAPTER 1

The Present, Amesport, Maine

She's crying.

He shouldn't give a shit.

He didn't want to care.

But unfortunately, he damn well did.

Jared Sinclair rested one muscular shoulder against the brick exterior of Shamrock's Corner Pub on Main Street, watching as Mara Ross left her doll shop and walked briskly across the road, swiping angrily at her cheeks. He held his breath as she passed within a few yards of him on her way down to the boardwalk, feeling like a damn stalker. Her gaze was focused straight ahead, and he released the air from his lungs as Mara walked right by him, completely unaware of his presence.

She never even saw me.

That shouldn't bother him, either, but somehow it rankled that he was so fascinated by Mara, enthralled enough by her that he stopped everything to watch her, and she never even acknowledged him.

Why is she crying? She's always smiling.

Pushing himself away from the building, he followed her, unable to resist the compulsion to chase after her, selfishly hoping her unhappiness wasn't caused by his actions.

She shouldn't know . . . yet.

It could be anything. Maybe she was just hormonal. That happened to women, right? Or perhaps her dog died. Tragic, but animals *did* have short life spans compared to humans, and they *did* die. He'd never had a pet, but Jared imagined losing a canine companion would definitely make Mara cry. Problem was, Mara didn't have a dog, and her only close relative, her mother, had passed away a year ago.

It could still be anything, some other reason.

He cursed himself for caring, his curiosity getting the better of him as he continued to trudge after her.

She'd disappeared from the boardwalk, obviously making her way to the sandy, deserted beach. The weather was dismal, and it had been raining all day long. Yeah, there was a temporary break in the storms at the moment, but all Jared had to do was take one look at the sky and he could see the next one quickly moving into Amesport. The dark clouds were coming straight toward the small Maine coastal town—which was the primary reason most sane people were indoors right now. The streets and beach were nearly deserted.

Cursing his fascination with the curvy brunette, he took a slug of his coffee from Brew Magic and headed for the boardwalk. Personally, Jared loved the darkness of the stormy day, the crashing of thunder and deluge of rain matching the agitating restlessness he felt inside himself. He didn't much care if he acted like a prick most of the time. It was better than trying to fake a happiness that didn't exist for him.

I wish I'd never left the Peninsula and come into town. I wish I had stayed indoors and dry like the tourists are doing today. Then I never would have seen her, never would have known she was even upset.

Since he was probably the worst cook in the world, he'd driven from his home on the Amesport Peninsula into town to get something to eat. Just as he'd been heading back to his vehicle, he'd stopped to stare across the street at Mara's store. Two very different, odd compulsions struck him deep in his gut whenever he saw the monstrous old structure that was Mara Ross's shop and home. Certainly, he was drawn to the old residence because it was part of the Sinclair history in Amesport, a house that had belonged to a sea captain who was his ancestor. Every time he looked at the home, he wondered what it had looked like two hundred years ago. Hell, he was an architect by education. Wasn't it normal to imagine seeing the rambling old structure as it had been in its glory days? Jared could shake *those* feelings off because of his education and occupation. He loved old houses in general, the sense of history he felt when he was near them. Understandable, perhaps—considering his background. What really disconcerted him was his obsession with the building's occupant, Mara Ross.

She helped me out a few times. It's normal to feel a certain amount of gratitude, right?

Jared was bullshitting himself, and he knew it. There were a lot of people who had helped him research the Sinclair history in the town of Amesport since he'd arrived there for a visit to his vacation house weeks ago. Intrigued because he'd never known just how entrenched the Sinclairs had been in this community historically, he'd sought information just for the hell of it in the beginning. The more he learned, the more he wanted to put all the puzzle pieces together of his family history. Although he was grateful to everyone who had helped him put the mystery of his Amesport ancestors together, he didn't feel any inexplicable pull toward a single one of them—except *her*.

Oblivious to the damage he was doing to his casual but expensive Italian leather shoes, Jared left the boardwalk and went down the small incline to the beach, his feet sinking into the wet sand.

Where the hell did she go?

His heart hammered in alarm as his eyes swept over the deserted beach, not seeing another living soul. The violence of the crashing waves hitting the shore increased his urgency to locate her . . . until he finally saw her, sitting alone at the end of the rock formations near the pier, her head bowed in what looked like defeat.

Leave. Don't get involved. It's none of my damn business why she's upset. She obviously wants her privacy. Go. Now.

He avoided emotional scenes like incurable diseases. The last thing he wanted to do was get involved in some female's problems, a woman he'd only talked to briefly a handful of times. He hardly knew her. And he didn't do drama. Staying in control of his own emotions was critically important to him. The only way he'd found to accomplish that was to avoid caring about much of anything. And that included sad, crying, beautiful women like Mara Ross.

She's trouble.

Jared tried to turn away. He really did. But for some unknown reason, he found himself drawn to her sorrow like a magnet. His brain might be telling him to go before she noticed he was there, to let her sort things out herself. But instead, he found himself striding across the sand and to the rocks, making his way stealthily to the end of the stone edifice where *she* was sitting.

Face it, man. You've been screwed since the moment you saw her big brown eyes, genuine smile, and curvy figure. For some reason, she messes with your head, and you can no more walk away from her pain than you can stop breathing.

But dammit, he wanted to. Badly.

Sure, he liked a good fuck as much as any guy who was almost thirty years old. He made it a point to deliberately find women who wanted something from him other than emotion. He gave them whatever they wanted materially in return for a night of hot, pleasurable sex for him with no strings attached. Jared didn't do relationships, and he didn't do emotional entanglements. The women he screwed didn't either. And he liked it that way.

Then what in the fuck am I doing here?

He halted behind Mara, wondering again if he was losing his mind along with his ever-present control. The rough seas were spraying his black jeans and button-down green shirt with moisture, slowly saturating his clothing. Mara looked like her jeans and T-shirt were already drenched, but as she stared blankly out at the Atlantic, Jared was pretty certain she hadn't even noticed that her garments were soaked. Despair seemed to be rolling off her body in waves, and it reached out and wrapped around his icy heart with a vengeance.

Shit. This has to stop. Whatever her problem is, I'll help her solve it. Then maybe I can get over this inexplicable obsession I have with her. She's throwing me off balance, and I can't afford to lose control.

Done fighting with himself, Jared admitted defeat for just for the moment and made his way to her side, sitting down on the rain-soaked rock next to Mara. Plucking the glasses from her face, he tried to dry them on his semiwet shirt. "Very few things in life are worth crying over." He'd learned that lesson a long time ago.

Startled, Mara finally jerked her head to the side to look at him, as though she was astonished to see him sitting next to her. "What are you doing out here?" she asked warily. "It's going to start pouring again any minute now." She glanced up at the approaching dark clouds.

Jared shrugged and perched her glasses carefully back on her nose. He could hardly tell her that *she* had drawn him here, that she'd pretty much seized him by the balls the minute she'd first spoken with him and had never let go—even though it was lamentably true. "I could ask you the same thing. This isn't the safest place to be right now."

Jared's jaw clenched as her previous comment about the weather reminded him that the ocean was incredibly rough, and yet another violent storm looked to be coming their way. His eyes swept over her, and a raw possessiveness surged tempestuously over his entire body. Mara looked small and vulnerable, and he didn't like it. Her dark eyes were swirling with sadness, and she wrapped her arms around her body protectively as she responded. "I wanted to think. This is where I come when

I need to figure something out. Sometimes it makes me realize how small my problems are when I see how vast the ocean is." She raised her voice so he could hear her over the loud surf slamming against the rocks.

Jared cringed at the vulnerability he could hear in her voice, wanting to snatch her up and take her somewhere—anywhere—to make her forget whatever her problems were. "And is it working?" Judging by her look of distress, it wasn't.

"Not today," she admitted with a large sigh, resting her elbows on her knees and clenching her fingers together, her gaze once again focused on the rough sea.

"Want to talk about it?" *Jesus, I sound like Dr. Phil.* When did he *ever* encourage anyone except his brothers and his sister to talk about anything emotional? And even *that* was rare. The Sinclairs weren't exactly prone to spilling their guts to anyone, or wearing their emotions on their shirtsleeves. He and his siblings had been born wealthy, part of an elite class of old money. Showing any emotion except polite social behavior was prohibited, and that trait had been pounded into every one of them since birth. They were loyal but rarely demonstrative in their affection for one another, even though it was there.

Strangely, he still wanted Mara to talk about whatever was bothering her, even though he was pretty sure he'd have no idea how to respond. Wanting to know her thoughts was a very strange impulse for a guy like him.

What the hell was she doing to him—besides giving him a perpetual boner? As he chugged down the rest of his coffee, Jared realized that he really *did* want to know what was wrong so he could help her fix it. Maybe then he could get some damn peace, maybe he'd stop feeling compelled to wring every single detail of her life from her gorgeous, plump lips.

Jared watched as Mara shook her head, her damp, limp ponytail swaying behind her head. "I don't really want to talk about it. We hardly know each other."

Barely able to hear her, Jared moved closer, his thigh brushing against hers as he replied, "Sometimes it's easier to talk to someone you don't know, get an unbiased opinion."

Then I can kill whoever is making you so damn unhappy. Problem solved.

Jared squirmed restlessly, unable to stop the incredibly uncomfortable protective instincts he was having toward a woman he barely knew. Truth was, he hated seeing Mara this way. The fact that she was obviously discouraged and unhappy was eating at him. Every time he'd visited her store in the last few weeks, she'd been unguarded and enthusiastic about helping him learn about the Sinclair history in Amesport, leading him to other sources to help him with his research. Hell, he'd just seen her yesterday, and she'd given him one of her bright, cheerful smiles—a genuine expression that told him she was glad to see him for no particular reason, a look he'd never had focused his way before by any woman other than his sister, Hope. In his world, almost everybody wanted something from him, and nobody was going to give without getting something in return. Mara Ross was pure light, and for a very short time, she'd illuminated the darkness that seemed to cling to him almost every waking minute of the day. She was so damn sweet, and always seemed so intoxicatingly innocent. When they had a conversation, he could sense that she was looking at him as a person, not a billionaire, her entire attention focused on helping him just because she wanted to. Not once had she expected anything in return. Those were traits that had Jared wanting to run the hell away from her as fast as he could, yet drew him inexplicably toward her at the same time. Something about her fascinated him, and for the first time in a long time, he was unable to exert the proper control to stop himself from exploring that unwelcome attraction.

After a long pause, she answered hesitantly, "Okay. Maybe you're right. Maybe I do need to talk about it, and I don't have anyone I can tell. I'm being evicted from my house. The owner is selling the property. I have to leave." Continuing to stare out to sea, she clenched her fingers together tighter. "My grandmother ran the shop, then my mother, and now me. Everything I have left of them is going to be gone."

Jared tensed. "You have a lease, right?"

"Nope," she answered abruptly. "It's always been a month-to-month rental. It's been that way since my grandma had the house. There's not even a written rental contract. The owners lived here in Amesport up until about twenty years ago. The house was passed from son to son. There was never any question about the rental of the property until the last son moved away. He hated it here."

"We can find you a new place. The house isn't safe anymore, Mara. It needs major renovation. The old place is like a ticking time bomb without complete renovation. Is the roof leaking from the rain?" Jared rasped gravely.

She looked at him, startled. "Yes. In a few places upstairs. How did you know?"

"I'm an architect. I can see the signs. How much repair have the owners done that you can remember?" *Fuck.* He hoped it was more than he suspected.

Her shoulders slumped as she replied, "Nothing that I can remember. The house needs a lot of work. I do what I can, but it's been hard since my mother died, and the owner now refuses to do any work to the house. I guess because he never planned on keeping it."

Jared knew from the town gossip circuit that Mara had lost her dad to a heart attack years ago, and her mother had just passed a little over a year ago. The shop wasn't making money, probably hadn't for years. Jared had already figured that out just by observation. Mara made incredible dolls, but how much could a doll shop really make in the current market? How many sales did it produce even during the busy summer months? Her rent for being on the main street in a coastal tourist town had to be sizable, even for a residence that was in desperate need of renovation. "You can find a new location," he grunted, refusing to believe there wasn't a solution to her problems. "You can't stay there anyway if the roof is leaking. It's not structurally sound."

Mara shook her head slowly and shot him a weak, defeated smile. "There is no place else. And it wouldn't be the same. I know I need to face reality. The business isn't making a profit. I was going to have to let it go sooner or later."

"What will you do?" Jared asked hoarsely.

Mara shrugged. "I'm not certain. Move to a bigger city. Find a job somewhere. Start over again. I guess that's what I was thinking about. It's just going to be really hard to leave Amesport."

Oh, hell no. She can't leave. Mara Ross's family has been in Amesport for generations. She knows every historical fact about the town and is pretty much the unofficial town historian. She belongs here, dammit. She obviously loves it here.

Thunder rumbled ominously before Jared could reply. He stood quickly and held out his hand to Mara, worried about her being out in the elements as the storm blew in. She took it without hesitation and let him haul her to her feet.

"We need to find cover," Jared ordered, urging her in front of him so they could get off the rocks and find protection from the rapidly approaching storm as quickly as possible.

She moved swiftly without saying another word, as though she'd navigated the rocks hundreds of time, which she probably had. Large droplets of rain started to fall, and she skidded once, but Jared wrapped an arm around her waist and led her off the rocks. Grabbing her hand as he dumped his paper coffee cup into the nearby trash, he pulled her with him as he ran for protection from the steadily growing strength of the rain.

By the time they reached the sidewalk by Shamrock's Pub, they were both breathless. The two of them stood under the protective canopy of the local bar and gathering place, watching as the rain started coming down in sheets.

Mara's eyes swept over him, and she laughed. It was a delighted, husky sound that made Jared instantly hard.

"You look almost human now," she informed him merrily with a mischievous grin.

Affronted, Jared asked abruptly, "What did I look like before?"

Mara shrugged, looking embarrassed. "Perfect. You always look immaculate and perfect."

Jared's gaze surveyed her appearance, her soaked hair, her T-shirt nearly transparent and clinging to her body like a second skin. Her eyes were shining with an openness he wasn't accustomed to as she looked up at him. Finally, he responded automatically, "You look beautiful." He'd blurted the words out before he could censor them. Dammit. She did that to him, made him say whatever he was thinking before he could think about it.

She's dangerous.

Looking at him skeptically, she replied, "I've heard you were a ladies' man, but that description is more than a little over-the-top, don't you think?"

He cringed inwardly. Being a billionaire and very much in the public eye, his every behavior was scrutinized. Okay. Yeah. He was always seen with a different woman clinging to his arm. Maybe he *did* go through his share of female companions, but it didn't sit right with him for Mara to actually be pointing out the well-known fact that he was reputed to be a man-whore.

"I meant it," he replied huskily, his eyes roving over her hungrily. He'd honestly never seen a woman more attractive than Mara was to him.

She crossed her arms and looked up at him disapprovingly. "In case you haven't noticed . . . I'm a little too plump, short, and plain."

She's curvy, petite, and completely fuckable.

Jared felt a low, reverberating sound rising up in his throat. He didn't like her making derogatory comments about herself. It pissed him off, especially since he didn't think he'd ever been this drawn to a woman. He maneuvered her against the brick wall, trapping her body with his, which was probably a mistake. She smelled like fresh rain and vanilla, a scent that made his dick harder than he thought was possible. He raised a palm to her cheek and ran it down her silky, wet skin. "You're soft and sweet, exactly the type of woman a man wants beneath him naked," he told her bluntly. Her scent was driving him mad, and his control was definitely slipping. In his current state, he was having a very hard time not telling her that he desperately wanted to be the man on top of her, sinking his aching cock into her sweet, soft body.

Jared's gaze locked with hers, and just for moment, there was nobody in the world but the two of them, their connection profound and unbreakable. Damned if he didn't want to take her hard against the brick wall, her legs wrapped around his waist, and pound into her until they were both sated.

I have to fuck her or I'll never get over this insane need. Somehow, he had to get her in his bed and have her until he got bored. Generally, that was directly after the first sexual encounter. His desire usually faded immediately after he bedded a woman, his interest gone.

Mara flushed bright pink as she stared up at him, shaking her head slowly. "You don't have to charm me," she informed him as she inched her way down the wall and away from his body.

"I'm not trying to be charming," he rasped irritably, damning his reputation to hell right at the moment. He might like women, but he was never, ever charming. He laid out the score before he ever fucked a woman, the deal struck before their bodies hit the bed. Women *always* wanted *something* from him, and it was never him or his body. It was always monetary in some way, although he'd never had a woman leave a session of hot sex unsatisfied. He made damn sure he got them off before he fucked them.

"I think you *are* charming when you want to be," Mara mused as she moved to the edge of the awning, looking like she was contemplating whether or not she wanted to sprint across the street to her shop.

"Beatrice and Elsie told me you were a very sweet boy. That's definitely a compliment coming from those two, and a testament to how charismatic you can be. I have a feeling it comes naturally to you."

"Then you don't know me," Jared grumbled, not happy that the two elderly women, the town gossip and the matchmaker, had referred to him as a damn boy. He liked Elsie and Beatrice, enjoyed listening to their stories and banter. But that didn't prove that he was the least bit amiable. Truthfully, he was usually an asshole. But he couldn't be that way with two aged women like Elsie and Beatrice. The pair of old ladies amused him, and even *he* wasn't *that* big of a dick.

Mara turned back to him. "You're right. I don't know you. And I have no right to make any assumptions. I'm just trying to tell you that I've enjoyed our few conversations and I already like you. You don't need to throw me false compliments. I appreciate your concern about my home. I really do. I guess I'm just not used to it." She hesitated before adding, "Not from a guy, anyway."

Holy hell. Did she think he was trying to blow smoke up her ass when he told her that he found her attractive?

"Get used to it. I'm going to help you whether you want my help or not. You need it." He clenched his fists to keep from reaching out to snatch her up and hold her damp body against his until flames of desire dried them and set them both on fire.

Every instinct he had was clawing at him to comfort her or fuck her, but his brain knew that she'd run like hell if he tried to do either one of those things. Besides, what the hell did he know about comforting anybody? His experiences with women were like business arrangements. He'd learned a long time ago that it was better that way.

"Why do you even want to help me?" Mara looked up at him, wide-eyed and curious. "We aren't exactly friends. You hardly know me."

"I plan on getting to know you extremely well," he informed her calmly, even though he was picturing her naked beneath him, screaming his name as she climaxed. Hell yeah, he wanted to know her . . . intimately. His fixation with her wasn't going to go away until he did.

"I doubt we'll ever get to know each other well at all. You're only visiting here."

True, his home on the Amesport Peninsula wasn't his primary residence. But really, he didn't actually *have* a home. He had houses all over the world, some he spent more time in than others, but they were just real estate. He'd initially come here to see his injured brother, Dante, but he'd lingered long after his police detective brother had recovered from his gunshot wounds. Dante was getting married to a local physician and taking a position with the police department here. "I'll be here. I'm staying until after Dante's wedding."

"Just a few more weeks," she reminded him, her brows narrowing in concentration, as though she was trying to figure out his motives.

She might as well give up trying to figure me out. I can't even reason out my own idiotic behavior right now.

"I'll be here," he repeated ominously.

Mara blinked rapidly, her eyes growing moist. "I appreciate the offer, Mr. Sinclair, but my problems are my own to solve."

Jared nearly growled when he saw the stubborn tilt of her chin and thought about her taking on the dismal situation all by herself. "Jared."

She nodded. "Jared. Thank you for the offer, but this is something I have to deal with on my own. My entire life is going to have to change, and so am I." She turned around without another word and sprinted across the street. Scurrying up the few steps to her door, she pushed against the wood and disappeared inside the house, never looking back.

I don't want her to change. She's perfect just the way she is now.

The sound of his name in her husky come-do-me voice had nearly tipped Jared over the edge, and he had to force himself not to follow her, grasping the wooden post that was supporting the overhang of Shamrock's to make his feet stay planted.

Christ. I am becoming a damn stalker.

Shaking his head in irritation as he stared at her door long after she had disappeared, he slowly made his way to his black Mercedes SUV, a vehicle that usually just sat in the garage of his Amesport home, his gut still gnawing at him to go after her.

Patience. I have to have some patience with her. I need my damn control back.

Restraint was something he had very little of at the moment, and his time to help Mara Ross was limited. Eventually she'd hate him. It was inevitable.

As Jared seated himself in his vehicle, he gripped the steering wheel hard and closed his eyes with a tortured groan, the thrum of the rain beating against his windshield almost sounding like a ticking clock.

How long will it take before she finds out the truth?

Jared opened his eyes and started the engine, realizing that he didn't have the fucking time to sit around moping. It wouldn't be long before Mara found out that *he* was the buyer of her beloved home and shop, the bastard ultimately responsible for her losing everything she cared about.

He hadn't planned on her finding out quite this quickly. Obviously, the damn irresponsible owner had jumped the gun.

As he did a quick U-turn from the curb he was parked on, heading back to his home on the Peninsula, he remembered his thoughts about just destroying whoever was causing her problems. Ironically, if he was going to deal with the situation *that* way, he'd have no one to kill . . . except *himself.*

CHAPTER 2

"I'm so sorry, Sarah. I can't walk down the aisle for your wedding on crutches," Kristin Moore moaned woefully to the other four women in her living room.

Mara frowned at the cast on her best friend's leg, the result of a bicycle accident during the rain. She and Kristin, Dr. Sarah Baxter's office manager, had been best friends since grade school, and her heart ached for the vivacious redhead. Mara knew how much Kristin had been looking forward to being a bridesmaid in Sarah's wedding. She also knew how restless her friend could be. Keeping Kristin down for even a short time was going to be hell. "I'm sure Sarah understands," she told Kristin adamantly, shooting a look at Dr. Sarah Baxter from across the room and seeing the pretty blonde nod emphatically.

"Of course I do. It's not your fault, Kristin. It will be fine. You just need to worry about your injury and healing," Sarah replied soothingly from her seat on the couch beside her best friend, Emily, Grady Sinclair's wife. Emily was Sarah's maid of honor. Randi Tyler, the pretty, dark-haired teacher seated on the floor, was one of the two bridesmaids for Sarah's wedding.

Mara tried to hide her frown, knowing that Kristin, the second bridesmaid for Sarah, was likely to cut off her own cast and limp up the aisle if she had to. Her flame-haired friend was just that stubborn and unwilling to let anybody down after she'd made a commitment.

Folding her arms in front of her doggedly from her position on a recliner, her casted leg propped up on the leg rest in front of her, Kristin muttered adamantly, "I am not going to ruin Sarah's wedding by making a spectacle of myself. Nobody wants to see some crazy redhead taking five minutes to struggle down the aisle on crutches."

"Nobody is going to care," Randi answered kindly.

"I care," Kristin replied, annoyed. "It's Sarah and Dante's big day."

Mara watched Kristin's unyielding expression from her own seat on the carpet. Kristin's tiny apartment didn't have much furniture, and seating was limited. She tried not to frown as she saw the obstinate look on her best friend's face, an expression she'd seen many times over the years. "You can't have the cast off before the wedding," Mara told her firmly. The accident had just occurred yesterday, for God's sake. But Mara knew Kristin was already looking for a way to get rid of the inhibiting plaster mold on her leg. "Not happening."

"Sarah's numbers won't be even. Grady is the best man, and Emily is the maid of honor. Evan is a groomsman with Randi, and I'm supposed to be across from Jared." Kristin sniffled, tears springing to her eyes from frustration. "Dante can't cut out his own brother from the wedding. Jared is already here. And he can't walk up the aisle alone."

"He most certainly can," Sarah replied decisively. "You, my friend, need to rest that ankle. Doctor's orders." She used her stern doctor's voice to make her point.

"What about Hope?" Randi asked inquisitively. "Can she do it?"

Sarah shook her head slowly. "Nope. We just found out that she's pregnant, and Jason is hovering over her like a mother hen because she's having really bad morning sickness that seems to be carrying over throughout most of the morning hours, and sometimes into the afternoon. She's miserable. He's bringing her to the wedding, but she isn't feeling well right now."

Mara grimaced as she heard the news that Dante Sinclair's sister was pregnant and sick. As the sister of the groom, Hope Sinclair-Sutherland would have been the perfect solution to the dilemma.

"Damn!" Kristin exclaimed. "There has to be somebody—"

Mara cringed as Kristin stopped speaking, her best friend's eyes landing on her with a calculating smile. *Oh, God. No.*

"Mara can replace me," Kristin said triumphantly.

"No, Kristin." Mara's eyes flew to the other women, who were all looking at her curiously and nodding. "I've never been in a wedding, and Sarah and I don't really know each other that well. I'm sure she'd rather have a friend." Honestly, they hardly knew each other at all. It wasn't that Mara didn't like the brilliant, friendly physician, but she couldn't exactly call her a friend. She'd thought about using Dr. Baxter as her physician if she ever needed one, since her longtime family physician had retired. But she hadn't needed a doctor in a while, and she barely knew Sarah. The only reason they were all together at Kristin's place at the moment was to visit because she was injured. She knew Randi Tyler casually because she volunteered as a tutor at the Youth Center, and Mara taught a class there occasionally on basic crafts during the winter. She knew Emily slightly better because Grady's wife was in charge of the Youth Center and arranged the classes.

I don't know any of these women well. I can't be a substitute in a wedding where I barely know any of the wedding party.

Oh, hell no. Kristin had led her into so many crazy things in the past, and she'd followed her vivacious friend willingly. But not this time.

"You're perfect to fill in. I already have my dress, and it will only take a little alteration," Kristin said excitedly.

"I think it's a great idea," Emily seconded.

"Me too," Randi agreed with an emphatic nod.

"I'd be honored if you'd do it, Mara," Sarah said, her tone genuine and slightly cajoling. "I know we haven't had the chance to get to know each other that well because I haven't lived in Amesport very long, but I'd like to be your friend. Honestly, I don't really have any other friends here."

Mara swallowed hard as she met Sarah's compassionate, understanding look. Since she'd spent most of her adult life taking care of her mom and running the doll shop, she hadn't had a lot of time to make new friends, or spend time doing anything with her old ones from high school. It was one of the reasons she valued her friendship with Kristin so much. They were tightly connected and hadn't ever drifted apart, even though Mara rarely had the time or money to do anything except hang out with Kristin. "Okay, I'll do it." The words popped out of her mouth before she could stop them, and she shot Kristin an I'll-get-you-for-this-later expression. Her best friend knew her all too well. Mara could never say no to somebody who needed something or had a problem to solve.

"Thank you. I really *am* delighted," Sarah commented with a gentle smile.

"It's going to be great," Randi agreed. "Dante hired a wedding planner, and it's going to be quite a party."

"Fantastic," Emily added.

"I think the dress is going to take more than a little alteration," Mara warned the women bluntly. While Kristin was slightly curvy, Mara was curvier, and Kristin was a good inch taller than Mara's five-foot-three height.

"It's not a problem. I'll have it altered," Sarah offered.

Kristin laughed merrily. "Mara is an incredible seamstress. She's just used to sewing very small doll sizes."

Mara nodded at Sarah. Because of her mother and her gran, there was very little she couldn't do when it came to sewing. "I can do it."

The other women all rose to their feet except for Kristin, and Mara got up hastily to accept hugs and expressions of gratitude for filling in for her best friend at the last minute. It felt strange to suddenly be pulled into this circle of friends, but it felt so very good to break her solitude. She liked all of these women, admired all of them, and her heart warmed as they each hugged her kindly.

"I guess I'll be paired with Jared?" Mara asked curiously.

Randi snorted. "Yep. I don't think it will be that much of a hardship. Just being paired with Jared Sinclair is worth the trouble. You have to admit, if you're standing through a wedding ceremony, he's great eye candy to have across from you."

Emily smiled knowingly at Randi as she commented, "I don't think you'll find Evan difficult to look at, either. Seeing all four brothers together is damn near breathtaking, although Grady *is* the best-looking Sinclair brother."

Sarah shot Emily a displeased expression. "Excuse me. I think you meant Dante."

Randi burst out laughing as she watched Emily and Sarah giving each other belligerent looks. "You two are pathetic. I think we can just leave it at the fact that *all* of the Sinclair brothers are hot. And I saw Evan at your wedding, Em. He's gorgeous, but obviously obsessed with his job. He dashed in just as the wedding started, and left right after the toast at the reception. I've never actually met him."

Emily sighed. "I know. Our wedding was planned so fast, and Evan had meetings he couldn't cancel. I'm glad he's coming to actually participate in the wedding party this time. Grady's afraid he's working himself into an early grave."

"Dante thinks so, too," Sarah admitted glumly. "Like Dante can talk about workaholics? He worked nearly every hour of the day when he was a homicide detective in LA. But he swears that Evan is even worse, that he never takes a break and has absolutely no sense of humor. I have to admit I'm a little nervous about meeting him. He sounds more than a little daunting."

Mara watched and listened as the women continued to banter about the four Sinclair brothers. To be honest, she didn't know any of them well, although she had to admit that Grady, Dante, and Jared were three of the handsomest men she'd ever seen. She had no doubt that the oldest brother, Evan, was just as hot.

How can any family be blessed with such incredible genetics?

She didn't know their baby sister, Hope Sinclair—now Hope Sutherland—but Mara was willing to bet she was as gorgeous as her brothers. Since Hope had recently married one of the most eligible and good-looking billionaire bachelors on the planet, she had to be a pretty extraordinary woman.

Mara tried not to think about her strange encounter with Jared Sinclair yesterday. Unfortunately, no matter what she tried to think about to wipe out the memories, it didn't help. So she was working on convincing herself that he had been kind to her, and that was all. She didn't want to remember how his damp shirt had clung to his broad shoulders and muscular biceps. Or how, for the first time since she'd met him, his smile had actually reached his incredibly sexy jade-green eyes.

Don't forget that he's a womanizer.

Jared Sinclair's reputation with women was well-known, and it was said that he was never seen with the same woman more than once. Mara knew that, but she somehow had a difficult time imagining Jared as completely wicked. She sensed he was restless, and he almost seemed . . . well, for lack of a better word, lonely. It was pretty much a ridiculous notion since Jared had four siblings, and apparently plenty of women to keep him company. But Mara couldn't shake off the notion that he was somehow . . . haunted. The bleakness she could see in his eyes even when he was outwardly smiling had made her wonder if there wasn't way more to Jared than people could see on the surface. Strangely, the only women she'd seen him with since he'd arrived in Amesport had been Elsie and Beatrice. The other times she'd happened to spot him around town, he'd either been alone or with one of his brothers.

Oh, hell, maybe she was just seeing what she wanted to see because Jared Sinclair was hot enough to melt almost any woman into a puddle at his feet—her included. His usual impeccable, sophisticated appearance had been blown away yesterday, his expensive shoes ruined by the sand and rain, his auburn-streaked hair mussed and damp instead of tamed into its usual sleek style. His shirt had been rumpled and dark with moisture, so green it had actually matched his eyes. For once, he had seemed so human, almost . . . touchable.

Sighing inwardly, Mara tried to concentrate on the female conversation going on around her and stop fantasizing about Jared Sinclair. A guy like him was definitely not for her. Granted, she wasn't exactly ugly. She saw her own face in the mirror every day. But she wasn't particularly attractive, either, and his words had been just that: *words*. Jared Sinclair had been born rich, and had made himself even richer by owning one of the biggest commercial real estate companies in the world. Obviously he knew how to be charming when he needed to, even though he denied it, and equally as ruthless when it was warranted for his business.

"Nobody knows why Jared has hung around Amesport for so long. Dante thinks some woman here has caught his attention."

Mara's heart skipped a beat at Sarah's offhand comment, wondering if Dante's fiancée was correct and Jared had stuck around for a female conquest. "Do you think that's true?" Mara asked breathlessly, cursing herself for sounding so interested. She wasn't dying to know, dammit. She wasn't. Who Jared Sinclair had sex with was absolutely none of her business.

"I'm not sure," Sarah answered, looking curiously at Mara. "If he's interested in somebody, he's hiding it well. I haven't seen him talking to anybody in town except Elsie and Beatrice, and I'm pretty doubtful he has his eye on either one of them romantically."

Mara let out a startled cough, and it turned into a delighted laugh before she answered, "They both adore him, but I don't think either one has realized he's a grown man. They refer to him as a sweet boy."

"That's truly mind-boggling since we all know he's anything but sweet," Randi said thoughtfully.

"He's always been nice to me," Mara replied, for some reason feeling she needed to defend Jared. After all, he had sat with her in the rain and listened to her problems. He'd even offered to help solve them, an act of kindness she hadn't expected. Of course, it was an offer she couldn't accept. Jared was almost a stranger, and she needed to make some major changes in her life. Still, just the fact that he had offered had been thoughtful and amazingly . . . sweet.

She squirmed as four sets of curious, feminine eyes focused on her.

"How nice has he been, exactly?" Sarah asked, smirking as she crossed her arms in front of her, pinning Mara with a questioning gaze.

"No. Oh, no. Jared isn't interested in me in that kind of way," Mara told the women hastily, knowing exactly what they were thinking from their expressions. "He just asked for some information on the history of the Sinclairs in Amesport."

You're exactly the type of woman a man wants beneath him naked.

Mara had to suppress a shudder as Jared's words from yesterday drifted through her mind. Really, he hadn't meant a word of it. She was fairly certain that it was a line he used without really thinking about it. Just the thought of Jared Sinclair really finding her fuckable was ridiculous. They were from two different worlds, and the type of woman he usually took to his bed was no doubt beautiful, privileged, and pampered.

Nothing like me.

Unfortunately, her face had flushed a bright pink just from thinking about Jared, which, unfortunately, made the women scrutinize her expression even more carefully.

"Um . . . I have to run. I have a million things to do." She grabbed her purse hastily and hightailed it out of Kristin's apartment as quickly as she could, giving Sarah her e-mail and phone number on the way out so she could contact her about the wedding events.

Mara took a shaky breath as she stepped outside Kristin's apartment building, hoping nobody had noticed how awkwardly she had handled the Jared discussion.

They noticed. I know they did.

Taking another deep breath, she trotted down the steps of the building quickly. She headed back to her home and shop, hoping no one ever figured just how uneasy Jared Sinclair could make her when he focused those hungry, liquid green eyes on her like he had for a few moments the day before.

Don't think about him. Don't think about him at all. You have a lot bigger issues to think about at the moment.

Mara sighed as she quickened her pace, anxious to get back to her house. She had a ton of work to do before she attended the Amesport Farmers' Market early in the morning. It was imperative that she make as much money as she possibly could. Very shortly, she'd be homeless, and she needed to gather the funds to find another place to live.

I'm going to help you.

Jared's promise floated through her mind automatically.

"I don't need help," she whispered softly. "I'm used to doing everything myself."

She blinked to keep her tears at bay. Crying wasn't going to resolve her problems. If only she didn't feel like she was failing her mom by losing the shop and the home she'd lived in since she was born.

Chin up, sweetie. Everything will look better in the morning.

She swore she could actually hear her mother's voice in those words. It's exactly what she would have told Mara if she were alive right now. Unfortunately, her mom was gone, and unable to give her advice on exactly how to handle her problems. Her life was going to have to change drastically. She needed to change careers, and probably leave the familiar atmosphere of Amesport. She'd been a doll maker from an early age. What kind of job did that qualify her for?

I'll find something. I'll have to.

Mara felt more alone than she had in her entire life, and it was going to be hard not to let the profound emptiness she was feeling swallow her whole.

CHAPTER 3

Jared cursed himself for wearing yet another pair of casual leather shoes as they became saturated from walking across the large, grassy field. "I'm going to need to buy my damn shoes in bulk if I can't get over my obsession to see her," he whispered irritably under his breath. "Who the hell gets up at the crack of dawn just for a farmers' market?"

Apparently, Mara did.

Sarah had mentioned that Mara came to the Amesport Farmers' Market every Saturday to sell products. That was all it took for Jared to decide he needed to investigate his first farmers' market. So here he was, traipsing across a wet field *before* Brew Magic even opened in the morning. So far, he was less than impressed by this particular Amesport event.

He needed coffee.

He needed his breakfast.

And he needed to have his head examined. Desperately.

As he ducked underneath a rope that was acting as a temporary fence for the market, he admitted to himself that he had to see her, had to know that she was doing okay after the news she'd gotten about losing her home. He hadn't completely worked out the details of exactly how to help her yet, but he would. Hell, he could very easily set her up for life with funds and not notice a dent in his net worth. But he'd scratched that idea almost immediately, knowing Mara well enough to realize she'd probably starve before she took money she hadn't earned. If she was already determined to solve her problems on her own, there was no way she was going to take his money.

He had to admit, the idea that a woman didn't want his money was . . . strange.

Wanting to fuck her as desperately as he did, making some kind of sexual arrangement had also been a possibility, but he knew she wasn't about to accept that, either. To be honest, the thought was actually distasteful to him for some reason.

Because I want her to want me as much as I want her. I need her to give herself to me just because she wants me.

It was another weird thought. When the hell had he actually cared *why* a woman screwed him?

"The market doesn't open until seven," an older gentleman called to Jared as he unloaded vegetables onto tables from his truck.

"I'm here to help a friend," Jared answered, annoyed.

The man nodded slowly, a doubtful look on his face as his eyes moved over Jared.

Did he look that damn useless? Okay, maybe he *didn't* look ready to work at a farmers' market. He had deliberately dressed in casual clothing, but he guessed a pair of designer tan slacks and a dark blue button-down shirt wasn't the usual farmers' market attire. Nothing fancy, but he still stuck out like a sore thumb compared to other men wearing old jeans and T-shirts that were already dirty, and sweating and disheveled from setting up their sales tables for the day.

You usually look immaculate and perfect.

Mara's words drifted back to him, and he wondered if looking immaculate and perfect was good or bad. Mostly likely, he did look different. In his world, he was dressed casually. For Amesport, he probably looked like a billionaire snob, and for some reason that bugged the hell out of him. He used to like doing manual labor, getting sweaty and downright filthy. There had been a certain satisfaction in feeling his muscles burning after working all day. Suddenly he missed that sensation and the pleasure of accomplishing something he thought was important.

"Jared! Yoo-hoo! Over here!"

His head turned sharply to the right as he heard a high, singsong female voice calling him. Smiling as he spotted Beatrice Gardener waving her arms in the air to get his attention, he made his way around other booths to the elderly woman.

"Beatrice," he acknowledged as he stood in front of her table and smiled at her. "Are you sure it's healthy to actually be up this early in the morning? What are you doing here?" It was a dumb question. Judging by the table in front of him, which was loaded with crystals, she was here to peddle her wares. She had polished stones and jewelry, some of it obviously from her Natural Elements store. Jared considered it a New Age store, but Beatrice had once told him she was a student of all philosophies and religions, and she was an original. In the weeks since he'd been here, and judging from the conversations they'd had, she was definitely unique. His eyes ran over her long, pink shorts, sneakers, and T-shirt with her store logo emblazoned on the front. "Where's Elsie?" Where Beatrice was, Jared could usually find Elsie Renfrew. The two old ladies seemed almost inseparable.

"Oh, Elsie refuses to get up before seven in the morning. Says she's retired and deserves to sleep in now," Beatrice said unhappily. "She'll probably drop by later."

"Did you set all this up yourself?" Jared asked with a frown. Beatrice was spry, but it didn't seem right that she had unloaded the van behind her alone.

Beatrice chortled merrily. "I might be old, young man, but I can handle a few boxes. I only bring my crystals out here on the weekends to help people."

Jared eyed the table. "The table is too heavy," he told her politely.

"George always helps me with my table. He's such a gentleman. He sells produce here every weekend."

Jared shot her conspiratorial smile as he asked, "Have you gotten yourself a beau, Beatrice?" He put a dramatic hand on his chest. "You'll break my heart."

The silver-haired woman shook her finger at him. "Save your flattery for someone who believes it, young man. Remember, I can read your aura." She raised her eyebrow at him knowingly.

"Then you know I'm telling you the truth," Jared replied, deadpan.

Beatrice considered herself the town mystic and psychic. She was also the unofficial Amesport matchmaker, apparently able to foresee matches before they happened. And . . . she could supposedly read auras. She'd told him more than once that he had a complex, mixed aura—whatever the hell that meant. Sure, Beatrice was different, and some people might find her peculiar, but she was adored by most of the people in Amesport because she was quirky but sweet, and Jared had liked her almost immediately. She and Elsie were completely harmless. Both of the women meant well, no matter how interfering or gossipy the ladies might be.

"You aren't telling me the truth," Beatrice argued, tilting her head first one way and then the other as she looked at him. "But something is changing with you." She continued to observe him pensively.

"What?" He was starting to squirm beneath the woman's intense scrutiny, feeling downright uncomfortable. Not that he really thought Beatrice could see into his inner thoughts, but damned if she didn't have the mystical look thing down pat.

Beatrice rifled through the stones on the table, finally lifting a dark, polished object. "You could use this one." She held out the long rock attached to a key chain. "Carry it with you. It can help you with your guilt and your grief. You have to get rid of your emotional blocks before you can be happy again," Beatrice informed him in a warning voice.

Instinctively, Jared reached out and took the key chain. He wasn't about to argue. Things were getting a little too weird for him. Digging into his pocket, he pulled out several bills.

"No, no!" Beatrice exclaimed. "The crystal is a healing gift. I don't want your money," she insisted.

Startled, he looked at the elderly woman's distressed expression and put the bills back in his pocket. "You're running a business, Beatrice. You can't give things away." Honestly, he was touched, even though the conversation was a bit eerie. Other than his siblings, no one had ever given him a gift. Although, he had to admit, this one *did* make him a bit uneasy. He certainly didn't believe in her hocus-pocus, but there was something about the way she continued to give him her fixed stare that made him want to fidget like a naughty schoolboy.

It's just a coincidence. She doesn't really know what happened.

"I don't need the money, Jared. My late husband was filthy rich in addition to being a stud. I'm loaded." She gave him a sly wink.

Jared chuckled, more amused than he wanted to admit. "You're still a businesswoman," he reminded her.

"And a very good one . . . most of the time. I only give gifts in special cases. You and Mara are both special." Beatrice went back to arranging her jewelry casually.

"You're trying to help Mara, too?" Jared asked curiously.

Beatrice nodded. "Of course. Both of you. You were meant for each other."

Jared shook his head adamantly. Beatrice was matchmaking, and it was terrifying the hell out of him. "I'm not meant for anybody," he told her flatly.

"Oh yes, you are. You two were incredibly easy to predict. My spirit guide channeled the information to me quite loudly and clearly. Maybe you aren't ready to believe it yet, but you will," she told him mysteriously.

"Um . . . okay," he said awkwardly, putting the key chain in his pocket. He'd let Beatrice have her delusions. She'd be disappointed when she found out she was wrong, but he wasn't about to argue with her. Frankly, she was too damn frightening sometimes. Fact was, he actually *did* want to fuck Mara. But out of all the women in this town, how did Beatrice know exactly who he was obsessed with having in his bed?

Coincidence.

Yeah, it was definitely a lucky guess.

"She's in one of the booths behind me," Beatrice informed him casually, waving her thumb to the back of her.

"Thanks," Jared mumbled, more than a little disconcerted. "I hope you have a prosperous day."

"The same to you," Beatrice answered, looking up at him with a knowing smile.

He hurried away from the elderly woman to go find Mara, sticking his hand in his pocket to rub the smooth stone unconsciously.

It's just a damn rock. And Beatrice probably saw me talking with Mara at her store. She absolutely is not a psychic.

Nevertheless, he clutched the stone in his fingers as he searched out Mara, wishing the rock could actually solve some of his problems as Beatrice had promised.

"I'd be willing to pay almost any asking price for that."

Mara startled, almost spilling the coffee onto her fingers as she filled a paper cup from her thermos. Glancing over her shoulder from her bent position, the first thing she noticed was that Jared Sinclair wasn't staring at the coffee. His eyes were trained on her ample butt, which was sticking up in the air as she filled her cup.

"Coffee is free," she told him as she straightened hastily, turning and holding out the cup. "It has creamer. I only bring it for myself, but I have plenty."

What the hell is he doing here?

Jared Sinclair looked about as at home here in the middle of the wet, open field for the farmers' market as he would doing any other everyday activity that the inhabitants of Amesport did on a regular basis.

He belonged in the corporate world, in an immaculate suit that he wouldn't get dirty, sitting in a high-rise office discussing business deals. The only casual things about him were the rolled-up sleeves of his button-down shirt, which exposed strong, muscular forearms lightly covered with reddish-brown hair, and the open buttons at the neckline collar, which gave her just a tantalizing glimpse of one very masculine chest.

Jared finally accepted the cup from her hand as he met her eyes with an intensity that made her shudder. Not letting go of her gaze, he took a large sip of the hot coffee, watching her over the rim of the cup before replying in his sexy baritone, "I think you know I wasn't talking about coffee, although if I can't have what I want right now, I'll take the caffeine. Thanks."

Mara looked away from him, embarrassed. Ignoring his innuendo, she told him curiously, "This doesn't exactly seem like your scene, and I'm surprised you don't already have a cup of coffee in your hand. I rarely see you without one."

"Brew Magic isn't even open yet. Why do they start this thing so damn early?" he grumbled unhappily.

"Having withdrawals? I'm sure you have a coffeemaker at your house." Already having set up her jars and containers for sale, she reached down for her thermos on the ground and straightened back up again, deciding to fill her own cup standing up this time. Honestly, she was having caffeine withdrawal, so she understood needing a cup of coffee. She'd been running late this morning and had skipped breakfast and coffee.

"The damn thing hates me," he rumbled, as though his coffeemaker had a personal vendetta against him. "My old one took a crap, and I bought one that's supposed to be top-of-the-line. I end up with half a cup of coffee grounds in my cup."

"Did you read the instructions?"

Jared shrugged. "Why? How hard can it be to make coffee? It must be defective."

Just like a man, he obviously didn't believe he needed directions. "It might help," she suggested lightly. She very much doubted the coffeemaker personally disliked Jared. It was more likely that Jared was impatient with the coffeemaker. "It's better than having withdrawals."

She knew it didn't escape Jared's notice that she was pouring her coffee in an upright position, and he smirked evilly as he watched her. "Now I'm definitely having withdrawals," he rasped. "Putting that gorgeous ass in the air can definitely give a man a lot of fantasies."

"I didn't know you were there," Mara answered defensively. Her ass was hardly her best feature, and she wouldn't have put it on display had she known anybody was behind her.

Jared crossed his arms in front of him, his coffee balanced in his right hand. "I know you were unaware that I was behind you. That just made the possibilities that much more tempting."

No doubt it made a large target for just about anything. My butt is too big, and I'm pretty doubtful that my old Patriots T-shirt and cut-off blue jean shorts are a major turn-on.

It had been so early when she was loading her battered pickup truck that she hadn't bothered with any makeup, and her hair was barely tamed in a clip behind her head.

Oh yeah, I'm definitely a real seductress. No wonder he wants me.

She rolled her eyes at him, letting him know she wasn't going to engage in his flirtation. "Do those sorts of compliments usually work for you?"

He raised a quizzical brow. "For what?"

Mara shrugged and averted her eyes, concentrating on arranging her jars and cutting up homemade bread and placing it into airtight containers. "Pickup lines."

"I wouldn't know," he informed her harshly. "I don't usually bother. The only thing women want from me is money."

Startled, she turned her head and openly gaped at him. "You don't really believe that."

Amazingly, Mara could tell from the look in Jared's momentarily expressive eyes that he not only believed it but was completely convinced that women were only after his money.

"What else would they want?" He shrugged as though he was resigned to the fact that he was pursued for monetary reasons only.

Okay, the man is either blind, or he doesn't look into the mirror every morning. This nearly flawless specimen of masculine perfection is actually insecure? "There are other things," she muttered quietly. Somebody had hurt him, rejected him. It was the only reason Mara could think of that he wasn't conceited about his appearance.

"What?" he questioned in a low, velvety baritone.

Seriously? Jared Sinclair didn't know he was hot enough to melt a woman's panties with a glance? Since yesterday, when those amazing green eyes had begun to actually show some of his emotions, he'd become nearly irresistible to her. "Everything," she admitted in a husky whisper, unable to keep her eyes from moving over him hungrily. "You're every woman's fantasy. Not only are you drop-dead gorgeous, but you're kind and funny when you want to be. What more could a woman want?" Nothing. Absolutely nothing.

"Money," he added gravely. "Lots of it."

Mara's heart melted. He really *did* think every woman was after him primarily for his money. "Believe me, there's plenty more of you to appreciate than your bank account." She hated that Jared actually believed what he was saying.

"I've discovered that a big bank account is their first priority. Other large assets come in last place," he replied, a hint of humor in his voice now.

His emphasis on the words "large" and "come" made beads of sweat break out on her forehead, even though the summer day wasn't particularly warm yet. She wasn't touching his comment. Having this conversation was uncomfortable enough. "Would you like a sample?" she asked desperately, determined to steer the topic of conversation in a different direction.

"I'd like more than a sample," Jared answered huskily. "I think when it comes to you, I'll want everything."

CHAPTER 4

Sweet Jesus, if he doesn't stop flirting with me, I'm going to jump over this table and devour him. Men don't try to seduce me with words or actions, especially not a guy who looks good enough to gobble up for breakfast. He's the type of man who doesn't have to try to be scorching hot. He simply . . . is.

"Jam," she squeaked nervously. "Wild Maine blackberry is the sampler today." She cut a full slice of the bread in front of her and hastily smeared a generous portion of her sample jelly on top of it.

Jared took it from her hand with a satisfied smirk.

He knows that he's getting to me. Dammit!

Mara tried to keep her hand from trembling as she let go of the sample. She had to control her reactions to him, but he was starting to become hard to ignore. His husky, low voice made her overheated no matter what he said. When he made innuendos that were probably second nature to him, she melted. Her panties were drenched just from the thought of him sampling any part of her, and her core was clenching, aching with a need she'd never experienced before.

Get a grip, Mara. He isn't seriously attracted to you. He's charming and likeable, but Jared Sinclair is about as likely to be genuinely attracted to you as your chances of winning the lottery. Remember? You don't even buy a damn lottery ticket. Don't fall into this fantasy. You're a realistic woman, and Jared Sinclair is way out of your league.

At the age of twenty-six, Mara was practically a virgin. It was embarrassing but true. She'd given her virginity away at the age of eighteen to her one and only steady boyfriend, who she'd met in her first and only year of college. When she'd had to leave the university after her freshman year because her mom had been diagnosed with cancer, her boyfriend had dumped her before she ever left the campus. Strangely, her heart hadn't been broken. At the time, she'd been too worried about her mother, and she had always been convinced that sex was highly overrated. Now . . . she wasn't so certain she was right. Jared Sinclair could do funny things to her body without even touching her. His clean, masculine scent and his husky baritone alluding to anything remotely sexual *was* getting to her. It was like he exuded pheromones from every pore in his body, luring her instinctively. Maybe for him the sexual references were just words, but Mara was beginning to picture him gloriously naked, his handsome face above her, his beautiful eyes filled with desire as he took her to some kind of nooky paradise she'd never experienced before.

"Holy shit, this is good," Jared groaned as he devoured the bread and jam. "You make this?"

He closed his eyes, and Mara clenched her thighs together as she noticed the look of ecstasy on his face.

Don't go there. Forcing her mind out of the gutter, she replied, "Yes. I make all kinds of things. Jams, jellies, relishes, and sauces are my favorite. Most of them are old recipes that I picked up from my mom. I keep trying to improve them or create new flavors."

Jared was silent as he chewed and swallowed, finally taking a sip of his coffee before he answered, "You're in the wrong business, sweetheart. You should be selling those." He hesitated before adding, "You do beautiful work with your dolls, but they aren't going to make you rich. It takes too much time and material to make them, and the profit on each unit you sell is too small. Sell these and you'll have a thriving business." Jared examined all of the jars, checking the labels. "Chocolate peanut butter saltwater taffy?" He read the label almost reverently as he set his coffee down on the table and opened the jar. Unwrapping a piece of the candy, he popped it into his mouth.

"That wasn't the sample today," Mara chastised him, but she was smiling. He looked too damn hot as he chewed, and released yet another low, appreciative groan when he swallowed, for her to lament over a lost sale. Watching him was worth it.

"I'm buying," Jared said greedily. "All of it. I've never had anything like it."

"I only have a few jars of the taffy."

"How fast do you sell out on market days?"

"Pretty fast," Mara admitted. "I'm usually only here for a few hours. Most of the people in the area have tried the jams and the taffy. That goes first."

Jared gave her a questioning look. "Let me guess . . . you can't make more because you run your store and make dolls all day and cook at night?"

Mara shrugged, uncomfortable because he had just summed up her work habits perfectly. "Pretty much. The kitchen needs some updated appliances. I have to pull the taffy by hand, so my ability to make it in larger quantities is limited. I make as much as I can for the market."

"Christ, Mara. You have this amazing ability, and you aren't doing this in mass? What the hell are you thinking?" Jared asked harshly. "This is the money you live on, right? This is how you actually survive? I know damn well you haven't kept yourself afloat on sales from your shop."

"The doll shop is a tradition in my family," she told him angrily. "And I hardly have the funds to start another business. The market works for me."

"Bullshit. You could be making good money if you'd switch your product, put a store online."

"That would require capital—"

"Which you'd probably make if you weren't letting your funds get drained by keeping a losing business," Jared interrupted.

She hated his words because he was absolutely right. "It was my grandmother's store, and then my mother's. Now it's mine," Mara answered stubbornly. "I know I failed and I'm losing the doll business. I went to a year of business school, Jared. I know it wasn't a good business anymore, and I couldn't really make money. But I wanted to hold on to a part of my mom. It's all I have left." Her eyes flooded with tears of frustration and leftover grief.

"You don't need the doll store, Mara. You have your memories. What do you think your mother would have wanted you to do?" Jared asked in a much calmer, gentler voice. "She wouldn't have wanted you to starve to keep the store going. I'm sure she wouldn't have wanted you to be working every minute of the day to survive. Times change, progress happens, and tradition isn't going to keep you in funds. You can't sell enough dolls to make a living anymore. It would be an incredible hobby, but you can't keep yourself solvent."

Mara's heart squeezed, the truth in Jared's words hitting her hard. It was nothing she didn't already know, but to hear it said out loud was painful. "My mom and I barely got by. When she got sick, I started doing the Saturday markets with some of the skills and recipes she passed down to me from my gran—making taffy, jams and jellies, relishes and sauces. It kept us afloat. I never knew things were as bad as they really were until Mom got sick and I took over the finances during the last year she was alive. I knew the outlook was depressing, but I wanted to keep it going for her." Mara swiped at her tears irritably, hating her own weakness. "She sent me off to business school, and she didn't have a penny saved. If I had known—"

"You didn't know," Jared growled. "Stop blaming yourself."

Mara looked up at him in surprise, shocked that he was defending her. She'd made some lousy business decisions and she knew it. "I can't help it. I was an adult. I should have known our situation. She never told me." Her mom had never given her a clue that she didn't have the money to send her only child to college. "I went for a year before she got diagnosed with cancer and I came back home. Seven years later, I'm still paying the student loans she took out to do it. And I never even finished." Mara vented her grief and guilt to Jared as if she'd known him forever, realizing how good it felt to talk to *somebody*. Kristin was her best friend, but Mara had never wanted to mention her financial woes to her. Kristin would have wanted to help, and her friend had it tight herself.

"Are you about done beating yourself up now?" Jared asked her patiently, folding his arms in front of him and leaning a hip against the metal folding table. "Because if you are done blaming yourself for your past, which were entirely understandable actions considering you lost your mother only a year ago, then I'm going to make you a proposition."

Mara brushed the last few tears from her eyes and stared at him blankly. His eyes were liquid and heated as he glared back at her. "What?" she asked curiously.

"I'm willing to put up the capital for a new business venture for you. I'll provide the equipment, space, and start-up capital if you want to start a business selling your consumable products," he told her briskly.

"You want to be an angel investor?" Mara folded her arms in front of her and looked him directly in the eyes. "You're a billionaire. What interest can you have in a small business?" Even if she was successful, the money made on her business would be peanuts to him.

"First of all, I'm not what anybody would call an angel of any type." Jared shrugged. "I like the products. One of the perks is I'll get unlimited supplies."

Mara rolled her eyes at him. "It's not like you can't afford to purchase them. Come on, Jared. You're trying to help me, and I appreciate it. But I need to figure this out on my own."

"Why? It's a legitimate offer."

His statement was laughable coming from a billionaire who did multimillion-dollar business deals, but she was curious now. "For what percentage of the business?" she asked doubtfully, watching as he scrambled to come up with an answer. Jared Sinclair wasn't offering to go into business with her. He was offering to help her. Her heart melted as she watched a flicker of indecision move across his face, his businesslike facade temporarily faltering.

"Ten percent, and unlimited product," he said decisively.

Mara snorted. "How in the hell did you ever become a billionaire? That's not a serious offer. It's a charitable donation to me."

Jared ran a hand through his hair, looking frustrated. "I don't need more money. I need a project I can believe in," he told her bitterly.

"You don't like what you're doing, owning one of the most profitable commercial real estate companies in the world?" What exactly did he mean by needing something he could believe in?

"It's big business. Big buildings. Big money changing hands. Big commercial buildings. It's not a challenge anymore. It never really was."

Jared had helped to build some of the most impressive, enormous buildings in the world, and that wasn't demanding enough for him? "You don't like it," she decided adamantly. "You don't like what you do."

"Maybe," he agreed grudgingly.

"But you believe in my products?" Looking at the tortured look on his face, Mara believed him. Maybe he *was* bored. Maybe he really did want to be her mentor.

"I believe in you," he snapped.

"Do you hate what you're doing that much?" she asked gently.

"I don't exactly hate it," he grunted. "But I don't like it, either. I have competent upper management who can do most of the work now. I'm basically a figurehead, the guy who makes the final decision. But everything has already pretty much been decided by research and professionals chasing the deals and the details, the pros and cons already figured out. All they need is my okay. Maybe I need the challenge of building a business from the ground up again."

"It's never going to be a huge moneymaker," she warned him calmly, moving back enough to place her coffee in the bed of the truck and hop up on the tailgate to sit. Jared was a lot safer from a distance. "I know I can turn a good profit, but it isn't the kind of money you're used to dealing with," she continued, relieved by the distance she'd put between them.

"I don't give a shit about the money. I never did. I had more than enough money to live a life of luxury for the rest of my life and never do a single day of honest work. Success doesn't always involve huge profits. I just want you to make enough to live comfortably. I want to teach you how," he admitted roughly, his graveled tone sounding like he wanted to show her much more than business. Moving around the metal table, Jared set his coffee down before he stalked her, slowly pursuing her until he finally pinned her body against the open tailgate of her battered truck with his much larger, muscular form.

Mara's breath hitched as she inhaled his masculine scent, feeling intoxicated by his nearness. He placed his hands on both of her knees and ascended slowly along the sensitive skin of her inner thighs with his thumb, stroking until he reached the tops of her thighs. Once there, he moved his hands up and gripped her hips in an urgent motion, pulling her forward until her saturated core was flush against his hard, steely erection.

Mara shuddered, her body melting into Jared's as she looked up at him. His expression was strained and hungry, like a starving predator that had finally spotted prey. "And what do you get?" she questioned shakily, her nerves raw from trying to pretend she wasn't ready to crawl up his big, muscular body and beg him to satisfy the ache he was causing to pulsate through her entire being.

"Satisfaction," he answered in a husky voice before his mouth covered hers.

He swallowed her needy moan greedily, and he plundered her mouth with a dominance that turned Mara inside out. Helpless to do anything else, she wound her arms around his neck, threading her hands into his coarse hair, luxuriating in the feel of Jared taking her over completely. He demanded. She gave. He tilted her head, grasping her hair to position her head, demanding better access to her mouth. His tongue surged through her lips and into her mouth, his teeth taking small nips at her bottom lip between the bold thrusts. Strong hands moved down her back with brazen, possessive strokes that finally landed covetously on her ass as he cupped it like it belonged to him. He wasn't gentle as he yanked her forward, bringing her core as close as it could get to his engorged cock with their clothes on.

His embrace was bold and volatile, and she responded to his wildness with an equally frantic need all her own. Yearning. Tasting. Touching. All things that she had wanted to do to Jared Sinclair in her fantasies.

For a few moments, Mara let herself go, forgetting everyone and everything as she submerged herself in the feel of Jared's mouth and hard body claiming her. In the back of her mind, she knew there were probably other vendors at the market watching curiously, but Jared's body was blocking her from anyone's view, all of the other stands now behind him.

Her body nearly imploded as he squeezed the cheeks of her ass, released her mouth, and his tongue starting exploring the sensitive skin of her neck. His ragged breathing, the feel of the warm puffs of air he was expelling against her flesh, nearly making her come undone.

"Jared. We have to stop," she panted with very little conviction. Her hands were raking over his scalp, fisting his hair and pulling his mouth against her neck for more even as she said the words. "People will talk."

"Let them," Jared rasped against her heated skin. "I don't give a shit. As long as they can't see you I don't care. I want them to know you're fucking mine, Mara."

Mara tilted her head back and wrapped her legs around his waist. "Oh, God. Jared. Please." The fact that he was temporarily staking his claim just made her even hotter, more desperate.

Her mind whirled as she tried to comprehend the fact that Jared really *did* want her. His passionate touch, the hard erection between his legs, and the seriously ravenous look in his eyes told her that he was doing more than just teasing her. She wanted more . . . and that need was mutual.

He nipped at her earlobe, and then soothed it with his tongue. "What do you want? Do you want to feel my cock inside you? Do you want me as much as I want to be buried as deep as fucking possible inside you?"

"Yes," she whimpered, tightened her legs around him so she could feel his length. "Please."

"Jesus, I love to hear you beg. Do you know what it does to me when you respond to me like this, to know that you want me as much as I want you?" His hands squeezed the cheeks of her ass tightly, possessively. "All I want right now is to lay you down in the bed of this truck, strip off those shorts, and bury my face between your legs, Mara. I need to taste you. All of you. Your taste would be so addictive that I'd keep licking that sweet pussy long after you'd already come screaming my name more than once."

Mara's already-pebbled nipples grew impossibly harder as they abraded against his chest. Sweet baby Jesus, she was ready to come just from listening to him talk, feeling his body and mouth taking control of her. "Jared," she whimpered, her entire body hot, tight, and needy. She let go of her death grip on his hair and let her hands explore his body. Cursing the material of his soft shirt, she molded her hands over his muscular back and strong biceps, squirming against him as she encountered a body that was completely ripped. "I want to feel your skin," she breathed softly, her voice vibrating with raw passion.

"Sweetheart, you're going to feel all of me if you don't stop rubbing that hot pussy against my cock," he warned ominously, finally ceasing his exploration of her skin to lean his forehead against her shoulder. "Fuck. The market must have opened." His chest was heaving, but he moved his hands from her ass to her hips.

Panting, Mara slowly came to her senses as she heard the volume of voices in the field increasing steadily, many headed directly toward them. "It's open." She dropped her legs from around his waist.

Mara caught a glimpse of Jared's face as he straightened reluctantly. He looked as ravaged and tense as she felt. She could sense the effort it was taking for him to back off, his whole body tight under her fingers as he backed away. He took a deep breath, and then released it, one of the muscles in his jaw pulsating as he looked at her darkly. "It's closed now for you. I'm buying out your stock, and you're spending the day with me."

She knew she should argue, but it would be pointless for her to do that. "I can't keep you from buying everything," she told him with more calm than she was feeling at the moment. Placing her trembling hands on her thighs, she met his flaming gaze with one of her own. "And I'll only spend the day with you if you actually ask me." His dominant personality might heat her blood, but she wasn't letting him get away with bossing her around. Telling her how she was going to spend her day was way too high-handed.

"I did ask you," he argued in a husky voice.

Mara shook her head. He was a billionaire, and she was pretty certain that people jumped when he told them what to do. But that wasn't *asking*. And she wasn't jumping. Folding her arms in front of her stubbornly, she informed him, "You *told* me. Can't you just ask?"

"Well, will you?" he grumbled hesitantly, like he was afraid she might say no.

She shot him a sunny smile. It wasn't exactly a polite invitation by conventional standards, but for him, it probably was. "I'd love to, Jared.

Thank you." Like there was ever any question? It wasn't often that she had a morning off, and she'd like to spend it with him. Actually liking Jared Sinclair was dangerous, and desiring him was even more so. But she wanted to examine the possibilities of a new business.

And I want to explore Jared Sinclair . . . in every way possible.

Mara's breath caught in her lungs as Jared shot her a genuine grin at her acceptance of his offer. He was handsome under normal circumstances, but when he smiled at her like that, his curved lips and that happy expression making it all the way to his gorgeous eyes, she was toast.

She exhaled shakily as he looked away and started eagerly packing jars back into boxes and loading them into the bed of her truck.

"I can pack the stuff up and drop it at my place," Jared drawled as he hefted several boxes easily into the back of her truck as she moved aside.

"You mean you'll actually be seen riding in my poor old vehicle?" Her truck was beyond old, and should have gone to the truck graveyard a few years ago. But it did run, and it got her where she wanted to go. However, she couldn't really see Jared Sinclair, billionaire extraordinaire from the elite Boston Sinclairs, riding in her beat-up pickup.

"I'll even drive," he agreed readily. "Are you trying to say I'm a snob? Believe it or not, when I was right out of college, I actually used to have a construction work truck similar to this one. I think I kind of miss it."

"But your other car was probably a Maserati?" she teased him playfully. "This is my primary vehicle."

"Actually, it was a Bugatti," he answered gruffly. "And a couple of others."

"How many vehicles can one guy have?"

He shrugged. "More than he can count. I have at least one in every residence I have. But not all of them are outrageously expensive," he added defensively. "I have an inexpensive vehicle here in Amesport."

Mara bit her lip to keep from smiling. How did one tell a billionaire that a Mercedes SUV wasn't exactly an economy car? She hadn't meant to imply he was a snob at all. He was just living his life as it had been handed to him, and how he'd gone on to earn the extravagant items that were normal for him. She'd actually never seen Jared as being conceited or full of himself, even though he'd been born rich and had become even richer. In fact, beneath his external facade of measured control that he usually showed to the world, she had a feeling there was a warm center somewhere inside him.

Don't forget that he discards women as fast as he picks them up.

Ignoring her negative thoughts, Mara reminded herself that what she had heard about Jared was gossip. She'd never had or seen any firsthand knowledge of Jared being a dog, and her mother had always taught her to judge people for herself rather than listen to what others were saying.

"No," she finally answered. "I don't think you're a snob at all. But you *are* just a little too pretty for my old truck," she told him cheekily, eyeing his gold watch, designer clothing, and his now wet leather shoes.

Giggling at his disgruntled look, she bent over to retrieve her coffee thermos.

Whack!

Mara squealed and dropped the thermos as his hand connected with her backside, and he wasn't particularly gentle. "Ouch. What was that?"

Jared leaned in close to her ear. "*That* was too pretty of a target, sweetheart, and it was payback for insulting my manhood." He rubbed the area he'd slapped discreetly before moving his hand.

Like anybody could deny he was entirely male.

Okay, maybe she *had* deserved *some* retaliation. Jared Sinclair was much too masculine to let her get away with calling him *pretty*. She gave him a mischievous smile and dug in her pocket for the keys, pulling them out and dangling them in the air.

Jared snatched them deftly. "You have one of these, too?" He was staring strangely at her key chain.

"The Apache tear stone? Beatrice gave it to me."

Jared dug into his pocket and dangled an empty key chain just like hers. "Me too," he confessed.

Mara sighed. "She gave it to me after my mother died."

"Did it help?"

She shrugged. "I survived. I figured it couldn't hurt." She didn't actually believe in Beatrice's healing, but she'd always found some comfort in the stone for some reason.

"My thoughts exactly," Jared answered as he shoved the key chain back into his pocket. After folding the heavy table she used for her displays and loading it into the back of her truck, he slammed the tailgate closed and snatched up her thermos and the tote lying on the ground. As he handed her the items, he asked, "Ready?"

That one little one-word question touched Mara's emotions on so many levels. Was she ready? Her entire life was changing right now, and she'd have a lot of challenges she'd never faced before. Was she done grieving over the loss of her mom and generations of tradition? Maybe not, but she had to move on with her life. Jared was right. Her mother would have wanted her to succeed, and would have been disappointed if Mara kept holding on to a losing business when she had better opportunities. Still, she wished it didn't hurt so damn much to let go.

Jared Sinclair inspired far different emotions, and she was fairly certain they were dangerous.

I need to start living my life sometime, taking some risks.

She'd spent her entire adult life looking after her mother, and she'd never regret it, but her mom would have wanted her to be happy, experience life. Jared was right about what her mother would have wanted for her only child. She had her memories of her mother, and her gran who had died when Mara was still in grade school. She'd hold those close to her chest and start living for herself now. She had to if she wanted to move on and survive.

She nodded at Jared. "I'm ready."

A look of understanding sparked between them as their eyes met and held. Mara shivered as she felt some kind of connection solidify.

Maybe he was dangerous to her.

Maybe he was troubled.

Maybe he had some of the same issues he needed to work through as she did. She'd begun to suspect he did, even before the strange coincidence that Beatrice had given them the same stone.

As Jared opened the passenger door for her, Mara wondered if maybe, just possibly, they could help heal each other.

CHAPTER 5

What in the hell is wrong with me?

Jared tried to focus on his driving, unable to forget his passionate encounter with Mara for even two damn seconds. He'd remember her needy little moans for a very long time, and they'd be echoing in his head later when he took himself in hand to take away the pressure of his aching cock.

I completely lost control. I don't lose control anymore. Not ever.

Kissing Mara had been his first loss of restraint in years. When he'd been devouring her, he couldn't have cared less if the entire world fell apart, as long as he could get closer to her, deeper into her mouth.

Mine.

That one word kept repeating in his mind, driving him closer to the edge of taking what he wanted, and damn the consequences of his actions.

She wanted the same thing.

Bullshit! He was kidding himself if he thought for a moment that Mara really wanted *him*. She had no idea what she was getting herself into, what kind of man he really was. Mara Ross was way too open, too sweet to realize what she needed, and that sure as hell wasn't him. Yet, it didn't stop him from wanting her with an intensity that caused him to forget rational thought.

"Sullivan's is better than Tony's." Mara's voice broke the silence.

Jared jolted himself into reality as she spoke from the passenger seat of the beat-up old truck. And dammit, he needed to talk to her about this damn vehicle. He didn't care what it looked like. He hadn't been kidding when he told her he'd had a work truck like this one. But it had always been in good repair. What really mattered was that the brakes were squealing, the engine was choking, and the tires were almost completely bald. "Sullivan's?" Jared had never heard of the place. He always ate at Tony's. The ambiance was good, and the food was decent.

"Turn right at the stop sign," she instructed. "Sullivan's has the best seafood in town. It's mostly locals. Tony's is fancier, so I guess the visitors figure the food is better. It's not."

Jared turned, letting her guide him to a different place to eat. After they'd dropped off the jars of taffy and jam he had purchased from Mara at his house and settled the bill, he was starving. He'd missed breakfast, except for the sample of her incredible homemade products, and was beyond ready for lunch. "Now what?" he asked, his tone impatient. There wasn't a food joint in sight.

"Find a place to park at the dead end. We'll have to walk to the end of the boardwalk," she told him calmly.

Jared turned into a dirt parking lot at the end of the street and maneuvered into a parking spot. "The shack?" He'd seen the rough old building at the end of the boardwalk, near the old pier that led to the lighthouse, but hadn't paid much attention. It hadn't even looked habitable.

"Sullivan's Steak and Seafood. It's been there for as long as I can remember. Best lobster rolls in the area." Mara unbuckled her seat belt and smiled at Jared.

"It looks like a dive," Jared grumbled.

"It is," Mara agreed. "But the food is the best in town. And I don't have to worry about being underdressed."

Hell, he *wished* she was underdressed, preferably beneath him naked right now. He would happily trade lunch for *her*. Jared suspected his irritable mood was caused more by his inexplicable need for Mara than food. Unfortunately, she was still wearing her ass-hugging jean shorts that were like a torture device if he was walking behind her, and the T-shirt she had been wearing at the market. He hopped out of the truck and pocketed the keys as he jogged to her side of the truck to open the door before she could get it. He'd noticed that the door stuck when he'd had to practically pry it open at his house. "I'm starving," he told her testily as the door popped open after he exerted considerable force.

"You won't be." She laughed and grabbed his hand, forcing him to close the door quickly as he followed her. For a moment, he considered whether or not he should have locked the truck, but discarded the idea. Someone would be doing her a favor if they stole it, and he'd have an excuse to replace it.

They passed the Lighthouse Inn at the end of the street, a lodging he'd become very familiar with during the time he'd been supervising the construction of homes on the Peninsula for him and his siblings. He designed and helped build every one of those homes except Grady's, who had built his own home at the very end of the Peninsula before Jared had ever set foot in Amesport. After visiting Grady, Jared had known every one of them needed a home here. There was something special about the small coastal town, something healing, and God knew every one of the Sinclairs needed a place like this to escape.

Jared let her lead him until they reached the boardwalk, and then they ended up walking side by side. She tugged to let go of his hand, but he entwined their fingers and kept a firm grasp, liking the feel of her palm against his, being connected to her somehow. It was a simple touch that he hadn't felt in a very long time, and he'd forgotten how good it felt. Honestly, he didn't think it had ever made his heart lighter just by touching a woman in such an uncomplicated manner. But with

Mara, it did. "It's raining," he observed, feeling a few droplets land on his forehead.

"That's why I wanted to sell my stuff fast at the market today. We're supposed to get more thunderstorms this afternoon."

It had warmed up considerably since his rude awakening early this morning, but Jared could see the clouds starting to roll in. Thankfully, they arrived at the shack, and Mara led him around to the front entrance, a door that wasn't visible unless a person walked toward the lighthouse, which few people actually did once they reached the end of the boardwalk. The pier leading to the large beacon for fishermen wasn't exactly picturesque, and neither was the old lighthouse, which looked weathered and in need of repairs.

Sullivan's Steak and Seafood.

The name of the place was carved on a piece of weathered driftwood hanging unevenly beside the entrance. "Classy," he mumbled, able to hear voices now coming from inside the hut. He plucked Mara's glasses off her face and dried them on his shirt, cleaning off a few droplets of water, before perching them back on her face.

"Thanks." She adjusted the glasses slightly. "Why do you keep doing that?"

"I wore glasses. It's irritating to try to see around the spots."

"You don't need them anymore?" she asked curiously.

"Nope. I had laser done." He looked at the lopsided sign on the door dubiously. "Are you sure it's safe to eat here?"

"Don't judge. Outward appearances can be deceiving. The food is amazing."

"I hope so." He reached for the door and opened it for her, waving at her to go in first.

Surprisingly, the place wasn't as bad as Jared had imagined, judging by the weathered exterior. There was a cash register inside the door and a bar with four chairs, where solo diners could sit and eat. The tables weren't exactly elegant, but they were serviceable, and most of them were full.

"Mara," a high, female voice called loudly from the service window behind the bar.

Jared looked at Mara as she waved at a pretty woman with honey-blonde hair, around the same age as she was, standing near the service window. "That's Tessa Sullivan. We went to high school together. She'll come out and say hello. Tessa is deaf, but she reads lips very well," she told him in a quiet voice.

The blonde came barreling out the swinging door to the kitchen and made a beeline for Mara, catching her up in a huge hug. "I haven't seen you in a while," Tessa scolded Mara as she hugged her.

Mara leaned back so Tessa could read her lips. "I've been busy, or I would have been here sooner. You know how much I love your food."

"As much as we love yours," Tessa replied, her voice lilting slightly from her inability to hear her own words. "Did you bring me anything?"

"Sold out at the market," Mara replied, sounding regretful. Turning her head to Jared, she quickly explained, "They use some of my products when I have extra."

Looking directly at Tessa, Jared asked, "Would you use them all the time if you had an ample supply?"

Tessa looked at Mara questioningly, as though she was wondering if she should answer a stranger's questions.

"Sorry. Tessa, this is my friend, Jared Sinclair. Jared, this is Tessa Sullivan, half owner of Sullivan's. Tessa and her brother, Liam, run the restaurant," Mara explained.

Jared had to let go of Mara's hand to hold it out to Tessa. "It's a pleasure," he said warmly, already liking the cheerful female who didn't seem the least bit troubled about the fact that she couldn't hear.

"Same here," Tessa answered, gripping his hand firmly and shaking it. "And yes, I'd use her products all the time if I could get my hands on them. Her jams and sauces are amazing. I'd love to have them all the time. I've based some of my recipes on her sauces, so I can only make them when she can get me a supply. And the customers love her jellies."

Jared smiled at the attractive blonde as he dropped his arm to his side, automatically reaching for Mara's hand again. "I'm trying to talk her into making her jams, jellies, and sauces into a real business. Then she could make them available all the time."

The fair-haired female bounced up and down, excited, clapping her hands together. "That would be fantastic. But what about your doll shop?" She looked at Mara with a frown.

Mara shook her head. "The owner is selling the house. I have to find something else. The shop isn't making money anyway, so there's no point in finding another location."

The blonde's face fell. "I'm so sorry, Mara. But you'll do great with the new business. Your edibles are unique and wonderful. If I could stock your taffy and jams near the register, I'd sell out in a day."

"That's what I keep telling her," Jared seconded the woman's encouraging comments when Tessa looked his way.

"Thanks, Tessa," Mara answered with a smile.

"Let me get you a table." Tessa went to clear and clean a table for them.

"You didn't tell me you already had customers in town clamoring for your products." Jared shot Mara an irritated look. Hell, her food products were obviously already in high demand here in Amesport. "Are there others?"

Mara shrugged. "Some. A few of the shops in town would like to carry them all the time. But I can never make enough to distribute."

"That won't be a problem anymore," he told her harshly.

"We'll talk about it. The offer you're making isn't acceptable to me. You should take at least half interest."

Hell, if he was thinking with the head above his neck, he'd take more than half so that he had controlling interest. Unfortunately, the head below his waist didn't give a damn about having the greater percentage in her business. The only place he wanted to control her was in the bedroom. Or up against a wall. Or just about anywhere that he could have some privacy. "We'll definitely talk about it," he ground out, his jaw clenched. Somehow, he'd talk her into seeing things his way.

Mara opened her mouth to say something, but she closed it again as Tessa came back to show them to their table.

Jared was agitated, and he wondered why it was so damn important that he make Mara see reason. It was a small business. It should be no big deal to him. However, for some reason, getting Mara to agree had somehow become the most important thing he'd ever done in his life. Her future depended on it.

Mara glanced around the restaurant and then at Jared as he looked over the menu. She didn't need to look. She knew Sullivan's menu by heart.

Maybe I should have taken Jared to Tony's restaurant. He definitely doesn't look like he belongs at a table with mismatched chairs and pictures everywhere of men holding up big fish.

God, Jared Sinclair *was* beautiful. He exuded power and confidence, even when he was looking at a damn menu. The auburn highlights in his chestnut hair appeared to almost glow in the dim light of the casual restaurant, and he just looked so damned . . . polished. It didn't matter that he was dressed fairly casually. He radiated control, sophistication, and dominance wherever he was, and no matter how he was dressed. It appeared to be as natural to him as taking his next breath, and that aura of strength was nearly impossible to ignore.

A teenage waiter took their order, and Jared sat back in his chair, his elbows on the table, watching her. "I'd like to get this business deal out of the way." He released a deep breath. "You're right in saying that I'm not doing it for the money. Obviously, I don't need more money. I want to do it to bring out your products to the masses. They're pretty incredible, and it will be a challenge and something different for me. I don't know much about making a business of consumables successful, but I'll learn. And I can help you with the marketing process and the business end of things."

Mara scrutinized him, noticing that his eyes lit up at the possibility of a challenge. "Why me? There are tons of small businesses trying to get a foothold." *And any one of them would kill to have the backing of a Sinclair.*

Jared shrugged. "I like you. And believe me, that's a novelty for me. I don't like very many people other than my family."

"Why?"

"Because most of them want something from me. You don't, which fascinates me."

Mara gaped at him, wondering what kind of world he lived in where he didn't have anybody who cared about him as a person. "You don't have friends? People that you trust other than your siblings?"

Jared's expression turned dark. "Not since right after college. I learned from those mistakes."

"You trusted somebody who burned you," Mara guessed. Someone had hurt Jared Sinclair . . . badly. She winced inwardly at just how much some person must have betrayed him. It was obvious he'd never fully trusted anyone except his family again. "I'm sorry." She wanted to ask who it was, and what they'd done to him, but she didn't know him well enough to pry. It was obvious he'd never quite healed from the betrayal.

His eyes burned hot as their gazes locked. "Why? You didn't do anything."

Yet.

Mara could almost hear the word hanging at the end of his sentence. "Nobody deserves to have their trust in another person shattered. It hurts."

"I got over it a long time ago," Jared snapped.

Mara shook her head slowly, not breaking eye contact with him.

"I don't think you have." In fact, she was pretty certain that he was still bitter. It showed in his lack of trust, his unwillingness to allow people into his controlled little world.

Jared smiled at her cynically. "Are you attempting to be my friend, Mara?"

"What if I am?" She wasn't sure *what* she was doing. All she could feel was the urgency to make sure that Jared Sinclair could trust someone other than his family again. There was a hidden sorrow somewhere inside him. She could sense it, and it was eating at her.

Jared averted his gaze. "I'm afraid that would be impossible."

"You want to do business together. How can we do that if you can't learn to trust me?" she asked him breathlessly.

"That's what legal contracts are for."

"Are you planning on having your lawyers draw one up?"

"No," he rasped, looking relieved when their lunch arrived.

Mara waited until the waiter had delivered Jared's lobster rolls in front of him, and her fish special to her. After she assured the friendly teen that they didn't need anything else, he departed.

She went through the motions, taking a bite of her fish and then the fries, wondering desperately what to say to Jared. "You need a contract," she finally told him adamantly. "And I don't see any reason why we *can't* be friends." For God's sake, he'd had his tongue down her throat not so long ago. She'd hate to think that he wasn't even a friend.

He began to devour one of the two lobster rolls he'd ordered, waiting until he'd finished it before commenting. "I think it would be very difficult to be friends with a woman who keeps my dick hard the entire time I'm in her company. I also don't think I'd be imagining a *friend* naked and begging me to fuck her every time I look at her."

Mara nearly choked on a sip of her water. She swallowed—barely— and coughed a few times after she'd gotten the liquid down. "I can't believe you just said that," she told him in a harsh whisper, more upset by her body's volatile reaction in the middle of a restaurant than the fact that he had no problem talking dirty to her.

He paused and gave her a sultry, dark look that made her core clench so tightly that she had to clamp her thighs together.

"Why not? It's the truth." He looked around the restaurant. "It's not like anyone could hear me."

Mara flushed, her face heating so much she was starting to sweat. While it was true that nobody was seated that close to them, she was squirming from him just casually declaring that he was having those kinds of carnal thoughts about her. And Jared had no problem letting her know about them . . . boldly. "I heard you," she squeaked.

"I know." Jared shot her a mischievous look as he bit into his second sandwich.

"It's not like I'm *trying* to make you think about . . . that." God, she got even more hot and bothered just from looking at his teasing, sexy smile.

"I know that, too," he admitted. "Doesn't matter. I think about it anyway."

Mara munched on her fish and chips, trying desperately not to let Jared Sinclair fluster her. "I'm not going to have this conversation with you in the middle of a restaurant."

"Then we can have it once we leave," he answered huskily.

"Business and pleasure don't mix." She *was* going to let him help her get a business off the ground. It wasn't like her choices were many, and she wanted to make something of her life. Her mother and gran's business was all but gone, and the business-minded part of her knew that she could have a modicum of success with her consumable products. Much as she didn't want to take advantage of Jared's generosity, she was going to let him be her business partner. She'd succeed; make sure she didn't let him down. She doubted her paltry business would ever add much to his net worth, but she'd make it prosperous.

"They won't mix," Jared agreed. "The business is yours. The pleasure will be ours." He wiped his mouth with his napkin and dropped it onto his empty plate. "Have you known real pleasure, Mara? Has any man ever made you come until you were so sated you couldn't move?"

Her eyes still on her plate, she answered, "I'm not a virgin, if that's what you're asking." She could feel the heat of his gaze caressing her, but she couldn't look up. "I had a steady boyfriend when I went away to college."

"What happened?" he grunted, his tone careful and wary.

"He dumped me as soon as he found out I was dropping out of college to take care of my sick mother," Mara told him informatively. She really didn't think about her one sexual relationship anymore. She'd still been a teenager, and she could barely remember what he looked like.

"Bastard," Jared hissed.

Mara shrugged. "It was college. We were young. Honestly, I didn't miss him all that much. I was too busy with my mom. Obviously, it wasn't real love." It hadn't even really been lust. Mara was pretty sure she'd hooked up with a boy in college just because she'd been lonely, and it hadn't helped.

"Is there any such thing as real love?" Jared mused skeptically.

Her head finally snapped up to look at him. "How can you ask that when you see Grady and Emily together every day? And Dante and Sarah. I also don't doubt that your sister loves her husband just as much as Grady and Dante love their wives. You have some wonderful examples of love, yet you don't believe in it?"

He was digging his wallet out of his back pocket as he replied blackly, "I think all of them are crazy. But it works for them, I guess." Jared dropped some bills on the table and took the check the waiter had left while they'd been talking.

"You pay at the register here," she directed him, distracted. "So you've never been in love?"

His beautiful eyes pinned her with a dark look. "Just like you . . . I thought maybe I was once. If you must know, I also thought I had a best friend back then, too."

"What happened?" she asked him breathlessly.

"I found my supposed best friend fucking my supposed girlfriend." Jared's expression grew darker, his green eyes swirling with emotion.

Oh, dear God. No wonder he was so cynical, so disbelieving. She couldn't imagine the pain of seeing two people you cared about so much betraying you together, finding both of them untrustworthy. Obviously, nobody had ever done right by him since, taught him anything different than the betrayal he'd experienced. Maybe it was because he'd never let anyone in again.

"What did you do?" Mara's heart was breaking as she asked the question anxiously.

"I killed both of them," he told her flatly, breaking eye contact with her abruptly and getting up to make his way to the cash register to pay the bill without another word.

CHAPTER 6

He was almost numb at the funeral, standing back from the crowd of mourners who surrounded the casket about to be lowered into the ground. Since he was the one responsible for the death of the woman about to be buried, he wasn't sure he even needed to be here. For some reason, he had needed to be present, the compulsion to be here too strong to ignore.

It was the second funeral he'd attended in the last two days.

He could hear the keening wail of sorrow coming from the young woman's mother, and he clenched his fists restlessly when the casket disappeared into the ground as a clergyman blessed the female who had died just days before.

Flowers were dropped on top of the casket, and he heaved a sigh of relief that it was over.

"I'm sorry." He whispered the same husky words he'd spoken at the funeral the day before. And he meant them, even though he'd been responsible for her demise.

Barely able to process the fact that she was gone, that she'd never again take another breath on this earth, he turned away from the grave site, ready to make his escape. A lone tear escaped from his eyes, and he brushed it away angrily. He couldn't show any emotions. Not here. Not now.

"You!"

He stopped, immobilized as he heard the voice of the deceased woman's mother. Unmoving, he let the older woman beat at his back as she wailed, "You killed my daughter. I hope you rot in hell for what you did."

Turning slowly, he let her slam her fists into his chest. It didn't hurt. Nothing she could dish out would match the anguish he'd suffered emotionally the last few days. "I'm sorry," he said to the grief-crazed woman right before she let her hand fly and slapped him across the face so hard that it jerked his head to the right.

"Sorry doesn't bring my daughter back. You killed her. You killed her. You selfish bastard." Her voice rose with every word she screamed hysterically.

The words rang through his head, the truth undeniable. His chest heaved with remorse as he let her take her anger out on him. He deserved it. Darkness started to blur his vision as he panted, unable to breathe, imagining the young woman in her casket beneath the ground.

"I killed both of them," he admitted brokenly, his voice filled with horror as he clawed at empty space to stay upright and conscious.

Jared woke sitting up, his hands clawing at the sheets on the bed, sucking in huge gulps of air. Shuddering, he tried to slow down his breathing as he swiped at the sweat on his forehead.

Not again!

Christ! He thought he'd gotten over his nightmares. It had been a few years since he'd had the one about the funerals, and he'd thought he was finally going to get a permanent reprieve from the fucked-up shit that tortured him while he slept.

He didn't talk about it.

He didn't dream about it anymore.

He'd stopped caring—or so he thought.

I shouldn't have talked about it today.

Jared cursed himself for screwing up as he lay back on his pillows, wondering why in the hell he'd blurted out his sordid secrets to Mara Ross. To her credit, she hadn't asked any more questions. She'd dropped him off to get his car where he'd parked at the farmers' market and had said a polite good-bye to him as he'd exited the truck, embarrassed for spilling his guts to her. Granted, his somber mood hadn't exactly invited any further conversation, but he was fairly certain that he'd probably frightened the shit out of her, rendering her silent.

Why the hell did I tell her? I found peace from nightmares, and I had my control back, dammit. I have for years.

Rolling over in bed, he pounded the pillow, trying to alleviate his jumbled thoughts so he could sleep again. Regardless of how he'd blurted out his dark past to Mara, he still planned on helping her, whether she wanted his help now or not. She was likely afraid of him now—what woman wouldn't be if he'd blurted out that he was a killer?

It won't keep me from helping her out, even if I have to do it anonymously now somehow because I opened my big mouth and told her the truth.

Flopping onto his back again, he scowled into the dark as thunder rolled outside, the wind starting to kick up as the rain began to fall. Jared could hear the fat droplets as they plopped against the glass of his bedroom windows.

I wonder if her roof is leaking. I wonder if she's okay.

He found himself actually counting the days until he could get Mara out of that house, a death trap disguised as a neglected home. Unfortunately, they hadn't been able to discuss their business any further because he'd been uncomfortable talking about anything after his confession, but he planned on tracking her down early in the morning. He'd stalk her if he had to until she agreed to his terms. Her ability to make a living depended on it.

"Fuck," he cursed in a harsh whisper as his house vibrated with the next roll of thunder, the lightning momentarily illuminating his massive bedroom. The storm just kept getting worse, the rain pounding against the windows as the howling wind made the droplets come down at an angle. "She's probably drowning in that damn old house."

Jared sat up in bed again, frustrated. He wasn't going to fall back asleep anytime soon. Leaning over, he clicked on the bedside lamp, got out of bed completely nude, and wandered over to the window. The only thing he could see was the beacon of the lighthouse in town, situated at the end of the Amesport Pier. Amazingly, the coastal town actually had a functioning lighthouse. In an era of GPS, radar, and other technology, so many lighthouses didn't function anymore. Hoping like hell there were actually no boats out in this ferocious storm, he focused his gaze toward the approximate area where he knew Mara's house was located.

Nothing but darkness.

It was well after midnight, and most people in town were sleeping. Even if they weren't, it was unlikely he could actually see lights that were any dimmer than the blazing glow from the lighthouse from this far away. Although he'd built his home on the side of the Peninsula closest to Amesport, and his bedroom window faced town and the Atlantic, downtown Amesport was still a few miles away.

Turning away from the window even more aggravated, Jared searched for his pants on the floor and rifled through the pockets until he found his cell phone. He crawled back into his bed, gripping the phone hard in his fist, willing himself not to call her.

She's sleeping. You aren't going to call her now.

But what if she wasn't? What if the house was leaking so badly that she *wasn't* asleep? What if she needed help and nobody was there to help her?

In the end, Jared dialed her number, contact information she'd given him back when he'd been researching his family history. Come to think of it, he really needed to talk to her about handing out her number so easily to anybody who might need information. But right at the moment, he hoped like hell that it *was* her home phone as well as her business.

"Hello?"

Mara's sleepy, husky voice made Jared's dick stand at attention immediately. Erotic visions filled his mind. They all included Mara in his bed with him, in various positions, and always coming hard.

He clasped the phone, knowing his greatest pleasure in having Mara here in his bed would be that he would know that she was safe, away from a home with a leaking roof and other possible safety hazards.

"It's me." Stupid response, but it was about all he could get out of his mouth when he was imagining her in his bed, naked and having multiple orgasms.

"Hello, *you*."

Jared listened intently, able to tell by her breathlessness that she was sitting up in bed, becoming more aware of her surroundings. "Is your roof leaking?" he asked abruptly, feeling like an idiot now because he'd given in to the urge to call. She'd obviously been sleeping comfortably. The last thing she needed was a middle-of-the-night call from a near-stalker acquaintance who'd just admitted to killing two people earlier that day.

"It's leaking pretty badly. I'm glad you called. I need to change out the buckets."

His heart was pounding as loud as the rain against his house, relief washing over him as he realized he hadn't scared her away because he'd opened his big mouth earlier. She didn't sound the least bit frightened of him.

I'm glad you called. I'm glad you called. Jared didn't much care *why* she was okay with him calling her, it only matter that she didn't mind.

She needed to change the buckets—as in more than one container? Jared wondered what the hell time she'd gone to bed. How could the leaks possibly fill a damn canister or pot that quickly? "You need to get out of that house," he growled, feeling even more protective of her because she wasn't uneasy with him. Obviously, the woman didn't have the smallest bit of instinct for self-preservation.

"I know," she agreed forlornly. "But I only have a little while longer to live here, and it's been my home since the day I was born. And I have no place else to go yet."

You can be with me. I want you to be with me.

Jared closed his eyes, almost able to feel her pain. His childhood home had been a prison, and he'd been counting the days until he could escape and go away to college. Mara's situation was completely different. She had loved her mother, and leaving her home had to be difficult. He didn't completely understand her sorrow, but he could reason it out. And for some fucked-up reason, he could *feel her*, even though he never let any of *his* emotions touch him anymore. "It will all work out okay. We didn't get to discuss business today, but I have a guest house that you can take over, and you can use the house to start production of your products. Hire whatever help you need. Get whatever equipment you want."

"You want me to live with you? Start my business there?"

Hell, yes.

"You wouldn't be exactly living with me. The guest house is separate from my residence. We can find the right property eventually, get you a shop. But it would take some time. You don't have time." She needed to leave that dilapidated house as fast as possible.

"I'm going to have to show you that I can turn a profit first, before you pour your money into a shop," she replied agreeably. "I understand that."

Jared opened his eyes and shook his head, even though she couldn't see him. "It isn't that. It will take time to find the right place, the right location. Since you don't have the luxury of time, we can use my place for now."

"But you aren't always here in Amesport—"

"I'll be here for a while," he cut her off abruptly. Leaving wasn't an option right now. He had Dante's wedding coming up, and he had no desire to leave Mara in the middle of her business setup. He hesitated before asking gravely, "Why haven't you asked me about what I said earlier?" She hadn't asked him a single question. Even now, when she could easily grill him from a safe distance on the phone, she hadn't mentioned his history or the secrets he'd revealed. Obviously, he could avoid the subject, pretend like he'd never mentioned it. She was going to allow it. But he needed to know.

Mara sighed. "Jared, what happened in your past isn't my business. I'm sorry for your pain, and I don't want to push you to talk about anything that causes you more hurt. You don't owe me an explanation."

He scowled. "I killed two people. That doesn't concern you just a little?"

"No. Whatever happened, I know you didn't murder them."

"How in the hell do you know what happened?"

"I don't know what happened, but if you ever want to talk about it, I'll listen," she answered gently.

Jared felt like she'd gutted him. "You trust me?" The certainty in her voice when she'd said she knew he hadn't murdered anybody made his heart clench and pissed him off at the same time. What in the hell was she thinking? He could be a serial killer, for all she knew. Still, knowing that she trusted him enough not to need any explanation of his earlier confession completely blew him away.

"Yes. I trust you," she answered simply.

"Why?" he asked hoarsely.

"I trust my instincts."

"I'm a jackass." He heard it from his siblings almost on a daily basis.

"Agreed. Sometimes I think you act that way to hide your pain. But that isn't all that you are, Jared. You're so much more," she said hesitantly.

"If you're trying to look deeper into my soul or something, forget it. There isn't much there. The asshole is pretty much all you'll get."

Of all the reactions Jared could have gotten from his comment, the last thing he expected Mara to do was . . . laugh.

But she did.

Continually.

She howled with amusement for a long time, and it really annoyed him that even though she was laughing at him, he loved the sound of her laughter.

"Murderers aren't usually into self-deprecation," she said, still half chuckling.

"They could be," he grumbled into the phone.

She snorted. "Are you *trying* to make me afraid of you?"

Yes.

No.

Maybe.

"No," he finally decided. "I just want you to know what you're getting yourself into. I *am* an asshole, and I'm not about to start looking into my goddamn soul." Jared shuddered at the thought. It was empty, just like the rest of him. There was no point in even looking.

"I think I can handle it," she answered a little more soberly. "I can work for a surly boss. And I still don't think you're a jerk all the time. I think you're protecting yourself."

Jared was uneasy with her observations, so he tried to ignore them. "I don't want to be your boss anywhere except in the bedroom." Looking down at his raging erection, Jared had to admit that he wanted her under his control just about anywhere: outside, up against a wall, on the floor, in the shower . . . the list could go on and on. However, it had nothing to do with her business. *That* he had no doubt she could handle on her own. She'd been holding up a struggling shop for years. Working on a business that could actually thrive should be a piece of cake for her.

"Jared, I can't—" Her voice cut off in a horrified gasp.

"What happened?" His heart thundering, Jared catapulted out of bed.

"Smoke. A lot of smoke. Oh God, the house must be on fire." Mara sounded panicked and anxious. "I have to call 911."

To Jared's complete horror, Mara hung up the phone.

"Shit. Mara? Mara? Dammit, talk to me." Racing to the window, he could actually see the fire burning in the distance, a faint glow in the dark sky. He disconnected the phone and tried to call her back again.

No answer. Was she on the phone with the fire department, or was she not answering for far different and more dire reasons?

"Fuck. No." He pulled out a pair of jeans and a T-shirt from his drawer and had them on in less than a minute. Shoving his phone in his pocket, he sprinted through the hallway and down the stairs, taking them two at a time.

It's raining. The flames will get put out quickly. She'll be okay. She'll be okay.

After cramming his bare feet into a pair of leather shoes, he stepped outside and realized the rain had all but subsided. His heart plummeted to the ground and sped up in total and utter terror.

Get the hell out of the house, Mara. Please. Get the hell out.

Hopping into his SUV, he drove like a madman toward Amesport. He tried to call her again and again as he raced toward her house, hoping like he'd never hoped for anything before that he wouldn't get there too late.

After notifying the emergency operator that there was smoke in her bedroom, and that it was possible that her house was on fire, Mara hesitated, her mind still trying to process what was happening. She snatched her mother's wedding ring from her jewelry box and grabbed the folder from her underwear drawer that contained critical papers like her birth certificate and some pictures, just in case. She had just turned to escape her upstairs bedroom and try to figure out where exactly the fire was located on her way outside when all hell broke loose.

The smoke was already heavy, but she'd been certain she'd have time to flee. She hadn't actually seen flames, but she saw them now as timbers came crashing down with a deafening roar, preventing her from exiting the house as what was apparently a portion of the roof collapsed, leaving the doorway to her bedroom blocked.

Trapped! Holy hell. This isn't a small fire or smoking old wiring like I thought it was.

The gravity of the situation hit her like a rockslide, making her move automatically into survivor mode. Dropping to her knees where the smoke wasn't as heavy, she crawled toward the door, her heart hammering in her chest as she felt the heat of the flames. Examining her options and trying not to hyperventilate, she realized there was no way out except straight through the fire. Her desperate, smoke-irritated eyes scanned the doorway frantically, finding her only escape route right in the middle of the door frame, a hole large enough for her body to get through. However, she had no idea what was happening on the other side of the door. How much of the roof had come down? Was she going to jump directly into more flames? Would she actually be leaping into her own death?

Don't panic. The fire department is coming.

Unfortunately, from the way the flames were now voraciously consuming the house, she knew she didn't have time to wait for them. Her life clock was ticking, and she could feel it with every frenzied beat of her heart. Mara clambered on her hands and knees to the bed and ripped off the comforter, standing when it was finally off the bed. There was no water source for her to use to dampen the heavy material. The house was old, and it didn't have a bathroom connected to the master bedroom.

She already knew the window was a no-go. She was too high up. If the fall didn't kill her, she'd certainly have some broken bones and other injuries. There was absolutely nothing to cling to on the side of the house. It would be a direct drop.

I have to get out of here. I have to get out of here.

She'd made a critical error in not fleeing immediately, but since she hadn't seen flames, she'd thought the fire or smoke was contained to one area upstairs. Apparently . . . it wasn't. Maybe those extra moments that she'd used to alert the emergency operator would have saved her. Or possibly not, and the roof would have come down on top of her as she made her escape. Her mind was murky from shock, and her entire body shook as she considered her options, her horrified stare fixed on her only means of escape as she dropped the folder she had paused to retrieve and shoved her mother's wedding ring into the small pocket of her pj's.

Doesn't matter now. Just get the hell out or you won't be alive to need any of it.

With the roof partially collapsed, Mara knew anything could happen in a heartbeat now. The rest of the ceiling could topple, cutting off *any* means of escape or killing her painfully.

Do it. Just do it. You have to take the risk or die.

Using the comforter as protection, she wrapped it around her body and covered most of her head before taking a leap of faith into the fire at the bedroom door, hoping that she'd be safe on the other side.

CHAPTER 7

If there was one thing Evan Sinclair detested, it was incompetence.

As he walked down the dark streets of Amesport, he cursed the lack of ability of the transport company that was supposed to have had his vehicle at the Amesport airport. He'd arrived on schedule in his private jet only to find that his vehicle hadn't yet been delivered to his location. Dammit, he didn't have time for the ineptitude of other companies. He ran his own business like a well-oiled machine, and he expected the same of every other company.

Damn his younger brother Dante and his unusual urgency to enter the state of wedded bliss within a few weeks' time. Evan really couldn't understand Dante's enthusiasm to have *that* event happen so quickly. He was already living with the woman, why did he have to marry her so hastily? *That* was the real reason that Evan didn't have his car, and his ever-present driver, Stokes, who never separated himself from the vehicle. Evan's own transport jet had been tied up doing a favor for a very important business client, unavailable because Evan hadn't known he would need it. He'd promised it months ago, and had scheduled accordingly. He didn't like schedule changes, and he never broke a promise once he agreed to something. So, he'd been forced to use a damn transport company that obviously couldn't deliver, even though they were the most expensive and supposedly the best company in the business.

"Amateurs," he growled angrily to himself.

It wasn't that he hadn't known that Dante would end up married to Sarah . . . eventually. After all, he made it his business to know exactly what was happening with his siblings . . . or rather, he should say all his *brothers*. He'd screwed up with his sister, Hope, finding out about her adventures way too late to prevent her from suffering the consequences of her rash actions.

My fault. I should have known better than to assume that Hope was living a quiet life in Aspen. Women were trouble, every single one of them, including his sister. Evan knew that he was the only Sinclair aware of all that she'd been through in the past, and it wasn't because she'd told him. No. She'd hid everything from her own brothers. The only reason he knew *now* was because he'd gotten a call from Grady that she'd gone missing in Colorado. He'd gotten an investigator involved, even after she'd been found by her now husband, Jason Sutherland, and the agent had subsequently uncovered the fact that Hope had been leading a completely different life than the illusions she'd maintained to all of her brothers. Presumably, her husband knew the real Hope and the trauma she'd suffered, but it didn't stop Evan from regretting that *he* hadn't checked up on her often enough to find out the truth sooner. She'd suffered, and Evan hated that.

Hope was a very important missed detail, even more critical than business for me.

He tried not to think about the horror of Hope's life, attempted to put it out of his mind since she was happy *now*. And she'd stay that way. He'd make sure of it.

The walk from the airport into town had calmed his temper somewhat, but he was still irritated by the time wasted for him to walk to his Amesport Peninsula home from the airport outside of town. Yes, he could have called Grady, Dante, or Jared, but it was late, and he was the eldest Sinclair. He wasn't about to make one of his siblings get out of bed to come pick him up. He'd never hear the end of it from his brothers if they had to come give him a ride in the middle of the night because his car hadn't arrived at the airport before he did. Such things just didn't happen to him.

Evan, the oldest and very anal Sinclair sibling.

Evan, the manager-of-every-single-detail brother.

Evan, the meticulous planner who never missed having anything prearranged, no matter how big or how small, had actually been stranded at the airport without a car?

Oh, hell no. He'd walk until he got to his home, even if it did mean a several-mile hike in the middle of the night and the possible destruction of one of his favorite custom-made suits and fine leather shoes. The rain that had been coming down off and on left him damp, pissed off, and ready to strangle the delivery team the second they arrived with his car. He couldn't blame Stokes. The elderly driver had never left the vehicle, and he couldn't control the inability of a company to deliver. Stokes was where he needed to be. The delivery service was not.

"I should have never trusted another company to deliver," he grumbled to himself, his hands in the pockets of his pants, shaking his head irritably as he trekked along the deserted Amesport boardwalk. He might not want to call his brothers, but he'd had no problem waking up his assistant to verify that everything had been confirmed. Of course . . . it had. His assistant knew if he failed at one single task, his job would be history. It had been the transport company's error. Evan would deal with them first thing in the morning, and he'd destroy the bastards who had left him out here walking in the fucking rain. If the CEO of the company couldn't get a simple delivery to the place it needed to be on time, his company didn't deserve to be in business anymore. It had been a very expensive botched job, and Evan Sinclair could make or break a company easily. When a company couldn't perform, he had no problem doing the latter.

Evan was just about to leave the boardwalk and turn onto the street leading to the Amesport Peninsula when he saw a burst of fire explode from one of the homes at the end of Main Street.

Was it a business or a home?

Evan had only been to Amesport a couple of times, but as far as he could remember—and he recalled nearly everything in detail—Main Street was all businesses.

Jogging across the street, he stopped in front of the old home, which had obviously been converted into a shop. He looked at the window and then looked up at the flames that seemed to be consuming the roof of the building.

Dolls and Things?

It was definitely a store, and it was highly unlikely that anyone was inside at this hour of the night. Digging into the pocket of his suit jacket, he pulled out his phone to report the fire just as he heard the wail of fire engines.

"It's already been reported then," he muttered to himself, ready to turn and get on his way to the Peninsula. There was nothing more he could do. The fire department was obviously alerted and on their way.

It wasn't until he turned that he heard a scream, a terrified wail of terror that sent chills down his spine. Turning back, realizing there actually *was* someone inside the building, he pushed his considerable bulk against the door.

Mara flung the burning blanket from her with a loud shriek of horror.

I'm alive, but the comforter is on fire. Everything is on fire. I need to get out.

Brushing frantic hands over her clothing from her position on the hardwood floor outside her bedroom, she quickly verified that none of the items on her body—her pajamas and underwear—were in flames.

Stumbling to her feet, she tried to get her bearings in the thick, blinding, gray smoke. Coughing harshly, she felt for the bannister of the staircase just as she discovered she couldn't put weight on her right leg. Mara crumpled to the floor again, whimpering at the pain in her ankle as she scooted toward her right and down the hallway, her hand out, searching frantically for the stairs.

The steps should be . . . right . . . here!

Her fingers connected and felt the edge of the first step just before she was bodily lifted into the arms of a very tall, very strong, and very male figure she couldn't recognize through the darkened haze of fog caused by the fire.

"Generally when one's house is on fire, one feels compelled to leave it," a low, arrogant voice commented, as though he were addressing a person of questionable intelligence.

Mara trembled with shock as she let herself be carried down the steep flight of stairs to the main floor. The mystery man wasted no time getting her outside and didn't lower her to the ground until he reached the tiny patch of grass in front of Shamrock's Pub across the street.

"I was trying to get out," she finally responded, her voice raspy from inhaling the smoke. She breathed rapidly, sucking the clean air in and out of her lungs frantically. Looking up at her rescuer from her position on her ass, she still didn't recognize him. It was dark, and all she could make out was black hair and mammoth proportions. Squinting through her dirty glasses as she panted for breath, she could see he was actually wearing . . . a suit and tie. What the hell?

He knelt next to her and took her by the shoulders. "Obviously you weren't trying very quickly or successfully," he commented nonchalantly. "A fire usually requires a little faster response."

Mara gaped as he came down beside her. She could see him now; the dim glow from the fire and the lights left on inside of Shamrock's at night illuminated his face as he positioned himself beside her. His raven-dark hair was damp and slicked back from his face, and his startling blue eyes were roving meticulously over her body clinically, as though he was trying to assess whether or not she was injured.

"W-who are you?" She'd never seen him before, and if she had, she would have definitely remembered *him*.

"Evan Sinclair," he snapped. "Are you hurt?"

"Evan? Jared's brother?" As he scowled at her and shook her lightly, she answered his question. "My ankle. I couldn't walk. I was trying to find the stairs so I could crawl down."

She flinched as her home starting crackling, and a deafening crash sounded as the roof fell completely into the first story of the house. Fire trucks pulled up just as the upper level fell, and firemen, police officers, and an ambulance screeched up to the house, swarming the residence immediately.

Evan's sharp eyes glanced at her feet, and he moved to palpate her ankles. "The right one is swollen. I'll let the medics check you out. I'm not particularly versed in emergency medicine," he said, as though it annoyed him that there was *anything* he didn't know.

"Mara!" an agonized male voice rang out from the front of her house.

"Jared," she said roughly, her throat still raw from inhaling smoke.

"Ah, yes," Evan acknowledged as he stood. "I'd recognize the bellow of my younger brother anywhere. You two are acquainted, I take it."

"Friends," she answered shakily. "He's worried."

"Surprisingly, I think you're absolutely correct. He does sound somewhat desperate," Evan replied calmly as he strolled across the street to direct one of the medics to her. As he moved toward the house, his large figure disappeared in a cloud of smoke.

Mara shook her head at Evan's retreating figure until he vanished. Sweet Jesus . . . and she had thought *Jared* was cold and arrogant. Evan Sinclair made Jared look like a warmhearted angel. She mused that Evan was also probably one of the few men who could make the other Sinclair brothers look simply . . . large. The eldest Sinclair was built like a Mack truck covered in an expensive suit, and he hadn't appeared to have one ounce of fat on his body. He was just . . . mammoth, his expansive shoulders appearing as broad as Atlas, the primordial Titan who could carry the celestial spheres.

Evan Sinclair had just broken into her residence, carried her out of a burning house where both of them could easily have perished when the roof gave way if he'd entered just a few moments later. *All without batting an eye.* Mara hadn't seen one single emotion reflected on Evan's face, his haughty demeanor staying fixed in place.

Mara's entire body was shivering with horror as one of the EMTs ran over to check her out. She answered his questions shakily, watching with despair as her childhood home went up in flames. Tears streamed down her face as she watched every meager belonging she had destroyed. Firefighters were working furiously to put out the flames, and concerned residents slowly started to crowd the street, most of them with businesses close by.

"Mara! Thank fuck!" Jared exclaimed as he dropped down beside her on the grass, his chest heaving.

"Your brother saved my life," she told him tearfully, her mind starting to finally process what had happened.

"He told me," Jared grumbled, wrapping her body in a blanket that must have come from his vehicle.

"Everything's gone," she sobbed frantically, covering her face with her hands to keep from watching the rest of the house destroyed.

"You're alive. That's all that matters right now, Mara," Jared rasped, gathering her into his arms and cradling her head against his shoulder.

She let Jared hold her, fisting his shirt to reassure herself that he was here, and that she actually *was* still alive. He was her anchor right now in this surreal, heart-wrenching nightmare.

Turning her face into his chest, she finally gave in to her sorrow completely and wept.

Hours later, Mara lay in the bed of one of Jared's many guest rooms, unable to sleep. Fatigue was overwhelming her, but every time she closed her eyes, all she could see was everything she owned, every memory she had of her entire life going up in flames.

In the end, she'd left the house with nothing except her mother's ring in her pocket.

Emptiness threatened to swallow her whole, and she shivered underneath the blankets even though the bedroom was warm.

"It's as though I don't exist anymore," she whispered in the darkness. Daylight had come hours ago, but Jared had pulled the heavy drapes closed so she could sleep.

Jared.

He'd never left her side after he'd found her, waiting in the emergency room while they X-rayed her ankle and took blood to make sure she hadn't gotten too much carbon monoxide from the fire. He'd sat beside her patiently, never leaving until he could take her from the hospital, bringing her home with him as though there was no question of where she was going. Physically, she was fine other than her sprained ankle, and the swelling was subsiding already, making the pain bearable. Even so, Jared had tended to her like she was fragile, finding her an old T-shirt to wear to bed after she'd showered, insisting that she sleep.

The fire was contained, no damage done to any other shops except hers. God, she was grateful that nobody else had lost anything, but even that knowledge didn't lessen her pain.

"I have nothing now," she whispered huskily, curling on her side in the bed. If she'd had very little before, the total of her belongings since everything had gone up in flames was zip . . . zero . . . zilch. Even the pajamas she'd been wearing had needed to be trashed.

"You have your life," a husky male voice said from behind her. "You're supposed to be sleeping."

"I can't," she said tremulously.

The bed dipped heavily as Jared moved onto it behind her and wrapped his arms around her waist. "Not one damn thing in that house mattered except you." He breathed a masculine sigh of contentment as he held her. "I couldn't sleep, either. All I could think about was how close you came to dying in that damn house."

Mara shook her head, but let Jared's embrace warm her. "My mom's stuff, my pictures—all gone. I don't even have my driver's license or an ID." The warmth of his strong, muscular body soothed her, and she let herself relax back against him. She could tell he was fully clothed, feeling the denim of his jeans against her legs and his T-shirt against her neck. "I don't even understand how this happened."

"I know what happened," Jared growled into her ear. "The fire investigators will look the place over, but I'm fairly certain they'll find out the wiring in the place sucked and that it was run up in the attic. The water from the leaking roof probably sparked the shitty wiring. That house should have been renovated years ago. Homes that old can become a goddamn hazard if they aren't updated right."

"I suppose that's possible." Mara sighed.

"Probable," Jared corrected.

"I feel . . . lost," she admitted, hating her own weakness at the moment. She was going to have to move on eventually, but for now, she was still mourning. "Empty," she added woefully.

Jared ran a soothing hand over her stomach. "Shhh . . . I'll help you. I swear I will. Whatever you need to come alive again, I'll get it for you."

I need you.

His soothing, masculine voice was pulling her out of her haze of loneliness, the touch of his hands on her body making her feel again. Leaning her head back on his shoulder, she asked in a hushed voice, "Will you make love to me?" She needed *him*, wanted *him* to make her come alive again. The adrenaline was still pumping through her body, and she needed . . . something . . . anything to make it stop.

Not just anything. I need Jared.

He groaned into her ear. "Not this way. Fuck knows I want you so bad I can't think, but I can't do it this way."

"Why?" she whimpered painfully, her core clenching as his palm moved slowly, gently over her belly.

"You've been through hell and back in the last eight hours. I might be an asshole, but I can't take advantage of the fact that you're in shock, you nearly died, and you think you've lost everything right now," he rumbled, his deep voice vibrating against her back.

"I *have* lost everything," she murmured.

"No you haven't. You still have me," he answered in a graveled voice.

"Then show me. I need something to hang on to." She moved her hips backward, rubbing her ass against his hard erection, proof that he wanted her as much as she wanted him right now.

"Mara." His voice was a low, ominous warning.

"Please, Jared." Her voice was needy, entreating. His clean, masculine scent surrounded her, and all she could think about was getting the hard length of him that was pushing against her ass inside her, filling her until she could think of nothing else but him. That's exactly how it would be with Jared. He'd dominate her senses, push everything else out of her brain until she didn't have to think anymore.

"Fuck," he exploded.

Mara moaned with satisfaction as he easily flipped her onto her back and covered her with his hard, muscular body. "Yes," she begged.

"Your ankle," he growled.

"It's fine," she argued. "Please." The twinge of pain in her ankle was nothing compared to the overwhelming longing that was clawing at her mercilessly.

He answered her plea by pinning her hands over her head and covering her mouth with a tortured, agitated groan.

CHAPTER 8

Yes. Yes. Yes.

Jared was doing exactly what Mara wanted: eliminating her ability to think of anything else but him. He assaulted her senses with his all-consuming kiss, taking what he wanted, but giving her what she needed in return.

His full-on invasion of her mouth had her moaning beneath him, tilting her head to give him better access as his tongue pushed past her lips and surged deeply, claiming her completely without a word spoken.

Every nerve in her body vibrated with tension as his hips rolled, and his hard cock rubbed against her saturated core. She jerked at her wrists, needing to touch him. Turning her head violently, she broke the embrace that was slowly incinerating her. "Please, Jared," she panted frantically. "I need to touch you."

"If you touch me, I'll lose control," he grunted harshly against her ear.

"I don't care."

"I care, dammit. I care." Jared loosened his grip on her wrists and rested his forehead against her shoulder.

The note of desperation in his voice nearly made Mara come unraveled. He sounded . . . defeated. Realizing his big body was shuddering above her, she slid her hands free and into his coarse hair in a soothing caress. "It can just be this once, Jared. I'm not expecting forever, or even tomorrow right now. I just want you now."

The last thing she wanted was for him to feel like he was hurting her. In reality, he'd be doing her a favor, giving her temporary respite from the negative visions and emotions flowing through her mind.

"You think that will be enough?" Jared ground out coarsely, close to her ear.

"It will have to be. I don't care about the future. I just want to get through today."

Mara moaned in protest as Jared lifted his body away from hers. "Please don't leave me right now," she begged shamelessly, needing the presence of another human right at the moment.

"I'm not going anywhere."

She heard the rustling of clothing, and it was so quiet in the room that she heard the zipper of his jeans come down, followed by more whispery sounds of clothing being discarded.

"Dark or light?" he questioned softly.

"What?" she asked hesitantly.

"Do you want the curtains open or closed?"

He was naked. She knew it as surely as she knew that he wasn't going to leave her right now despite her fears. For just a moment, she wished for her glasses, which had been badly damaged during her escape from the fire. Mara ached to see Jared as clearly as possible. But her vision wasn't bad without them. She wore them mainly because she did intricate work and she had a slight astigmatism in one eye. Her vision sharpened up to perfect with glasses. Right at the moment, she longed for the clearest eyesight possible, but she'd deal with what she had.

"Light." She wanted to see him so urgently that she didn't care if he saw her less than perfectly toned body.

Wincing as he opened one of the drapes and the room flooded with sunlight, Mara finally got her eyes full of Jared Sinclair. Blinking fast as her pupils adjusted to the brightness, she stared unabashed as he walked back to the bed without a stitch of clothing on. She sat up, her mouth now as dry as a desert, her gaze lovingly adoring his sculpted, masculine body. His biceps and abs were ripped with solid muscle, and it was obvious he worked out on a regular basis. His powerfully built chest had a light dusting of auburn hair, exactly the same color that highlighted the locks on his head. As her eyes moved downward, she licked her parched lips as she saw a narrow happy trail of the same hue snaking down the lower part of a rippling six-pack that had her itching to trace over it. Finally, her curious stare landed on his groin, and her core clenched as she tried to find the right words for his engorged cock.

"Huge," she choked out, stunned. She'd only seen one other naked man in her life, and he hadn't been built anywhere near Jared's size. Anywhere.

"Are you done looking?" Jared asked huskily.

"No," she answered honestly. Really, she could stare at him forever and never get tired of gawking at his sinfully delicious body. Her glance eventually landed on his face, and she melted when his eyes flared with heat.

Leaning down, he grasped the hem of his own T-shirt that she was currently wearing and tugged it upward. "If I have to get naked, so do you."

"I don't look nearly as hot as you do," she told him reluctantly, but she lifted her arms so he could strip away her only item of clothing. She sat in the middle of the bed silently as Jared's expression grew hungry and heated, his eyes caressing her breasts like he wanted to devour them.

"Sweetheart, you look like a damn wet dream to me right now." A muscle in his jaw twitched as his long, surveying stare roamed over her possessively. Tearing his gaze away, his eyes met hers, his deep green irises turbulent as he held out his hand. "Here. You'll need this."

Mara took the condom from his grasp, watching him move with the grace of a predator as he crawled into the bed. She waited as her breath hitched with anticipation, but he surprised her by lying on his back beside her, kicking the covers to the foot of the bed, and locking his hands behind his head. "If you want it, take what you want."

Holy hotness, he looked like a gorgeous male sacrifice laid out for her pleasure, and she was itching to lick every inch of his solid, hard body with her tongue. But at the last minute, she balked.

Something was wrong. She doubted Jared Sinclair ever gave up control, and his behavior was just . . . wrong.

If you want it?

His desire was evident, but he looked almost angry . . . and slightly . . . injured? After his display of alpha male take-no-prisoners passion a few moments ago, something about his actions now was off.

If you want it.

Recognition of what he was thinking hit her like a bolt of lightning. "You think I'm using you." He might be more than willing, but he wasn't liking the fact that he thought that she would take a man—any man—right now to distract her.

If she had blinked, Mara would have missed the validation of her suspicions shadowing his expression for an instant. And then it was gone, replaced by a stoic look. I wasn't like she didn't know that Jared had insecurities buried deep inside that drool-worthy chest of his, but her selfishness hit her like a brick to her head. People always wanted something from him, used him. She'd acted no better than any other woman in his life by trying to rationalize what she was doing by saying she needed the distraction. She did . . . but only Jared could give that to her. She needed . . . him. Somehow, she needed to make him understand.

He shrugged. "It's not like I'm not willing. More than willing, actually."

Jared Sinclair was doing something Mara suspected he rarely did, because he knew she was vulnerable. He was letting her take control, letting her use him to escape from her own pain.

I don't want just anybody. I need him. Jared. I wouldn't be reacting this way with anybody else.

Dropping the condom she was holding on the pillow beside his head, she straddled him, biting her lip to hold back a moan as her saturated pussy connected with his sinewy, hard abs. She was no seductress, but his split second of insecurity made her bold. "I don't want *it*, Jared. I want *you.*" Spearing her hands through his hair, she leaned down, her pebbled nipples chafed by the light sprinkling of hair on his chest. "Only you. I wouldn't have asked for this with any other man." She pressed open-mouthed kisses against his neck and along his strong jaw. Grinding her hips against his stomach, she let him feel her wet heat slide along the hard strength of his groin.

"Jesus, Mara," he rasped. "You're so fucking wet. There's only so much control I can manage right now."

"No control," she insisted, inflamed by his response. "I need you right now, Jared. You."

Jared's arms wrapped around her as though he had finally snapped, his hands stroking greedily down her back and to her ass. "You're so soft. So damn sweet."

Mara knew she was too soft. She carried more weight than she should, and her ass was entirely too big. But the way that Jared was squeezing, worshiping her body, made her feel like a goddess.

Unable to stop herself from wanting to be more connected to him, she met his tortured gaze briefly before lowering her mouth to his. Mara savored the taste of him, and his delectable masculine scent as he responded, taking control of the passionate clash of tongues and teeth as they devoured each other. Her breath was coming unevenly between her lips as she finally lifted her head.

His fingers reached between their bodies from behind, meeting her wet heat with a low groan. "Have you had a man my size before, Mara?"

No. But she wanted to. She needed him so damn desperately that she was ready to start begging again. "No," she admitted breathlessly.

"Not like this then." He grasped her around the waist and flipped their position slowly, careful not to twist her injured ankle. "I don't want to hurt you."

Mara's heart clenched as she wrapped her legs around his waist, her ankle twinging in protest, but she ignored it. "I already hurt. I ache, Jared." All she wanted was to feel their bodies joined, that gorgeous cock of his filling her until she no longer felt empty.

"You won't," he promised, his voice graveled with desire as he pushed his body up to kneel between her legs, causing her feet to drop to the bed, her thighs spread wide to accommodate him. "You won't feel anything but me." Running his palms up her torso, he cupped her breasts and lowered his head to one of her hardened, sensitive nipples.

"Yes," she hissed, her hands fisting in his hair to keep him there. "Please."

His mouth nipped and sucked, tortured and soothed until Mara was lifting her hips, pleading for his cock to fill her. Without letting up on her breasts, one of his hands slid down her body and between her thighs, stroking through the folds of her pussy. She quivered as his fingers brushed her engorged clit, setting off a chain reaction of pulsation that stimulated every nerve ending in her entire body. Slowly, he stroked his way inside her channel with two of his fingers. "Christ, you're so tight," he growled against her breast, his fingers curling and finding a sensitive area inside her that she didn't know existed.

"Fuck me, Jared," she whimpered, lifting her hips, her need for him so intense that she nearly sobbed.

Leaning up on his knees, he pumped his fingers inside her, rolling his thumb firmly over her clit. "I need to watch you come for me."

Mara's eyes met his, the feral expression on his face arousing an answering wildness inside her. She tried to hold his gaze as her fingers clutched at the bottom sheet on the bed, desperate to hold on to something before she was hurled into space. As he stroked inside her harder, deeper, the expression on his face becoming even more intense and focused on her pleasure, she closed her eyes, and her back ached as wild pulsations flowed over her body. Her sheath clenched around his fingers as she climaxed, the volatile orgasm squeezing his fingers tightly.

Thrashing her head from the unfamiliar pressure and release sensations pounding at her body, she moaned, "Oh, God. Jared."

As her body relaxed and she started spiraling downward, she watched as Jared ripped the package of the condom with his teeth, rolled it on, and came down over her. "Watching you come is the hottest damn thing I've ever seen," he told her huskily as he eased his large shaft inside her. "I can't wait to feel you tighten like that around my cock," he told her desperately, his lips against hers.

"Don't try to be gentle. I need you too much," she mumbled against his mouth right before he kissed her. Jared's cock might be a little larger than the average size, but it was hers for this stolen moment in time, and she wanted to feel it, own it.

As his mouth ravaged hers, Mara wrapped her legs around his waist and surged her hips upward, wanting him to take her completely. Feeling his entire body shudder as she palmed his rock-hard ass and tried to pull him deeper, Mara felt him finally give himself up to the red-hot passion that was beating at both of them, unrelentingly demanding to be sated.

Gasping as he seated himself completely inside her, she felt the walls of her channel give way to him slowly, and clench tightly around him. The momentary pain of being stretched was nothing compared to the feeling of having him fill her. "Yes," she encouraged, wrapping her arms around him tightly, their bodies sliding together, both of them coated with a fine sheen of perspiration.

"You feel so damn good. Better than my wildest fantasies," Jared admitted harshly, pulling back and thrusting again to bury his cock inside her. "Can't. Hold. Back," he grunted.

"Then don't," she whimpered, thrusting her hips up.

Jared reached beneath them and grasped her ass as he started a ruthless, merciless pace of strokes with his cock, bringing her pelvis up to meet every entry after he retreated, pumping into her furiously. "Mara," he groaned. "Come for me, sweetheart."

Seconds later she imploded, screaming his name. "Jared!" She dug her short nails into his back, trying to find purchase as she spiraled out of control.

Jared entered her one last time with a tortured groan, letting her milk him as he found his own release.

Trying to catch her breath, Mara protested as Jared started to lift his body from hers. "Stay," she said softly, breathlessly. She wanted to feel his hard, masculine body surrounding her for a few more minutes, so she tightened her arms and legs around him. "You feel good." She wasn't ready to give up their exquisite connection.

Jared kissed her neck and the side of her face, making his way to her lips. He kissed her slowly, thoroughly, as though he was relishing the feel of them skin to skin. "Be right back," he said in a low, hushed tone.

He disentangled their bodies and went to dispose of the condom, pulling the heavy drape back into place before he slipped back into the bed. Lying on his side, he pulled her back against his front, spooning her protectively. "Sleep now," he insisted, burying his face in her hair. "We'll figure everything out when we wake up."

Her body sated, Mara realized how exhausted she was, and she had to stifle a yawn. "Thank you."

"For what?"

She sighed as she relaxed into his protective embrace and wriggled against him, luxuriating in the afterglow of being thoroughly pleasured. "For this."

He kissed her temple and chuckled. "It was my pleasure, baby. Literally."

Mara's eyes started to flutter closed, fatigue starting to take over. "Mine, too," she murmured quietly, his comforting hand stroking possessively over her hip, soothing her into sleep.

CHAPTER 9

The following few days went by in a blur for Mara. Several days after the fire, she was finally moving into Jared's guest house, which was in truth right next door to his mansion and might as well have been considered part of his gigantic residence. Except it didn't share a wall with the main home, and the separate dwelling had its own entrance. The so-called guest house was ridiculously large, a three-bedroom ranch that was fully furnished, including an excellent cook's kitchen with all the accessories she needed to make her products in much larger quantities than she ever had previously. Looking at the kitchen area, Mara was almost giddy with excitement.

She'd tried to get started on arrangements to get supplies, really wanting to make some jams and taffy for the next farmers' market on Saturday. Jared had nixed the idea with a fierce scowl when he looked at her ankle the evening after their passionate encounter. She'd woken up alone late that evening after the fire and limped downstairs, much to Jared's irritation. He'd picked her up and plopped her on the couch, warning her not to move until the swelling in her ankle came down. She was pretty sure he had been chastising himself for letting her be so physical in bed with him, thinking it had made her ankle worse.

Maybe it had . . . but Mara wasn't about to complain. She'd do it all over again if she could. Nothing would ever compare to such a tragic night turning into such a journey of discovery for her. Learning that her body could burn that hot had been an epiphany, and she'd never think sex was overrated again. In fact, it could probably be highly addictive. Having Jared close, as close as she could get to him, had taken away the devastating emptiness of that night for her. Honestly, it had taken away *all* of her loneliness.

Even though it was only for a short time, I'll never regret it.

Neither one of them had brought up the topic of their frenzied sexual activities that night. Jared appeared to be more determined to protect her than he was to fuck her ever since that incredible day. Obviously, there would be no repeat performance, and Mara wasn't sure if being together like that again would even be wise now that she had her head more together again. She was coming to like and understand Jared more and more the longer she spent time with him, learning new things about him every day. Getting too close to him, being with him again like she had that day, could prove disastrous. She could very easily become infatuated with him, and Jared wasn't the kind of man who wanted attachments.

Mara chuckled softly as she familiarized herself with her new temporary home, thinking about some of the more humorous things she'd learned about Jared in the last few days of staying with him in the big house. The guy was a complete and total sweets and coffee addict. He didn't function well without his coffee, and he ate sweets like they were an orgasmic experience. She'd laughed outrageously when she read the directions for his coffeemaker, quickly figuring out that Jared was yanking off the tops of the little containers of coffee rather than putting them into the device intact. The appliance made a perfect beverage; Jared had not. She'd snickered as he'd looked at her like she was a goddess because she could make a perfect cup of coffee. Since then, he'd mastered the simple task after he'd laughed at himself for the highly uncomplicated error. Of course, he'd grumbled when she'd teased him about everything being in the directions for the electronic device.

The taffy he'd gotten from her had been gone within the first day, and his supply of jam was dwindling since he seemed to pile it on his toast or bagel in the morning liberally. He usually preferred to watch movies or read in lieu of regular television shows, and he had a preference for classical music. He did indeed work out every single day, hitting his gym in the basement after he'd woken up with at least two cups of coffee and toast or a bagel slathered with her jam in the morning.

However, her most important discovery of all was that he cared about people, whether he wanted to show that side of himself to others or not. He'd coddled her for days, helping her fill out the forms to get her important documents replaced. One of the few things that *had* been recovered was her charred, soot-covered purse. It had been in the kitchen, and she'd been able to save her cards, checkbook, and her driver's license, so it left her fewer documents to replace. But with the fire investigation ongoing, and all of the things she had to do to prepare to take Kristin's place in Sarah's wedding, she was going to be busy.

She and Jared had scanned the Internet, looking at website designs, logos, equipment, and all of the other online details that needed to be discussed if the business was going primarily on the net.

Mara had wanted "Sinclair" to go into the business name. After all, Jared was financing it. He'd insisted that the business was hers, he couldn't cook worth a shit so the "Sinclair" would be a lousy endorsement, and he wanted to name it Mara's Kitchen. After an afternoon of furious debate, the Mara's Kitchen name had stuck, and he'd won, giving her a reasonable list of reasons why the name would be better and more focused toward their target customers—women. The business was going to be hers by name, and her efforts would either succeed or fail. Luckily, she had no intentions of failing.

It's going to bear my name. My reputation will be on the line.

It was frightening and exhilarating at the same time.

Now, three days after the fire, the swelling had gone down on her ankle and she could move around comfortably, which had prompted her to search out her own space. Well . . . okay . . . maybe it was *still* Jared's space, but it would get her out from under his feet in his own home. Staying immobile had been difficult for her, and Jared had insisted on carrying her everywhere, even to the bathroom, like she was completely incapable of walking on her own.

Kneeling down in the kitchen of the guest house, she opened the large cupboards beneath the countertops, smiling happily as she eyed the large kettles stored there. They weren't commercial size, but they'd make twice as much—if not more—than she could make at home. And she could do one batch after the other because she had the time now. Pulling the pots out of their resting place, her heart again aching because she really no longer had a home of her own, she set them on top of the stove in preparation for cooking the mixtures she was going to need. Regardless of whether Jared objected or not, she *was* going to the market in a few days, and she wanted as much product to sell as possible to start infusing her own cash into the business. Looking at the costs for commercial equipment and all of the other expenses there were to starting up even a small business like hers had made her queasy. She'd cringed as she'd watched Jared order more and more stuff for her new business without a moment's hesitation. Sure . . . he was a billionaire and this start-up was pocket change for him, but spending that much money had scared the bejesus out of her. Ultimately, her business would be in debt to Jared until he was paid back. Then, they could share profits. Mara didn't care if the money meant nothing to him. It meant something to her, and she'd never feel right taking the majority of the profits and not seeing him reimbursed for everything he was pouring out for her business right now. They *would* make a contract, and she'd bust her ass to see those conditions met. That was one battle she planned on winning.

I'll make it successful. I'll pay him back. This is just a business loan. A partnership.

Granted, it was an opportunity that almost any business-minded person would kill for, but Jared had offered it to *her*, and she'd be a fool not to make the most of it.

How many people get the opportunity to do business with one of the billionaire Sinclairs?

Her jaw set stubbornly, she made her way into the bedroom and opened the closet in the master with a gasp. Sarah had told her on the phone that she'd picked up some clothing for her and left it in the guest house, along with some other items to replace what she'd lost in the fire. A gift, she'd said, a thank-you from her because Mara was replacing Kristin in her wedding. Sarah had told her that Dante had once provided her with a new wardrobe when her own clothing had been destroyed and had refused any payment for it. She'd gone on to say she knew how lost she had felt then without her belongings, and she hoped the clothing she, Emily, and Randi had selected would help her feel a little better.

Mara started to hyperventilate when she saw the massive amount of clothing in her closet. The storage space was full of jeans, shorts, skirts, tops, dresses, shoes, jackets, and accessories. As Mara moved across the room to open the dresser drawers, she found they were no less crowded with underwear, lingerie, and every undergarment Mara could imagine.

"She shouldn't have done this," she mumbled anxiously under her breath. These weren't cheap clothes, and the gift was far too much. For her, a few pairs of jeans and T-shirts would have sufficed.

Closing the top drawer of the dresser, Mara sighed. Did any Sinclair, even one just marrying into the family, do anything in a small way? Having anyone care for her as an adult seemed awkward and strange. Most of her adult life had been spent tending to her sick mother. Mara couldn't call anyone other than Kristin a real friend since she'd been consumed with her mom's slowly debilitating illness. After her mother had passed away, she had grieved, living in a bubble of despair while trying to keep the shop afloat. Now, she wasn't sure what to do or how to feel.

Sad?

Disconnected?

Scared?

Excited?

Or free?

Feeling somewhat guilty for feeling *all* of those emotions, Mara realized that by an incident of fate, she was unencumbered and able to seek out something new for herself. She was no longer tied to a dying business she felt obligated to continue. It was a frightening yet exciting notion that she could carve out her own place in the world instead of following tradition.

Looking back, she was fairly certain that her mother had wanted something better for her, which was why she'd tried to send Mara to college. "Maybe she didn't want me to carry on the family tradition. She knew the store wasn't making money. Maybe it was *me* who just wanted to hold on to a piece of my mom," she muttered to herself as she wandered out of the bedroom.

After quickly donning one of the new outfits Sarah had bought her so she didn't have to wear Jared's T-shirts anymore, she left the house and walked outside, limping a little as she made her way down to the beach. Her injury was almost painless now, and the ice that Jared had applied to the strained outside muscle of her ankle and keeping it elevated had taken away the swelling completely. It was nothing more than a nuisance now, and Mara was happy to be walking again.

The weather was warm, bright, and sunny as she kicked off her sandals and waded into the ocean, sighing as the cool water washed over her feet.

I love Amesport. I'm so grateful that I don't have to move.

Her heart still ached with the losses she'd suffered from the fire, but Jared was right . . . she had her life. The near-death experience had jolted her into the reality of how fleeting and fragile that life could be, and she was determined to appreciate every new day now.

I'll make a success of this business. Mara's Kitchen will put out some of the best products on the East Coast. Jared is giving me this chance, and I'm going to run with it, make it as good as it can possibly be.

Flopping into one of the low, wooden chairs at the edge of the water, Mara stretched her bare legs out in front of her. The red shorts Sarah had selected for her were a little shorter than she usually wore, but the matching red-and-white-striped shirt was comfortable. The water beckoned her, but she had to treat her ankle gingerly for a while, give the stretched muscle a chance to completely heal. Work came first, and she needed to be able to get around well without restrictions. Reinjuring it would delay all of the ambitious plans she was forming in her mind.

It seemed so strange to be planning a business of her own, something that would be entirely new for her. Although she liked using the skills her mother had taught her to sew and make dolls, cooking was actually her first love. She was never more at home than when she was in the kitchen trying to improve on the already-incredible recipes that had been handed down from generation to generation.

She was just wondering what time Jared would be back from town when she saw a lone figure walking down the beach toward her. Squinting and shading her eyes with her hand, she noticed the male figure making his way slowly toward her. Gaping shamelessly, she acknowledged that the enormous male was actually wearing a suit and tie. Who in the heck would be wearing a suit in this heat, and on the beach, no less?

Not Jared. This guy is even bigger than Jared, which is saying something because Jared dwarfs most normal men.

The Peninsula was private, as were the beaches here, so it had to be a Sinclair, a guest of one of the family, or a trespasser.

Evan Sinclair.

She recognized the eldest Sinclair brother's purposeful stride and jet-black hair before she could actually see his features. Mara had wanted to thank him since he'd rescued her, and it appeared she was going to get her chance.

"Ms. Ross," he drawled haughtily, stopping a few feet from her chair. "Evan." She looked up at him with a hand still shading her eyes. A long way up. One of the first things Jared had arranged for her was a new pair of glasses, but Mara wasn't wearing them at the moment. That didn't present a problem, as he was definitely big enough to see clearly. The only thing obscuring her vision was the blazing sun. Mara refused to call him Mr. Sinclair. There were definitely way too many Sinclair men in Amesport at the moment, and this particular male had saved her life. "Would you like to sit?" She motioned to the chair next to her. "Why are you wearing a suit on the beach?" She stifled a laugh as she noticed that he was carrying a pair of shoes that were obviously intended to match his clothing, the socks tucked inside. His pant legs were rolled up just enough to keep them from getting wet. He was quite a sight, the rest of him looking absolutely pristine and much more suited to be in a boardroom than at the beach.

Lowering his big body into the wooden chair, he answered irritably, "This happens to be my everyday attire, Ms. Ross. I work. I don't normally go for any kind of strolls on the beach. It's a waste of time."

"Mara, please." Good grief, the man was edgy, and she hoped that he was joking.

Evan nodded. "Fine. I suppose since you're a friend of the family and in the wedding party, it's appropriate to use first names."

To his credit, at least Evan had been smart enough to wear a pair of dark sunglasses to shade his eyes. Mara couldn't see his expression, but she didn't hear a single note of humor in his tone. He was completely serious. "Are you always this uptight?" she asked curiously, staring out at the water again.

"I'm not uptight," he disagreed adamantly. "And yes, this is my usual personality. I have responsibilities. A lot of them. That leaves me no time or inclination to be jovial." He changed the subject. "I didn't realize you were cohabiting with my brother now." He sounded unhappy that there was anything he didn't know.

Mara shrugged. "I'm not. I'm using his guest house. I don't have much of a choice right now. My best friend is laid up with an injury, and her place is very small. I can't intrude on her right now. I'm pretty much homeless."

"You lived in your shop?"

"Yes."

"And how exactly do you know Jared?" Evan asked sharply, his head turned toward her.

He was staring at her, and just imagining the icy stare behind those dark glasses made her want to squirm. She supposed that Evan was suspicious of *any* person that his billionaire brothers hung out with, unless they were equally as wealthy, but she was more than a little insulted. Jared was a grown man, and she didn't need to explain her relationships to a near stranger. But because he was Jared's brother, she answered, "We're friends. He's helping me start up another business, so I guess you could say we're also business partners." Except for the fact that Jared was absolutely adamant about getting as little as possible in profit—not a single penny if she'd allow it. But she'd take care of that. "I can't seem to talk him out of getting the short end of the business." She caved, hoping maybe Evan could talk some sense into his brother. He was obviously all business, and Mara doubted Evan wanted his brother to make a crappy business deal, no matter how small. Maybe he could help.

"Why?" Evan sounded puzzled.

Mara proceeded to explain her business, her plans, and exactly how Jared had discovered her products to Evan. She also admitted the terms Evan's younger brother was insisting on.

"The whole thing is frustrating," she admitted candidly. "I can't take advantage of him that way."

"Most people would," Evan observed. "Jared might not be as good as I am at business, but he's ruthless when he needs to be. Unfortunately, it appears he's still merging personal relationships and business. They don't mix." He exhaled loudly in frustration.

"Jared runs a commercial real estate business worth billions. He might have been wealthy before he started, but he's done that all on his own," Mara answered fiercely. "He's brilliant."

"His backup plan," Evan snapped back at her. "He never planned on doing commercial real estate. He got screwed by a so-called friend in several different ways."

"One of the ones who died?" Mara asked quietly.

"How did you know about that?" His voice was calmer, but he sounded surprised.

"Jared told me. I know he was betrayed by a friend and his girlfriend. And I know they died. He didn't explain completely." No doubt Evan knew the whole truth, which Mara found interesting.

Evan released an exasperated, impatient sigh. "Jared's a different person since that happened. He and his friend were going to start their own business after college, an architecture venture specializing in renovating old homes. My brother had the capital, of course, and was able to do it on his own, but he wanted his friend and classmate, Alan, to be his partner. Jared was already rich, and it was his passion. He wanted to share it with his best friend. He didn't need the money, so he was free to pursue whatever dreams he had. Unfortunately, his friend wanted more than just Jared's business."

"He wanted Jared's girlfriend," Mara said flatly, her heart aching for the younger Jared, who had been betrayed.

"Selena was flighty and completely wrong for Jared," Evan stated arrogantly.

"He blames himself for their deaths," Mara told Evan as she turned to look at him, surprisingly unafraid of his fierce words and seemingly snobby indifference. He cared about his family, so the guy couldn't be all bad. Fascinated, she watched Evan's face as his jaw tensed and a muscle pulsated with frustration. "He emulates you now," she added, suddenly seeing the similarities between the two brothers. Jared wanted to be like Evan, cut off from his emotions, making it highly unlikely that he'd ever be hurt again.

"My siblings are nothing like me," Evan replied, his tone ornery. "And Jared didn't cause either one of their deaths."

"I know. He isn't capable of it."

There was a silence then, nothing but the sound of the waves hitting the sand. Evan was thinking, but Mara found the man confounding. She had no idea what thoughts were going through his obviously razor-sharp brain.

Finally, he spoke. "Jared went on a six-month bender after Selena and Alan died. He was never a drinker, but I found him in an alcoholic stupor that nearly killed him. I sobered him up, and he may no longer wear his heart on his sleeve, but inside he's still the same person. So as you can tell, he's nothing like me." Evan's voice was stoic.

Mara gaped at Evan, letting the information that Jared had nearly killed himself by self-neglect because two people he loved had died sink completely into her brain. "Oh, God. My sweet Jared," she whispered huskily.

Evan shrugged. "I think you're the only one who thinks he's sweet anymore. He lived through it. I *had* hoped that he learned not to mix business with friendships anymore. He gave up doing what he wanted because he associated it with the death of his . . . friends." He choked out the last word as though it was hard to say.

"And you think I'm going to screw him." Mara already had a grasp on Evan's suspicions. For a brother who supposedly didn't give a damn about anything or anyone, he seemed awfully tenacious as to her intentions.

"Are you?" he countered insolently.

"No. We argue about the business arrangements constantly. He's being stubborn. I planned on giving him more than half the profits."

"Ah . . . so that makes you just as ignorant in business as my brother is pretending to be. You're both putting emotion into business. And it doesn't belong there." He turned his head to look at her.

"I—I suppose," she stammered. She knew she was thinking with her emotions right now, and giving Jared *more* than his share was bad business. "But I owe it to him for helping me."

"Emotion again," Evan grumbled impatiently.

"This isn't business for him. He's trying to help me."

Evan shrugged. "Then let him. It's not like he can't afford it."

"I can't," she admitted. "I can never feel good about anything I achieve if I'm not doing it fairly, whether Jared is rich or not."

"Admirable," he answered grudgingly, drumming his fingers on the wooden arm of the chair. "Then do it properly. You've run a business before. It would be a simple enough contract and incorporation."

It would be, if Jared would just agree. Was Evan not hearing her? Jared refused, and that was no small problem. "He wants it his way, and I owe Jared for what he's doing for me."

Frustrating man! But there was very little point in arguing with Evan Sinclair. No doubt he'd bested many people a whole lot more knowledgeable than she was. He was toying with her, but for what purpose she didn't know. Obviously, one of his best weapons was doing business without emotion. She glared at him and crossed her arms in front of her, even though she couldn't see his eyes through his dark glasses.

"You owe no one if you're making them a profit," Evan observed calmly.

"I will make a profit," Mara retorted with a confidence she didn't quite feel . . . yet.

"Very well," Evan replied briskly. "Then I'll have the contracts drawn up, and you can make me your partner in this venture."

Mara's brain worked furiously as she frowned at Evan. "Are you offering this to prevent your brother from mixing business and personal emotions?"

"My reasons are my own. Yes or no?"

It could work. It would get Jared out of the picture. He was much too generous, and he was determined to let himself be taken advantage of to help her. She had no fear that Evan would do something that didn't benefit him. "Fine. I accept." She glowered at Evan. While she admired his business sense, she didn't like his meddling tactics when it came to his family. Evan was no more interested in this business than Jared was, but he'd make a deal with her to keep his brother from making a business mistake. Nevertheless, he'd be doing her a favor in every way except one. "You know Jared will be hurt." Mara hated that. It was the only downside of this deal.

"He'll be murderous," Evan agreed. "Perhaps it might be better if you just let Jared think you're accepting my deal unless he takes a fair cut. I believe it will solve your dilemma."

Mara eyed Evan suspiciously. "You were testing me?"

He turned his head and rose to his feet. "Not exactly. But if it was a test, you passed."

She rose to her feet quickly, so fast that she forgot about her healing ankle. "Ouch!" she exclaimed loudly, forgetting all about the fact that she was going to tell him off.

"Careful." Evan put his powerful arms around her to steady her.

Mara clutched the heavy suit jacket he was wearing. "What the hell are you doing out here in a suit anyway?" Evan smelled like fresh air and crisp, starched linen, a scent that was oddly pleasant. For a huge man, his hold was gentle.

"Grady's idea," Evan grumbled. "He called me an uptight asshole because I interrupted a conversation with Emily to take a business call. He suggested a very long walk on the beach as a cure. I've seen no medicinal value to getting my feet wet and sweating from the humid air."

Mara smiled up at him. "It helps if you wear something more comfortable."

He scowled down at her. "This is my most comfortable suit."

"I meant shorts, maybe a T-shirt," she suggested with a smirk. "Something you'd wear when you're not working."

"I'm always working," he snapped back.

He doesn't own anything but suits? Good Lord . . . Grady was probably right. Does Evan never stop working?

"You can cut across to your house by taking Jared's driveway and crossing the road that runs down the Peninsula."

"Excellent," he replied, sounding relieved. Evan let her go for a second and swooped down to pick up his shoes.

To Mara's horror, he picked her up bodily and carried her until they reached the grass. "What are you doing?" she squeaked.

"Making sure you don't turn your ankle. You really shouldn't be walking in soft sand when your ankle is weak. It's rather careless considering you aren't completely healed yet," he informed her casually. "We seem to be making a habit of doing this carrying thing."

Just like Jared, only his brother had carried her everywhere for several days.

"Thank you for saving my life," she told him gratefully as he lowered her to the ground, suddenly remembering that she hadn't said a word about the fire and his role as her rescuer. Once again, Evan had picked her up and carried her as though she weighed nothing at all, just like the night he'd saved her life. She rested her hands on his massive shoulders as she glanced up at him. Jesus, he was handsome. He might be as cold as a glacier in Greenland, but he was a breathtakingly gorgeous chunk of ice.

"A bit of advice, if I may," Evan commented loftily. Without waiting for permission to dole out his advice, he added, "Next time you may want to actually *leave* a house that's on fire."

"Thanks so much for your profound wisdom." She mimicked his haughty tone. Mara scrutinized his expression for a moment, watching as the side of his mouth twitched like he wanted to smile, but wouldn't. "You're not as big of a jerk as you want everyone to think you are. You want to manipulate things the way you want them, but I think your intentions, although somewhat misguided, are in the right place," she told him, contemplating him as she let her hands drop from his shoulders.

"You're wrong, Mara," he replied coldly. "I'm exactly what you see before you . . . a total and complete asshole." He turned on his heel and walked away, his confession still hanging in the air.

After a few steps, he hesitated, turning back to her. "Mara?"

"Yes?"

"I'd really prefer not to see Jared in the state he was in when he went on his bender ever again."

She could feel his eyes on her even though she couldn't see his stare. Were his words a warning, or just a statement? Mara very much doubted that Evan said anything just for the hell of it. "I don't ever want to see that," she answered honestly.

"Good." He turned around without another word and went on his way.

Mara propped her hands on her hips and watched as Evan swaggered between the mansion and the guest house, disappearing as he went toward Jared's driveway.

She shook her head as she walked toward her temporary home, still not completely certain what to make of her whole conversation with Evan Sinclair.

CHAPTER 10

"She's off-limits," Jared growled. He caught Evan's arm roughly as his sibling walked to the front of his house and out of Mara's line of vision.

I am not jealous. I am not jealous.

Jared let the mantra run through his mind as he confronted his eldest brother. He'd just taken his load of groceries to the kitchen when he caught sight of Evan and Mara on the beach. He'd gawked as Mara jumped out of her chair and Evan put his arms around *his* woman, holding her just a little too long for Jared's liking. He'd seen Mara stumble because of her ankle, but that didn't mean that Evan had needed to hold on to her as long as he had, and he certainly didn't need to cuddle up to Mara and carry her once she was steady. Jared reminded himself that he'd carried Mara everywhere for the last several days. But *that* was different. Evan was a stranger to Mara, and she to him. What right did his brother have to even touch her?

"She said you were just friends," Evan said disdainfully. "I didn't get any indication that you'd staked some sort of claim on her. Isn't that a little barbaric?"

Jared gritted his teeth and let go of Evan as his elder brother shook off his grip. "We *are* friends." *And we're also lovers. Okay . . . maybe lovers only once, but I obsess about it day and night.* "She's been through a lot. The last thing she needs is a man like you."

Evan folded his arms gracefully in front of him. "What exactly does that mean? I certainly have the funds to give her everything she needs."

"She doesn't need funds," Jared ground out, trying to hold back his temper. Mara would succeed with Mara's Kitchen, and he planned on making certain she did. Jared knew he owed Evan a lot, but he wasn't about to sit back and watch while Mara slipped away from him.

"What does she need?"

"She needs someone to give a shit about her. After spending her whole adult life taking care of a sick mother, and then losing everything to a fire, it might be nice if somebody took care of *her* needs for a while."

"And if I'm willing to do that?" Evan questioned.

"Just. Don't." Jared knew he was being territorial, and the last thing he and his brothers would usually fight over was a woman. But this was Mara they were talking about, and Jared *would* fight his own brother if necessary. "And don't touch her again."

Evan strolled over to a bench in front of Jared's house and sat down to put his shoes and socks on. "You're being irrational."

"I don't give a damn if I sound fucking insane. Leave her alone."

Evan brushed off his foot before putting on his socks. "Are you claiming her then?"

Was he trying to tell Evan that he wanted Mara exclusively? His dick certainly did, the damn organ seeming to prefer only her. "We haven't talked about it," he admitted reluctantly.

His shoes back on his feet again and his pant legs back in place, Evan rose. "Then it isn't agreed on," he observed. "Actually, I like her, and I haven't been able to say that about many women in my life. She's smart, ethical, and she isn't afraid of me."

Jared clenched his fists to keep from striking his annoying, arrogant eldest brother. "She's also warm, caring, and strong. And she belongs to me." Goddammit! No way was he going to let Evan snatch Mara out of his grasp. He fucking needed her. And she needed somebody who really cared about her.

"Then I suggest you claim her," Evan said reasonably. "Or somebody else will." He turned without another word and started walking down the driveway.

Jared wondered furiously what the hell that comment had meant. Was Evan trying to tell him that he wanted Mara, too? He watched his brother's retreating figure get smaller and smaller as he moved farther and farther away.

Irritated that he couldn't quite figure out where he and Mara stood, he stomped up to his door and into the house.

It took him less than five minutes to realize that Mara wasn't in his home. He'd glanced outside and she wasn't on the beach, either. After searching and bellowing her name until he was hoarse, Jared stepped onto his massive back porch, took the steps two at a time, and strode determinedly toward the guest house, the aroma of food drawing him to the smaller home almost immediately.

She's there. She's in the guest house.

What the hell is she doing there? Yeah, he had told her she could use the guest house, but he didn't actually *want* her there. In the last few days, he'd become accustomed to hearing her voice on a regular basis, and her laughter, a sound that made him instantly hard. He wanted her in his home, and in his damn bed.

After their first night together, a night that shouldn't have happened until she was healed, he'd fantasized about being inside her again. And again. Now it was damn near all he could think about. She'd been so damn tight, wet, and perfect. He was a well-endowed man, and he knew he'd probably hurt her. She hadn't exactly been complaining, but when he'd seen the furious swelling to her ankle the next day, he'd been pissed at himself. What had happened to his carefully cultivated control? He'd definitely lost it with Mara.

Not. Happening. Again.

The last thing he wanted was to hurt a woman who had already suffered enough pain and heartache.

What happens when I'm done with her?

A low growl reverberated in his throat as he approached the door of the guest house. He'd never be done with her. Usually once he'd screwed a woman, he'd had his fill. For some reason, he knew he could have Mara in every way imaginable and he'd still crave her like an addictive drug.

Because she wants me, too.

A woman couldn't fake a reaction like Mara's. Her body had trembled when he touched her, her desire as fierce as his own.

She was vulnerable. She needed me then.

Turning the doorknob as he acknowledged that it might be *him* who ended up hurting over his obsession with Mara, he was pissed all over again to find the door unlocked.

I'll make her need me just like I need her.

"Mara," he called irritably.

"In here." The feminine voice was coming from the kitchen off to his left.

"The door was unlocked," he informed her, his tone annoyed as he walked into the kitchen.

"I've lived in Amesport all my life, and I never lock my doors except at night. The Peninsula is private. Nobody will come here except family."

Jared opened his mouth to tell her any tourist or transient could wander onto the property. Or a nosy, gossip-seeking reporter could find her if they were trying to probe into his personal life. Just her association with him made her a target for almost any crazy, and it was something he had to make her understand. But he halted near the entrance and became suddenly mute, fascinated as he watched her moving from one place to another gracefully, even though her ankle was injured. Her face was flushed from the warmth of the kitchen, but she flowed from one place to the other with a confidence that made every other thought fly out of his brain. All he wanted to do was watch her.

She's so damn beautiful.

All it took was for her to look up and smile at him for his cock to stand up and greet her with rampant enthusiasm. His heart began to race with some kind of deeply buried longing that he'd never experienced before.

Jesus. I'm so damn screwed.

"What are you doing?" he asked hoarsely, shoving his hands into the front pockets of his jeans. He leaned a shoulder against the door frame, trying to look more casual than he felt.

"Cooking," she replied happily. "Lobster stew, corn bread, and blueberry cobbler. I realized that Sarah stocked more than just clothes. She also filled the fridge, the freezer, and the cupboards with food."

Jared shrugged. "She owes it to you. You are filling in for her wedding."

Mara scowled at him. "I'm doing her and Kristin a favor. Sarah doesn't owe me, and I feel guilty because I know it cost a lot of money for what she bought."

Jared smirked. "I can personally assure you that her husband-to-be is beyond loaded."

"You're awfully nonchalant about Sarah doing all this," she said suspiciously. "Did you pay her?"

"Unfortunately, no, I didn't," he answered in a disgruntled voice. "I tried, but she wouldn't take it. She wanted to do this with Emily and Randi as a gift to you. Something about passing on something that had been done for her, and she likes you. Believe me, if I would have arranged this, your clothes would have been in my house. Why did you move?" He wasn't going to mention the fact that he'd offered the money for Mara's clothing to Dante, too, and his brother had adamantly refused it. Sarah was using her credit card, but Dante had laughingly told Jared that he'd pay it off the minute she finished buying for Mara and never miss a penny of the money. Dante might be obscenely wealthy, and it shouldn't bother him that his brother wanted to help Mara, but it still annoyed him. Jared had only closed his mouth on the subject when Dante asked him *why* it mattered. Jared hadn't had an answer.

"This is where I'm supposed to be. It's what we agreed on. I'll be out of your way."

I want you to be in my way, and I want to be inside you. You're supposed to be in my bed.

It didn't matter what he'd said before, he wanted her with him. "It wasn't inconvenient for me," he said, trying not to sound desperate.

"That doesn't matter," she chastised him, looking back at her pot on the stove and giving it a stir.

It did matter, but at least she was right next door. "Smells good." The scents in the kitchen were beyond *good*; they were tantalizing, and making his mouth water. "I didn't know there was a lobster stew."

"You'll love it," she answered without looking at him.

"I'm invited for dinner then?" Jared's mouth started to turn up in a smile.

"You're always invited. Now that I can get around, I'll cook for both of us."

Good. Then he'd pretty much be living here instead of his larger home. He wasn't happy with her not being with him, but if he could keep her right next door with an open invitation, he'd take advantage of it. Every. Single. Day. "I saw you on the beach with Evan. Do you really think you should be walking around already?" *Do you really like my brother?* He left that question unsaid, but damned if he didn't want to ask her what she thought of Evan, or if she was attracted to him.

Mara's feminine laughter flowed over Jared like a balm to his soul.

She snorted as she said, "I wish I still had my cell phone. I would have taken a picture. I've never seen a guy as uptight as your brother. I don't think I'll ever forget seeing him walking on the beach in a custom suit and that unhappy expression on his face. He's hilarious."

Hilarious? Evan? Jared wondered how his eldest brother would feel about that description of himself. He could guarantee that the words "hilarious" and "Evan Sinclair" had never been used in the same conversation. "So you liked him?"

Mara gave him a contemplative look, a spoon still poised in her hand. "He's . . . complicated, I think."

Actually, everyone except his siblings found Evan Sinclair terrifying, annoyingly cold, and a downright son of a bitch. Jared had never heard his eldest brother described as "complicated." Only Mara would try to see anything more than the bastard Evan usually was to nearly everyone in his life. "Why do you say that?" He moved over to her and took off her new glasses, cleaning them on the soft material at the hem of his short-sleeved shirt. They were fogged up from the humidity of the kitchen, and he could see tiny spots of liquid that had dried on the lenses. He put them back on her face once they were clean.

"Are you ever going to stop doing that?" she asked hesitantly.

"Cleaning your glasses?"

"Yes."

"Probably not. I told you that I used to need them." He shrugged. "I wore glasses for a long time, since childhood. It drove me crazy when they had spots. I finally had the surgery to correct my vision after I became an adult. Are you nearsighted?"

"Astigmatism. It isn't bad. My vision is just bad enough to be annoying and make me need the glasses when I'm working."

"Then it could be corrected," Jared mused.

"It could. But it hasn't been a priority. Glasses work fine for me, and the procedure is expensive."

"Glasses don't work fine if you never clean them." Jared smiled, loving the indignant, stubborn look she got when she was being practical.

"I clean them," she answered defensively. "I just look around the spots until I have the time to do it."

He was getting her eyes fixed so she could see well all the damn time. She just didn't know it yet. Mara was stubborn, but little by little, he'd make sure she had everything she deserved and needed. As Mara moved to the refrigerator, he grasped her by the arm and spun her around slowly, pinning her body against the metal appliance before she could open the door. "So you could see me just fine the other night without your glasses."

She didn't even pretend not to know what he was talking about. "Yes." She licked her lips as she glanced up at him.

"I'm big, and I wasn't gentle. Tell me the truth. Did I hurt you?" Jared wasn't sure he wanted to hear the answer, but he had to know. He *had* lost control, something he never did with a woman.

His heart started to settle into a slower rhythm as she shook her head. "No. And you gave it to me exactly the way I needed it, Jared. I needed to forget, and I did. I needed to feel close to you, and I did. I'll never forget that night because I finally know how pleasurable sex can be. You showed me that."

He hated hearing her refer to them being together in past tense. Jesus. He had a feeling he'd always need her, and there was plenty he *hadn't* shown her.

"No pain?" he questioned harshly.

"Just the stretching of having a man your size inside me. After that it was incredible. And you weren't rough. You were perfect." Mara sighed.

Jared shuddered as she put her arms around his neck, pushing her ample breasts against his torso and laying her head on his shoulder in a gesture of complete trust. "I want that again, Mara. I want you again," he rasped into her hair, inhaling her clean, intoxicating fragrance. "But I want it to be different this time. I want you to be with me for no other reason than because you want me. I want to lick every inch of your soft skin, bury my tongue in your pussy until you come screaming my name. I want to savor every moment of your trembling body while you come."

She tensed, but she didn't move. "I haven't . . . I don't—"

"No man has ever satisfied you with his tongue," he guessed, primitive instinct now pounding at him to be the first.

"No," she whispered. "But we can't do it again, Jared. It was one night, and I'll never regret it. It was the most pleasurable experience of my life. But I can't."

"Why?" If she'd enjoyed it so much, why couldn't it happen again? To hell with that. It *had* to happen again. And again. He'd lose his mind if it didn't.

"Contrary to what you might have believed that night, I really don't just screw anyone. You are and were special. I've been attracted to you since the moment I met you."

"I know that you don't," he growled, entangling one hand in her silken hair and resting the other on her delectably rounded ass.

"I don't think I can be your fuck buddy," she murmured. "I think it would hurt too much. You don't have relationships, Jared. You have sexual encounters. And I knew that when it happened. But I'm starting my life over, and I want everything to mean something to me. I'd get attached."

Her words were like a knife to Jared's gut. Truth was, he *wanted* to mean something to her. He wanted her attached to him more than he'd ever wanted anything. He wanted to be a hell of a lot more than a fuck buddy to her. Problem was, he didn't know exactly *what* he wanted from her. But hell, he was already obsessed with her, and he wanted to bind her to him.

Don't be a selfish prick.

Gripping her ass, he thrust one of his thighs between her legs and hissed softly as her heated core connected with the denim of his jeans. Even through the material, he could fee her heat, the dampness of her pussy. "You're wet."

"Whenever I'm close to you," she admitted tremulously, lifting her head from his chest and staring up at him.

Satisfy her!

Primitive instinct gripped him by his balls, and all he wanted was to see her beautiful face contorted in ecstasy, the tension building and then leaving her body in the throes and aftermath of her climax. "No fucking then. But give me your body. Let me teach you how good my tongue can feel exactly where you want it." Swooping down, he captured her mouth with his, heart hammering triumphantly as she capitulated and moaned against his lips.

Jared tasted and plundered, unable to get enough of her, doubting if he ever would.

CHAPTER 11

Mara was lost, caught up in Jared's sensual, heated assault. He was conquering. Captivating. Dominant.

She couldn't help the instinctive movement of her hips, rubbing her pussy against his thigh as her need for Jared held her steadfastly in its ironfisted grip. The peaks of her nipples rubbed sensually against his powerful torso, and she whimpered as he nipped erotically at her bottom lip and then soothed it with his tongue.

"Jared. Please." Mara didn't know if she was begging for mercy or for more of the sweet torture he was giving her. She squirmed against him as his mouth trailed down her neck, his tongue leaving a trail of fire on the sensitive skin.

"Tell me you need me, Mara," he rasped against her ear, his hand still tangled in her hair, manipulating her head the way he wanted it.

"I do. You know I do," she murmured, closing her eyes.

"This?" He squeezed her ass and pulled her pussy more snugly against his rock-hard thigh.

"Yes," she admitted shamelessly. "More."

"Ride me. Imagine my tongue licking that hot pussy, and all over your clit," he demanded harshly. "Maybe you're not ready for that right now, so think about it."

Mara had no idea how that would feel, but in her mind, she *could* imagine it.

Jared's handsome face buried between her thighs.

Jared's tongue abrading her engorged, throbbing clit.

Jared lapping at her sensitive flesh.

"Oh, God. It would be good," she moaned, pressing her core hard against Jared's leg in a sensual, frenzied motion. "So good."

"It is good, baby. My only goal would be to make you come," he told her in a husky whisper, grasping her hair tighter and pulling her head back so he could run his tongue up the sensitive skin of her neck.

The lash of his tongue sent her careening over the edge as she ground against his thigh, sensation spreading out from her core to the tips of her fingers as her sheath pulsated violently. "Jared." Her gasp turned into a long moan.

He covered her lips with his own, capturing her pleasure with his ravenous mouth. Fisting his hair, Mara clung to him as her climax vibrated through her body.

He ended the kiss with a muffled groan, burying his face in her hair. Sliding his leg from between her thighs, he held her body tightly against his, cradling her head against his chest. "You okay?"

"I'm doing fine for a woman who just climaxed without ever taking her clothes off." She panted heavily, her heart pounding so hard she felt like it was about to leap out of her chest.

Jared chuckled and held her tighter. "I'd be happy to do it again with your clothes off."

"You're dangerous," she muttered, her brain not quite clear. She could feel his persistent erection pressed against her belly, and she felt guilty that he hadn't found his own release. "That wasn't exactly mutually pleasurable."

"It was for me," Jared answered calmly. "There's nothing better than watching you come, Mara. And I'm not pushing you for more than you want to give me right now."

Her heart melted. If Jared only knew that she'd wanted to give him everything, make him as crazy as he'd just made her simply with his voice, his touch, and his kiss. Chances were, if he'd stripped her naked and taken her right here in the kitchen, she wouldn't have stopped him. She might have even begged him to do it. He hadn't done that because she had reservations, because she might end up hurt when this was all over and his attraction waned. "Thank you. But I don't feel right that you still haven't . . ." Her voice trailed off.

"That I didn't come." Jared pulled back and looked down at her with heated eyes. "Don't. A hard-on isn't fatal. Plus, I have plenty of fantasy material now when I take care of the problem myself."

She bit her lip to keep from moaning, visions of Jared stroking himself to completion, his head thrown back as he came, were now floating erotically through her mind. "I'd like to watch that," she blurted out before she could censor herself.

Jared gave her a mischievous smile. "I don't generally sell tickets to that particular event, but you're welcome to an exclusive showing."

She pulled away from him regretfully. "Sounds like trouble," she answered, trying to appear nonchalant when she was anything but aloof right at the moment.

"The best kind of trouble," he agreed in a hopeful voice.

"You're a wicked man, Jared Sinclair," she admonished playfully, her hands still not completely steady as she grabbed a pot holder and took the corn bread out of the oven. Truth was, she loved his kind of trouble, and his sexy voice saying erotic things to her drove her half-crazy.

"Baby, you haven't begun to see me misbehaving," he drawled in a husky voice.

No? Oh, God, then I'd really like to see you completely wanton.

Her wayward core flooded with heat just at the thought of Jared abandoned and wild. Something about his raw sensuality called to a carnal side of her that she hadn't known existed.

"Time to eat," she squeaked, needing to change the subject.

"My thoughts exactly." He leaned against the kitchen counter and sent her a wicked, heated grin.

Mara stirred the mixture in the pot on the stove furiously, fairly certain he wasn't talking about lobster stew.

"These are terrible," Mara giggled later that evening as she looked at the long string of photos that had spit out of the machine at the Amesport Arcade. "I look like a confused owl. I should have taken my glasses off." She'd been squashed beside Jared in the picture booth, laughing at his dry jokes as the pictures were taken.

"I like them," Jared said indignantly, snatching the strand of images from her hand.

Mara rolled her eyes as they waited in line to turn in their tickets. They'd wandered to the arcade hours ago when they'd driven into town. She'd finally convinced Jared that she was perfectly able to do the farmers' market this week, and she wanted supplies. Reluctantly, he'd agreed, but insisted on driving her into town to carry anything she needed.

He'd spotted the small arcade along the boardwalk while he was waiting as she'd ducked into one of the shops along Main Street. She'd seen him jogging back from the bank across the street, his hands full of rolls of quarters as she'd exited the store.

After depositing her supplies in his SUV, he'd nearly dragged her down to the arcade, and they'd been there ever since. She'd learned he was an expert at Skee-Ball, and he could trounce her at almost any video game. Collecting tickets like a madman, he'd hit every game in the small arcade more than once.

Munching on a bag of popcorn he'd bought for her, she sighed. "I love it here. This place has been here as long I can remember." The old building could use a paint job, but it was loud, colorful, and just as happy as she remembered. "This is where my mom taught me how to play Pac-Man."

"She must have been good," he grumbled.

"She was," Mara answered with a smile, loving the fact that there was at least one game that she was better at than he was. "Where did you learn to play all of these old games so well?"

Jared smiled at her as he folded the photos carefully and put them in his pocket. "I have three older brothers and three male cousins. We used to spend some time with my cousins in the summer, who were raised near Salem. We snuck out of the house as often as we could to play at the arcade, sometimes every day."

"There are more Sinclairs?"

"Yep. They scattered around the country, too, just like we did. Offspring of my father's younger brother, but they're close to us in age."

"You never see them anymore?"

"I think they're all coming to Dante's wedding. It's been a while since we've all been together. A long time," Jared answered, his voice holding a note of regret.

"Please don't tell me they're wealthy and handsome, too," Mara begged.

Jared shot her a puzzled look as he moved forward in line. "Loaded. They're Sinclairs. I think they're all ugly bastards, though," he added hastily, as though he was afraid she might be interested in any of them.

Mara groaned. "Cousin rivalry. What you really mean is they're as gorgeous and rich as you and your brothers."

"Are you interested?" Jared asked irritably.

"No. But Elsie and Beatrice will have a field day. Can you imagine . . . all of those rich Sinclair men in Amesport!" she exclaimed. "Please tell me they're all married with a gazillion kids."

Jared grinned and the tenseness in his body began to relax. "Bachelors. Every one of them. Micah, Julian, and Xander have never been married. I'm sure they'd love to meet Elsie and Beatrice. " He snickered evilly.

"Seriously? Even their names are hot," Mara complained loudly. "Beatrice will have them matched before they even get here if she finds out."

Jared grinned even broader. "Good. I think I'll swing by her shop and let her know they're coming. I want to see them all because it's been a long time, but I'd like to see them all squirm. Beatrice can be a scary woman when she wants to be."

"That's terrible." She swatted him on the arm. "You have no idea what it's like to be matched by Beatrice. She's persistent. I was her target several years ago, when she thought I and one of the accountants in town would be a good match."

Jared frowned. "What happened?"

"Turns out that he's gay, but the poor man was nagged to death by Beatrice until he finally had to tell her the truth. She swears she just read her spirit guide wrong and it was one of her few mistakes." Mara blew out an exasperated breath.

Mara shivered with delight as Jared's booming laughter exploded from his throat and vibrated through the air around them. He looked young, happy, and so incredibly sexy when he was like this; no longer a billionaire playboy, and more like a regular guy. Granted, he was just as panty melting, but he looked so touchable. "Go ahead and laugh. Just wait until she gets her claws into you. I'm surprised she hasn't already." She loved Elsie and Beatrice to death, but when one of them decided to meddle, they were relentless.

"Actually, she's already found my match," Jared informed her playfully.

"Who?" She tried not to sound anxious or jealous, but she was just a little of both.

He trained his deep green gaze on her, his lips turned up sensually before answering. "You."

Mara almost dropped her popcorn, and she gawked at Jared as he stepped up to claim his prize.

After turning in his tickets, he presented her with a tiny stuffed tiger, an adorable toy that Jared probably could have bought at a discount store for five bucks. Instead, he'd probably blown through fifty dollars in quarters to win it, but it was one of the most precious things she'd ever received because he looked like a young man who was proudly handing his girlfriend a prize. He'd won it for her, and that made it special.

"Thank you." She kissed him on the cheek, flinching as she stretched on her tiptoes. *Darn ankle!*

"It's hurting?" Jared asked perceptively.

"A little. I forget about it until I move wrong."

Jared wrapped his arm around her waist and plucked her up and into his arms, carrying her outside.

"I can walk, Jared. Put me down. I'm not exactly a lightweight. I'm surprised you haven't thrown your back out already." She swatted at his shoulder.

"You're fucking perfect, sweetheart, especially when you're like this," he answered huskily.

Exasperated, she wrapped her arms around his shoulders to make it easier for him to carry her to his vehicle. Judging by his insistent grip on her body, he obviously wasn't relenting, and he didn't look the least bit strained from carrying her weight. "I'm fine," she argued uselessly. "And please tell me you were joking about Beatrice matching us."

He stopped at his SUV parked on Main Street and lowered her gently to her feet as he took the keys from his pocket and flipped the automated switch to unlock the doors. "No joke. And after the lunch you fed me today, I'm seriously considering begging you to marry me."

She took his comment as the joke she knew it was. "That good, huh?"

"Hmm . . . yeah. I'm beginning to think Beatrice might be right on the money this time." He opened the passenger door of the vehicle for her.

The light from his car illuminated his face, and Mara smiled back at him as she saw the teasing light in his eyes. "You'd marry me for my Maine wild blueberry cobbler?" she cajoled, playing along with him.

"And the lobster stew," he reminded her. "Incredible stuff."

"What about the corn bread?"

"Perfection."

"And the coffee?"

"Better than Brew Magic," he said emphatically, taking her by the waist and lifting her effortlessly into the plush leather seat.

"You're such a food whore." She burst out laughing.

"Guilty," he admitted readily as he fastened her seat belt. "Not only was it the best I've ever had, but you made it for me."

"Nobody's ever cooked for you before?"

He shook his head as his gaze met hers. "We had a cook when we were young and at home, but it was her job. This is different. You did it just because you wanted to."

No wonder he came into town to eat every night. Jared really *didn't* know how to cook. That was incredibly ironic since he was definitely a man who loved his coffee, sweets, and food so much. Reaching out a hand, she palmed his cheek. "I'll cook you anything you want." She knew Jared Sinclair didn't like to admit to any weakness, and she wasn't going to tease him about not being able to cook. God knew he did everything else to perfection. It seemed to mean a lot to him that she'd done such a simple task for him, and her heart ached for all the little things that Jared had never had, things that told a person that someone cared about them. The starkness, the void of his life without tenderness squeezed at her heart. Sadly, she had a feeling he was right. None of the women in his life were interested in much except his money. Maybe he sought those kinds of women out, but it seemed so unfair that he was so willing to give and got nothing but a reluctant screw in return.

"You might regret saying that. What if I demand everything?"

"Then you'll get it," she told him stubbornly. "You deserve it."

He speared his hand into her hair and lowered his mouth to give her a gentle but emotionally devastating kiss that took her breath away. He explored her mouth leisurely, thoroughly before finally releasing her. "My fierce little tiger. So willing to defend me, are you?"

"Until you don't deserve it," she answered, tilting her head to look at him.

A haunted look passed over his face before he asked, "Are you hungry?"

"I have plenty of food at home. And tons of leftover cobbler."

He kissed her on the forehead before he straightened. "Then let's go home."

Mara sighed after Jared had closed the door and started moving around the car to the driver's seat. There was nowhere she'd rather be as long as she was with Jared.

She kept the stuffed tiger in her grasp all the way back to the Peninsula, realizing that the smallest of things really did mean the most.

CHAPTER 12

The farmers' market was a huge success that week for Mara. She ended up preparing three times as much product as she usually did, even with limited time, and sold out within a few hours. Jared worked along beside her, doing all of the lifting and moving required, making her sit her ass on the tailgate while he worked. Her ankle was getting stronger, nearly back to normal, but he was still insistent that she could reinjure it. She gave him instructions while he worked, and even though he let her do very little physical work, they managed to function as a team.

Orders from stores in town and from a few restaurants like Sullivan's came rolling in. She and Jared made the deliveries after the farmers' market, the profits considerably more than she'd ever seen before from her products. It wasn't big money, but it was a positive start for her.

The trouble came the next day when she tried to give Jared half the profits.

"No," he grumbled. "The profits can go back into the business. I don't need or want the money. You need to pay yourself, and then put it back into the business to keep growing. The website will be up soon."

Mara rolled her eyes as she pulled out the stitches at the seams of Kristin's bridesmaid dress, working on the alterations it needed to fit her fuller body. They had picked it up at Kristin's house on the way home from the farmers' market, and the sly look her best friend gave her as she introduced Jared to Kristin hadn't escaped her notice. Thank God Kristin hadn't said anything. She'd simply winked at Mara as she handed her the dress.

"You have to take a fair deal, Jared." It was well past time for them to discuss their business issues. They needed a contract soon, a business plan that was fair to him. She didn't give a damn if he didn't need the money. For her to feel like she'd accomplished something big, she needed it to be professionally done.

"I gave you my terms," he reminded her, shooting her a stubborn look from his position in the recliner across from her.

They'd just finished dinner, and he was working on his laptop while she was altering her dress. Jared lingered more and more at the guest house, slowly moving some of his essentials into the residence and leaving them there. Not that she minded. The moment he left to go back to the mansion at night, she was lonely. She was getting used to his company, craved it when he was gone. It hadn't escaped her notice that he was also slowly replacing all of her belongings with new items, bringing her a new computer that he just happened to have lying around. Not so coincidentally, it was brand-new in the box and top-of-the-line. He'd looked so pleased with himself every time he gave her something new that she hadn't had the heart to refuse the items. And she did need them. But his thoughtfulness made her uncharacteristically weepy. No guy had ever wanted to do things for her, or anticipated her needs. It felt strangely . . . good.

However, the business was a whole different thing, and she was willing to play hardball if she had to. And she knew she was going to *have* to do it. "Your brother made me an offer." Damn! She really didn't want to play this particular card or play any games with Jared, but the stubborn man wasn't giving her much of a choice.

"He what?" Jared questioned cautiously.

"He made me an offer to be my partner. Complete with a contract and controlling interest. If we can't make a deal, I'm taking him up on it," she said, trying not to look him in the eyes.

"You're not doing business with Evan. He's a damn shark. He'd eat you alive without a second thought," Jared snarled. "It wouldn't matter to him if the money was nothing to him. He's a goddamn anal perfectionist. He'd be bossing you around every minute of the day, working you until you dropped."

"But it would be a fair agreement. And I don't mind working hard."

"It would be in his favor. It always is."

Mara shrugged. "A major investor gets controlling interest."

"I don't want him controlling you," he bellowed, angry now.

"He wouldn't be controlling me. He'd be in control of the business."

"No."

"Then draw up a fair contract," Mara insisted, finally meeting his gaze unyieldingly. "This isn't fair, Jared." She had to be strong. This *was* a business deal.

"Life isn't fair, Mara. Is it fair that monetarily I've always had everything and you had nothing? Is it fair that you lost your mother too damn young and spent most of your adult life taking care of her? Is it fair that you're so damn talented but can't fund your own business? None of this shit is fair. For once in my life, I just want to help. Let me do it." His stare was intense, his eyes dark with frustration.

Mara nearly caved in. Underneath Jared's carefully constructed veneer of sophistication and coolness lay the heart of a generous man. However, she couldn't give in to this. Jared talked tough, but she was fairly certain that many people had taken advantage of him in the past. She wasn't going to be just another woman who used him. "Make the contracts or I walk. I understand that the money is peanuts to you, but it means something to me. It's not ethical, and I can't live with that."

He scowled at her, silent for a moment before replying, "Fine. I'll do the damn contracts. As long as you're not doing business with my brother," he rasped. "Happy?"

She dropped all pretense of working on the dress, letting it drop to her lap. "Yes. I'm excited about starting this business. The only thing bothering me was how unfair it was to you. I want us to be equal partners once the business gets going."

"What woman worries about being fair to a billionaire?" Jared rumbled.

"I'm not dealing with the billionaire businessman right now. I'm dealing with somebody I care about," she told him huskily. Knowing it was important that they put one more ghost to rest, she asked quietly, "Are you ever going to tell me about how your friends died?"

His expression turned dark as he closed his laptop and set it aside. "I killed them. I already told you that."

"How?" Jared desperately needed to let go of his guilt and past pain, and Mara felt close enough to him to push now. And she'd do everything she could to release him from the prison he'd built for himself. She had no idea what had happened, but she didn't have any doubt that he didn't deserve to carry the blame that he'd carried for years. Evan had said Jared had changed after the deaths of his friends, and she wanted to see him find himself again. No matter what crap he spewed about being an asshole, deep inside, he wasn't.

"By being young, stupid, and thoughtless," he spat out flatly. "Because I was a selfish prick."

Mara didn't believe that for a minute, but she stood up, the dress she'd been working on drifting soundlessly to the carpet, and walked across to him, unable to stop herself. Gingerly, she slid into his lap, and Jared's arms slipped immediately around her waist, cuddling her close as she rested her head on his shoulder. "Tell me."

For a moment, he didn't speak. He just held her like she was the most precious thing in his life. Haltingly, he started to talk. "It happened right after Alan and I graduated from college. He wasn't rich, and he took a lot of student loans to get through school. I had the money to put up the capital for the business, and he wanted to be part of it. We both loved old homes, restoring them back to their original condition. I wasn't joking when I said I actually had a work truck like yours. I bought a few old homes while we were still in college, and we spent a lot of time restoring them ourselves. We didn't decide to make it a real business until our last few months of school. The planning stage wasn't quite over, but we were working on it. Selena and I dated all through college, and she still had one more year to go before graduation. I introduced them, and they'd known each other for several years by the time Alan and I graduated. I have no idea how long they'd been screwing each other." Jared stopped for a moment and swallowed hard. "We were all attending a Fourth of July party that summer after Alan and I finished college. Pretty much everyone was drunk except me. I didn't drink much then. My old man was a drunk, and the last thing I wanted was to be like him. So I volunteered to be the designated driver. The party was in full swing when I realized Selena and Alan were missing. I went to find them, and I found them making their own fireworks in a bedroom upstairs." Jared broke off speaking, breathing hard as though he were living through the whole experience again.

Mara stroked his hair back from his forehead. His eyes were closed. "Don't think about that. What happened *after* you found them?" He looked so vulnerable that she almost wanted to stop the entire conversation, but Mara knew he needed to talk it out, no matter how painful.

"I left," he admitted hoarsely. "I took off, and they ended up catching a ride with a drunken student. They crashed not long after they left the party. The driver was going too fast and swerved off the road and hit a tree. All three of them died instantly." His voice grew stronger, angrier. "I was supposed to be their driver. I should have gotten them home safely. I was pissed, and I never gave one fucking thought about how they were getting home."

Her heart ached because he was so willing to take the blame when it wasn't warranted. "It wasn't your fault, Jared." She pulled his head against her breasts and rocked him like a child. "Your reaction was no different than anyone else's would be if they were betrayed. They were adults. Nobody forced them into that car. They could have called a taxi. What happened was a tragic accident, but none of it was your fault. How drunk were they?"

"Barely above the legal limit, according to their blood alcohol. The driver was plastered."

"Then they still could have made the right decision, but they didn't. Nobody can blame you for what happened, and you can't blame yourself." Mara's voice was pleading. She had to get through to him, make him really believe he wasn't responsible. His torment was evident now, and she couldn't stand to see him this way.

"Her mother blamed me," he replied gravely. "She always liked me, thought I was good for Selena. She was grateful that I was helping her daughter through school. Until the funeral. She let me know that I killed her daughter, and she hoped I went to hell. She never knew that I was already there."

Oh, dear God. Selena's mother never knew. "You never told her what really happened," Mara said softly, her heart skittering as her brain furiously worked out what had occurred.

"I couldn't tell her. I couldn't tell anyone," Jared choked out harshly. "All she knew is that I left the party without her daughter. There were plenty of friends who saw me leave. There were only three people who knew what really happened, why I left when I shouldn't have, and two of them were dead," he rasped. "How in the hell could I tell her mother that she was screwing another man, after Selena was already dead? That was her daughter. I couldn't leave her with those kinds of memories of her daughter. It was better to let her think that I killed Selena and Alan without the details. It didn't really matter."

"You didn't kill them," Mara answered angrily, defensively. Sweet Jesus, Jared had taken the blame alone, too kind to tell his girlfriend's mother or anyone else that he'd had a completely legitimate reason for leaving that night. The sheer selflessness that it had taken for Jared to shoulder all of the blame to let everyone else keep good memories of two people taken away so young nearly made her heart beat out of her chest with empathy for him. Jared had been young, but had still taken every criticism, every bit of blame to cover up for two dead young people who had betrayed his trust in every way.

"If I would have stayed—"

"You don't know what would have happened. They would have been embarrassed. They knew you saw them?"

He nodded slowly. "Yes. Selena saw me."

They wouldn't have gone with you anyway, Jared. Please believe that. Jesus, he'd been so damn determined to take the blame and let everyone else grieve that he'd actually convinced himself that it was really true, that he'd really been completely responsible for their deaths. Just the thought of his girlfriend's mother condemning Jared to hell when he was trying to actually save her and other people close to Selena and Alan from additional pain made furious tears flow from Mara's eyes. Her heart felt like it was being torn from her chest as she imagined what it must have been like for him during that time. He'd been alone, without a single soul to talk to about his own grief and betrayal. That was why he'd gone on a bender, the emotional pain so severe that he'd needed to escape.

"Do you really think they would have calmly ridden home with you?" she finally asked him gently.

"I don't know," he answered huskily. "I don't know."

"You need to stop blaming yourself. They made several bad choices. None of them deserved to die. But you don't know if things would have turned out any differently, and your reaction was perfectly normal. I would have done the same thing. I would have been upset, and I would have left." Mara took a deep breath, tears still streaming down her face. She found it amazing that years after the incident, Jared still blamed himself. Not only had he needed to deal with the betrayal and the death of two of the most important people in his life, but he felt he had to take the blame for his girlfriend and friend getting killed on top of it.

"I wish I could believe that things wouldn't have turned out any differently had I stayed and insisted on driving them."

What person does that? What young guy that heartbroken was going to keep a cool head and calmly drive two people home who had betrayed him? "They wouldn't have gone home with you. How long do you think they were involved?"

Jared released a masculine sigh. "Looking back, they may have been screwing each other for quite a while. They weren't drunk enough that night for it to have been a first-time fling, and I heard them before I actually saw them fucking. Selena was rambling about how much she loved some of the things that Alan did to her. It wasn't a new thing." He paused and took a deep breath before continuing. "They started doing things together about halfway through my last year of college. I thought they were just friends, and I was trying to get the business together, so I was busy. Selena and I just kept growing more and more distant. I thought it was just because I was so busy."

So it was Jared's fault for that distance between them, too? He worked too much so his girlfriend found someone else to screw her?

The whole incident was beginning to make Mara pissed off and defensive for Jared's sake. "Why didn't she just break up with you?"

"Her family was happy we were together then. She came from a family who didn't have much. After we met, I helped her pay for all her college fees. They were grateful. I think Selena was just waiting until she finished school to make the break," Jared answered flatly. "She had one more year, and Alan didn't have the funds to help her."

Bitch! Mara didn't know if Selena had ever cared about Jared or if he was just convenient to pay for her education. But she sounded like she was a user. And his so-called friend? What kind of guy did the horizontal mambo with his best friend's girlfriend, a friend who was completely funding their start-up partnership in business together? Okay . . . neither of them deserved to die because they were users, but she wished they were still alive so she could bitch slap both of them. "So this misplaced guilt caused you to go over the edge?"

His body tensed. "How the hell do you know about that?"

"Evan told me."

"Fuck! He hasn't mentioned that to anyone. He promised he wouldn't. My family never even knew," Jared growled. "Yeah, I went on a major bender. I just wanted to forget. Fuck! I just wanted to get rid of the images and sounds of the two of them together. I wanted to forget the scorn of their families and the whispers behind my damn back. I wanted to forget their funerals, and I really wanted to forget that they were gone forever because I'd done something stupid."

"And did you forget?"

"Hell no. And I hated Evan for a while for forcing me into reality again."

She stroked a palm over the stubble on his jaw. "I'm glad he did. What happened?"

Mara knew she was done fighting her attraction to Jared, finished trying to defend herself against getting hurt. This man had once loved and had been completely betrayed. Since then, he'd been torturing himself about what else he could have done to save the lives of the very people who had deceived him, and he'd shouldered every bit of blame. Jared might have been with a lot of women, but they were females who hadn't cared what demons lurked inside him. She did. And if opening her heart to him completely was the only way to heal those wounds, she'd do it. She didn't care about the risk anymore. She just cared about . . . *him*.

"I don't remember most of those months," Jared admitted in a hesitant, graveled voice. "Every time I woke up, I started thinking, so I got drunk again. It's pretty much lost time for me until Evan showed up."

Mara didn't even have to ask how Evan had known that Jared needed him. While Jared's eldest brother tried to act like he didn't care about anyone or anything, he seemed to have an almost scary way of knowing what was going in his siblings' lives. "So he sobered you up?"

"The hard way," Jared grumbled. "He tossed my ass in the shower because he said I stunk. A cleaning staff showed up almost instantly to clean my condo, and he forced coffee and food down my throat. He got rid of every drop of alcohol in the house. I guess the main thing I remember is that he stayed, even though he badgered the hell out of me day and night."

"Tough love," Mara murmured.

"With Evan, I don't think there's any other kind," Jared rumbled.

"How long?"

Jared shrugged. "Weeks. He took over my office and worked, but he never left me alone."

Mara could imagine the two gruff brothers in each other's company, snapping at each other, and caring so very much while they were doing it. "Your siblings love you, Jared."

"They don't even know me anymore," he growled. "They don't know what happened, or how naive and selfish I was."

"Evan knows, and he still cares." Mara could still remember Evan's words of warning that he never wanted to see Jared suffer like he'd suffered after the deaths of his friends. "I'm not one of your siblings, but I know, and I still care."

Jared threaded his hands through her hair and tilted her gaze down to meet his. "Do you? Can you really look at me and not see an irresponsible, selfish asshole who killed his friends?"

Mara turned her body and straddled him, letting her legs dangle off both sides of the recliner. "Yes," she told him truthfully, holding his eyes with hers. Her heart clenched as she saw the momentary confusion and hope in his eyes. "You need to stop torturing yourself. Please. The. Accident. Was. Not. Your. Fault." Mara put her arms around his neck and stroked the coarse hair at his nape. "I'm sorry they died. They were both way too young, and it's sad. But you aren't to blame."

"You care?" he asked hesitantly. "About me? Even after everything I just told you?" He looked endearingly confused.

"I do," she whispered softly, swallowing a huge lump in her throat. "I'm not going to try to protect myself from getting hurt anymore, and I'm never going to be less than honest about how I feel. I admire how you pulled yourself back out of the darkness and made yourself even more successful. I hurt for you because you gave up your passion and your dreams of restoring old homes because of bad memories. It kills me that you took the blame so others could keep their happy memories." Mara was pretty certain not many people would have done what Jared had done. Honestly, it was probably the right thing to do with a mother who had lost a daughter, but she hated that he'd had to be the scapegoat. She absolutely wished Selena's mother hadn't been so desperate for someone to blame that she'd made Jared the villain, especially after all he'd done for her daughter.

"It was Evan who pulled me back."

She pulled playfully at a lock of his hair. "It was *you*. Evan eventually left you alone to do what you wanted. You could have gone back to drowning in a bottle. You didn't. It takes a lot of strength to choose to change your life. You did that, and built one of the most successful businesses in the world." If she could do just a tiny fraction as well as Jared had done at changing his life after a tragedy, she'd be grateful.

Jared searched her face with a desperate expression before pulling her mouth down to meet his.

Mara sighed into his mouth, opening to him, returning his kiss by meeting his tongue as it pushed insistently between her lips. His kissed her breathless while she slowly slid her hands down to unbutton his shirt.

"What are you doing?" he asked as he pulled away from the fierce embrace, his voice crackling with desire.

"Seducing you. I've never actually done this before, so be patient with me," she requested in a sultry voice. She could feel his rock-hard erection pushing against her ass, straining to be free. Mara wasn't lying. She had never actually seduced a guy before. In her limited experience, they had both undressed and gotten right to it. Honestly, her sexual experience before her night with Jared had been so long ago and so unmemorable that she couldn't even say how it had started.

Right now, all she wanted was to do something for Jared. It wouldn't make his pain go away completely, but she hoped she could get through to him with time. There was no way she was going to let him live this way. He'd been there for her. Now she wanted to be there for him in whatever way would convince him that he was special. So damn special.

Opening his shirt after it was unbuttoned, she sighed longingly. "You're so beautifully made, Jared." He definitely worked at being fit, and it showed in every defined muscle on his chest and abdomen. "So smoking hot." Leaning down, she nipped at his flat nipple and soothed it with her tongue as she slid between his legs to the floor. Palming his cock through the denim material, she smiled against his chest as he groaned, loving the way his body responded to her touch.

"I don't have much control right now," Jared warned her ominously as his hands threaded roughly through her hair.

Exactly! Mara wanted to break through his control, make him understand that he didn't need it. Not when they were together. Her finger moving slowly down his happy trail of hair leading to what she already knew was an enormous cock, she looked up at him for a moment. "If this goes as planned, in a few minutes you'll have absolutely none."

CHAPTER 13

Jared's head thumped against the back of the recliner. He closed his eyes and hoped he wouldn't wake up from what had to be a fantastic wet dream before he had a chance to fuck the woman between his thighs. Jesus, he needed her, needed her warmth surrounding him right now.

Maybe I really am having a wet dream.

The attention Mara was lavishing on his body was too intense, too surreal, too damn everything to really be happening. The way she touched him—like she really wanted nothing more than to be caressing him, like she *needed* to feel his body beneath her fingers—drove him completely insane. It was real, and it was massively addictive.

Confusion and rapture clouded his brain. How the hell could she want him this much, still be willing to even touch him after what she'd just learned? How could she *not* blame him for the deaths of his friends? How could this even be taking place?

It's happening. It feels just like the last time, only better because she is actually trying to seduce me with a completely clear head. It wasn't happening because she was desperate to forget some tragedy, or because she was escaping. She actually just wanted to . . . please him, lure him into a state of desire. Really, like he needed any encouragement? His dick was always ready for Mara, even when she was doing absolutely nothing to tempt him. All she had to do was smile . . . or fucking breathe, for that matter, and his cock was rock hard.

Shuddering as her palms stroked down his chest and stomach, his breath caught as he felt her tugging insistently at the buttons of his jeans, her ferocious determination to get at his cock the hottest thing he'd ever experienced. Once she had liberated him and he felt her fingers tighten around the shaft, Jared nearly leaped out of his chair. "Bedroom. Now." If he didn't get inside her tight heat right now, he was going to embarrass himself right here in the recliner.

"No," she told him fiercely. "I want to taste you. Here. Now."

Holy. Fucking. Christ.

Control.

Control.

Control.

His eyes were wild with hunger and dread. His mantra wasn't working, and his usual mastery over his body and emotions was quickly abandoning him.

It's her touch.

It's her strength to move me like no other woman ever has.

Mara was killing him with her willingness to care about him, even after she knew what a bastard he'd been years earlier. Hell, he was still a bastard, but she was *still* giving herself to him. He knew he didn't deserve her, but he'd lost the will to resist or regain his all-important control again. Not now. Not with her.

"I won't last," he ground out between clenched teeth. There had never been a woman who had wanted to go down on a man his size, and it had never really mattered to him. He got off either way, but this . . . this was different. Oddly, it seemed that Mara actually *wanted* to do it, like she was dying to taste his cock. It was the most erotic thing he'd ever experienced.

"I don't care how long you last. I just want you to enjoy it," she answered earnestly. "You're so big, Jared. So hard."

Her husky reply caught him off guard, her adoration clear in her voice. It blasted him straight in the chest that Mara was accepting him exactly the way he was. Correction . . . she actually seemed to *like* him exactly as he was. Her unconditional acceptance was Jared's undoing.

The first touch of her mouth on him brought a pleasure so sharp it was almost painful. He tried not to grasp her hair and bury himself in the moist heat between her lips, take everything she was willing to give. He fisted her hair as she left a trail of fire over the head of his cock and started sucking in the large shaft.

Control. I don't want to hurt her when she's giving me something no other woman ever has.

It was damn hard not to lose it when she cradled his balls in her soft fingers and stroked them gently, never pausing in her effort to take his cock into her mouth as deeply as possible. Every nerve in Jared's body was throbbing, begging for relief. Sweat started to trickle down his face as Mara wrapped her hand around the root of him and began to stroke every inch of him with her hand and mouth.

Opening his eyes, he glanced down at the erotic sight of her between his thighs. Her eyes were closed as though she was enjoying every lick and suck, and the carnal vision induced such a visceral reaction that Jared had to close his eyes. His head fell back against the headrest of the recliner, and he gave up the fight.

He relished every stroke of her tongue, every vibration that her moans caused along his member. "Good, sweetheart. So fucking good," he growled as she sucked harder, started moving faster. He stroked over her scalp rhythmically with his fingers, ignoring the primitive instinct to thrust his hips up. For the first time in his life, he let go completely, trusting her to bring his ecstasy to completion. "Get me off, baby," he encouraged gutturally. "Suck me harder."

She responded immediately, increasing her suction and her pace until Jared's head was ready to blow . . . both of his heads, actually. His hips arched instinctively as the tension in his balls and gut tightened unbearably. "Oh, fuck, yeah," he groaned. "I'm going to come."

"Mmmm . . ." she moaned around him.

The vibration set him off, and his entire body pulsated as his powerful release pounded through every fiber of his being. "Mara!" He grasped her hair tighter than he meant to, panting as she left him sated and sweating.

Holy. Fucking. Hell.

He opened his eyes and watched as she slowly crawled back up his body, her tongue tracing the muscles in his abs and chest, before she settled carefully back into his lap.

She looked beautiful as she shot him a naughty, sultry look, her hair mussed and her lips moist. Snaking one arm around her waist and the other behind her head, he brought her talented mouth down to his, savoring the taste of himself on her lips as volatile emotions bombarded him.

I need her so damn much.

His heart swelled as she responded to him so sweetly, so automatically that it was difficult for Jared to pull his lips from hers. "You just rocked my world," he admitted huskily, looking into her sexy, dark eyes. The words were way too mild for the way he was actually feeling, but he didn't know what else to say.

She lowered her forehead against his and gently stroked back his hair. "Good," she answered, sounding vulnerable and relieved. "I was afraid I wouldn't do it the way you usually like it."

"I don't like it any particular way. It's never happened before." She'd given him something special. *She* was special. The least he could do was throw away his manly pride and tell her the truth.

Lifting her head, Mara looked at him, astonished. "But you've had a lot of women—"

"I've *fucked* a lot of women, Mara. But not a single one of them has ever wanted to go down on me." Usually, Jared figured they just wanted to get off and collect whatever they could from him. *That* was the type of woman he usually sought out. They were safe. He knew what to expect, and he knew what he had to give in return. He had no idea exactly what to do with a woman like Mara. "And I haven't screwed every woman I've ever been pictured with. A lot of them are just casual dates for charity functions or acquaintances. Contrary to what a lot of people think, I'm not a total man-whore. I've had my fair share of women, but I usually stay far away from women as sweet as you."

She gave him a puzzled look. "Why? You deserve a woman who cares about you."

Jared didn't have an answer, and he stared at Mara darkly. It took him a moment to form a reply. "Maybe I don't think I deserve that kind of woman." Subconsciously, he'd probably always sought out exactly what he thought he deserved after being responsible for the deaths of two people.

Kissing him on the forehead gently, she wrapped her arms around his neck. "You do," she muttered tenderly. "I think you need it, and you're probably even more entitled to it than a lot of men. You're special, Jared."

He stood, taking her with him before lowering her to the floor and sprawling his body on top of hers. "What about you? You deserve so much more than I do. You've spent most of your life taking care of other people, ignoring your own needs." Hell, Mara was the most self-less person he'd ever known, male or female.

Recovering from the change in position quickly, she smiled up at him. "You're a lot hotter than I am," she joked, twining her arms around his neck again. "And much too hard to resist."

Jared swallowed hard as he came to his knees between her thighs and shrugged out of his shirt impatiently, tossing it aside. "If you think that, you aren't seeing what I'm seeing right now." Everything about her was impossible to ignore. She was a temptress and an angel. She was wicked and an innocent. Her dark eyes were fathomless, deep whirlpools filled with emotion, and she touched Jared in ways that terrified the hell out of him. She was a temptation beyond his ability to control, and she belonged to him.

Mine.

Evan was right, he needed to claim her completely before someone else did.

"I need you naked. Now." Possessiveness filled him, and he needed to make her tremble with need for him until she could think of no one else *except* him.

She didn't protest as she sat up and he made short work of her clothing, his heart thundering when she was finally sprawled out on the carpet, completely nude.

"Like I said . . . I'm not as hot as you are," she mumbled, her entire body flushing pink as Jared looked his fill.

"Sweetheart, you have no idea how sexy you really are." His mouth was dry as his eyes swept over her body lovingly. Her raspberry-colored nipples were hard, the peaks beckoning him. Her ivory skin was flawless, and her curvy body beckoned him to explore every portion of it. "I want to lick every inch of you with my tongue."

Standing up, he shucked off his jeans and briefs, kicking them to the side impatiently.

"Jared, I—"

"Shhh . . ." He put a finger over her lips as he came back down on top of her. Mara looked embarrassed and beautifully aroused. "I want to taste you as much as you wanted to taste me. Probably more."

"I haven't—"

He pressed his finger harder against her lips. "You will. And you'll be moaning my name while I'm doing it. I need to make you come." He'd already known that no man had ever had his head between her thighs, and he loved knowing that he'd be the first. No doubt the only thing she'd experienced in the past was a fumbling boy who would let her give him head but offered nothing but an inept screw in return. "Lay back and enjoy it, baby. I know I will." He couldn't wait to touch her soft skin, lick her into orgasm. This generous, smart, gorgeous creature in front of him was now his, and he'd make damn sure she was begging for mercy before he was done. He needed her to remember nothing except him from this day forward.

No other man was going to touch her—ever!

She. Belongs. To. Me.

The words repeated in his mind over and over as he began concentrating on making her forget that anyone ever existed before him.

The first touch of his mouth on her made Mara cry out incoherently, her body so ready for Jared that any inhibitions she had were already gone. He looked at her like she was a goddess, his eyes an eddy of pure fire as he gazed at her body. No man had ever looked at her with as much longing as she saw on his face, and it increased her arousal to the point of carnal insanity.

Moaning as his tongue slid between her folds and leisurely licked her pussy from bottom to top, Mara speared her hands through his hair and urged him for more. He parted her thighs wider, taking his time like he was savoring every moment of her arousal. "More, Jared. Please."

"Patience, sweetheart," he groaned against her pink flesh. "It will make your orgasm so much more satisfying."

"I'll be satisfied now. I swear," she told him huskily, ready to lose her mind as his tongue brushed her clit lightly and she whimpered. It wasn't nearly enough.

Mara thought she heard a muffled, low chuckle rumbling out of his mouth, but she was too enthralled by the touch of his tongue to really decipher what was happening. She felt bared, shattered in a way she never had before. Everything he was doing was so much more intimate than anything she'd ever experienced, and her body was trembling with need.

Jared teased, flicking his tongue over the tiny bundle of nerves that were begging for his attention. He provoked, lapping greedily at every inch of her sensitized flesh, spreading her folds with his fingers, exposing her blatantly to him.

"Yes," she hissed as he finally rolled his hot, wet tongue over her clit with more pressure in a flowing, stroking pattern that had her hips rising off the floor.

Grasping his hair, she writhed desperately, trying to pull him closer, harder. "Don't stop. Please don't stop," she pleaded hoarsely, needing him to keep giving her the pressure she needed to come.

She was close. So very close.

Her climax hit her the moment he thrust two fingers into her sheath, searching for and finding that sensitive area inside her, caressing it with bold strokes while his tongue laved her clit.

"Jared. Oh, God." Mara's head thrashed wildly, her orgasm rolling over her with so much power it was almost frightening. She held on to his hair like it was her lifeline, her channel clenching around his fingers with spasm after spasm as she lay there helplessly riding the storm of sensations that overwhelmed her completely.

Her body relaxed slowly, cognitive thought coming back to her as she panted breathlessly on the plush carpet.

"Okay?" Jared asked as he moved up her body, his fingers swiping gently over her face. "Did I hurt you?" His voice was urgent and demanding.

Mara realized that tears had escaped from her eyes and were trickling down her cheeks. "No," she answered him hurriedly, removing her hands from his hair to dash away her tears. Wrapping her arms around his neck to reassure him, she tugged him down to kiss him tenderly. "I guess I got overwhelmed," she said as she finally broke the embrace.

"Is that good or bad?" he asked curiously, his intense eyes still watching her face anxiously.

Smoothing his hair away from his forehead, she answered, "Good. So amazing that I couldn't help crying. I guess I just realized all that I've been missing because I haven't had a guy in my life for so many years." Mara tried for some levity to lower the intensity between them, knowing that not just *any* guy would have alleviated her loneliness and set her body on fire. It had to be *him*. It had to Jared. "Or maybe I've just been waiting for you," she mused, entranced by the ferocity of his expression.

"You've been waiting for me," he said in a gruff, possessive voice. "I don't deserve you, Mara, but I need you."

His tortured look, the emotion in his voice made Mara's heart ache. This was a part of Jared Sinclair that she knew he never revealed, yet he trusted her with his vulnerability. The one woman he'd loved had thrown his trust aside and stomped on it, and then she'd died, leaving Jared empty, nothing inside him except guilt and grief. "I need you, too." She sighed softly, knowing she'd just given Jared Sinclair her heart. She'd been fooling herself to think that she could even fight it. From the moment he'd walked into her shop, Jared had been different from every other man she'd ever known, her attraction to him instantaneous. Before, she'd been able to call it lust, a balm for the loneliness she'd felt since her mother's death. But he was more than that, and she knew it. Beneath his I-don't-give-a-shit facade was the heart of a sensitive, generous man. An incredible, exceptional man who'd sacrificed so much for others, including his self-worth and belief in himself.

"If you need me, take me then. Take everything you want." He wrapped his arms around her and lifted her on top of him so she was straddling him.

"I thought you didn't want it this way," she squeaked.

"Oh, I want it any way you'll give it to me, but you can control it, take as much of me as you're comfortable with. Condom is in my pocket."

"I asked Sarah to start me on birth control when I went to her office for a checkup," she told him, feeling suddenly shy. Sarah Baxter, soon-to-be Sarah Sinclair, was officially her physician now. She'd been using Sarah for follow-up care on her injured ankle, and she'd be using her for everything from now on. Mara had asked Sarah to put her on birth control. Maybe she always subconsciously knew that what had happened with Jared was going to happen again. Pragmatically, she'd told herself it was just a precaution, but her heart knew that she and Jared would never stay away from each other if they were working together. Yes, there were other reasons to use the condom, but she wanted him to know that she trusted him. "It was exactly the right time. I'm covered, and I'm clean."

Jared's eyes shot to her face, astonished. "You trust me? Granted, my female count isn't as big as it's reputed to be, but I've fucked a lot of women, Mara. I won't lie to you about that. But I've never had sex unprotected, and I'm free from any diseases. I haven't been with anyone but you since I was last checked out."

She nodded slowly. "I trust you. You've never given me any reason not to. Just promise me that if you decide to be with somebody else, you'll tell me."

His eyes grew dark and he sat up with lightning-fast movements, wrapping his arms around her waist. "There won't be anyone else. Ever." Jared's voice was guttural and deep as he buried his face in her hair.

Mara told herself not to believe what he was saying. Someday there would obviously be other women. He wasn't staying here forever, and they were in a moment of passion. Nevertheless, her heart starting racing from his fervent declaration, wanting so desperately to believe it was true. Gut instinct told her she'd never be with anyone like Jared again. "Then fuck me, Jared. Now. Please." She'd worry about changes in their relationship when that time came. Nothing in life was guaranteed. For now, this was all about them, and all about Jared healing from some wounds so deep that they hadn't mended with the passage of time.

His hands moved possessively down her back and cupped her ass, repositioning her to accept his cock. "You need to let me know if I hurt you."

"You won't." Mara gasped as he filled her, but she was still so hot and wet from her climax that he entered her naturally and beautifully, as though they were made to fit together like this.

Jared groaned into her hair, moving a covetous hand down her back while he held her ass in place to accept his thrusts. "You're so hot, so wet. You feel so damn incredible that I'm not going to last very long."

Mara smiled as she wrapped her arms around his shoulders, their bodies skin to skin as he stroked into her sheath again and again. The position was intimate, every part of them touching as they flew higher and higher together. She tightened her legs around his waist, luxuriating in the affinity flowing between them, feeling every rapid beat of his heart against her naked flesh every time he thrust and retreated again.

I'm not going to last very long.

What was with his obsession about taking forever to come?

Control.

She knew she was right. The mask he wore was one of complete authority over himself and his actions, rigid restraint probably to make up for his emotional decision that had left him bleeding inside for years.

"I don't need you to last. I just want you. I need you, Jared. Fuck me harder." She nipped at the side of his neck, knowing she was daring him to lose his discipline and conditioning, the wall he'd built up around himself for protection. "You feel so good," she panted into his ear, rotating her hips sensuously, taking his cock deeper with every thrust.

"Can't. Lose. Control." His voice was guttural and determined. "Need you to come with me."

Mara had no doubt she was going to come hard. She was on the edge, her body already shivering with sensation. Being entwined with Jared like this, her hard nipples abrading against the coarse hair on his chest, feeling his hard, hot breath on her neck as he struggled for dominance over his orgasm—every single sensation intoxicated her.

Jared pumped into her harder, as though he couldn't stop. Mara leaned her head back and closed her eyes, her belly clenching as her climax hit her. "Jared!" She screamed his name as the internal walls of her channel clamped down hard on his cock as though they never wanted to release him.

"Fuck, yeah. Come for me, baby." Jared grasped her hair and pulled her mouth roughly to his, his tongue spearing through her lips and dominating her, sweeping her away with a reckless abandon that had Mara moaning as she came, squirming to get even closer to him.

"Mine," Jared groaned as he moved his mouth from hers. "You're mine, Mara."

Mara dug her short nails into his back as she milked him of his orgasm, taking everything she could get, feeling as possessive of him as he was of her right now.

My Jared. My sweet, tormented, stubborn man.

Cradling her head against his shoulder, Jared rocked their bodies together, his fingers still gripping her ass. "I knew you were trouble from the minute I saw you," he muttered huskily with a touch of amusement in his low rumble. "And I was right."

His voice was teasing, and she smiled against his damp, sweaty chest. "You're trouble, too. But only in the very best of ways," she answered breathlessly, mimicking their earlier conversation and savoring the afterglow of her mind-blowing intimacy with Jared for a very long time.

CHAPTER 14

"I'm wrecked," Jared confessed to all of his brothers the next day at Grady's house. Leaning back in his chair, he ran a frustrated hand through his hair and took another slug of his beer.

All four of them were having a bachelor party that Jared was fairly certain Dante didn't even want, sitting at Grady's kitchen table and killing off a whole lot of beer. Dante and Grady roared with laughter, while Evan simply stared with his usual icy control.

"Bastards," Jared mumbled irritably as Grady and Dante continued to chuckle.

"Welcome to the agony and ecstasy of love, little brother," Dante told him jokingly.

"I don't love her," Jared answered hastily. Maybe a little too hastily.

Hell, maybe he shouldn't have mentioned his involvement with Mara, told his brothers how it was getting to him, but he needed a male to talk to. He figured maybe more than one was needed for this particular situation.

Grady and Dante starting chortling again, and Jared shot them both a dirty look.

"Perhaps he doesn't love her," Evan observed, taking a sip of his bottled water, which he'd insisted be served in a real glass. "Not everyone is cut out for obsessive love."

Dante glared at Evan. "You might be capable of it if you'd take the poker out of your ass. When did you get so damned uptight anyway?"

Evan glanced back at Dante stoically. "The poker was put there by one of the best at torturing other people. And not everyone is cut out for love."

"Who put it there?" Grady asked curiously.

Evan's eyes fixed on his water, he replied, "Our father."

Jared swallowed hard, remembering how Evan had always been the caretaker of every one of them when they were younger. His eldest brother had never let go of that particular habit. Maybe Jared *had* hated his oldest sibling when he'd dragged him back into reality, but Evan had been there for him, asshole or not. Sometimes actions were more telling than words. Evan might be frigid, but he wasn't completely frozen all the way through.

Being the eldest, Evan had always been expected to take over their father's business. Their old man had died while Evan was still in college getting his business degree, but his older brother had been forced into their father's company almost every moment he hadn't been in school. From the time he was a young child, the heir apparent was being trained up by the biggest bastard in the country as soon as he could walk and talk—their abusive, alcoholic father. Remorse hit Jared hard and fast, suddenly realizing that Evan was a product of the way their father had treated him. His oldest brother had saved most of his other siblings from spending much time with their disparaging and particularly vile parent. But nobody had ever been there to give Evan a break. He'd been his father's target, a victim just because of his birth order. Evan just hadn't ever complained. Sometimes, Grady had been his father's main target because he'd been socially awkward as a child and adolescent, and he'd stuttered quite badly. Even then, Evan had done everything he could to deflect their father's wrath away from Grady.

"I'm sorry, Ev," Grady finally spoke, his voice full of regret. "I know the old man was a bastard, and you spent a hell of a lot more time with him than we did."

"I'm sorry, too," Dante interjected quickly.

"And me," Jared added hoarsely, his throat tightening as he tried to imagine what his father had put Evan through as his eldest child and heir.

"I obviously survived," Evan replied unemotionally. "The business has thrived, and I've doubled my own wealth over the last twelve years. I have nothing to complain about."

Jared wanted to call bullshit on Evan. If his suspicions were correct, Evan had plenty of things he could bitch about that could have made him as bitter as he pretended to be.

"Was it bad?" Grady asked hesitantly. "The time you spent with him alone. Was it really bad?"

Evan shrugged nonchalantly. "You were all there most of the time. It's ancient history now. We're all happy." He hesitated before adding, "Except possibly Jared right now."

Jared knew that Evan was denying the real truth, but he wasn't going to push his sibling right now. He knew Evan, and if he didn't want to talk about his childhood and adolescence, he wouldn't.

"Because our little brother doesn't want to admit he's in love with Mara," Dante commented right before he slugged another gulp of his beer.

"Because I'm not," Jared argued vehemently. He wasn't, right? Just because he lusted after Mara every waking moment of his day, wanted to be with her when he wasn't, thought of her all of the time, wondered if she was okay. Surely, that wasn't exactly all about love.

You don't believe in true love?

Mara's question drifted through Jared's mind as he tried to sort out his emotions. Nope. He didn't believe in love. Or he hadn't. Now he didn't know what the hell to think. Was he any less obsessed than his brothers were about their women? At one time, he'd thought they were all crazy. Now he was the one acting like a lunatic.

"Would you walk through fire for her?" Grady asked quietly.

Evan shot him a questioning glance, and Jared almost squirmed as he answered grudgingly, "Yes."

"What would you do if she didn't want to see you anymore?" Dante queried.

"I'd seduce her." *I'd fucking beg for the very first time in my life.* Holy shit. He wasn't saying *that* out loud. Just thinking about it made him shudder, but he knew it was true. He needed Mara just that damn much. "She's mine. She's not going anywhere," he added gruffly.

"Primal instincts," Grady observed.

"Unable to function without her," Dante added.

"Staking his claim," Grady mused.

"Probably thinks about her all the time," Dante interjected.

"You're screwed," Dante and Grady said in unison.

Jared looked at the knowing smiles on Dante's and Grady's faces and grumbled, "Assholes."

"Leave him alone," Evan ordered commandingly. "I doubt either one of you would have wanted your weaknesses pointed out when you were struggling through your own relationship difficulties."

Grady and Dante sobered after a moment of thought and nodded slowly, both of them muttering an apology to Jared.

"I thought we were here to play poker," Evan said evenly. "So far I haven't seen any of you putting your money where your mouth is or dealing out the cards."

Even though Jared was irritated, he almost smiled. Nobody could beat Evan at poker, and no doubt Grady and Dante knew they'd get their asses kicked. Not one of them had ever learned to really read Evan in poker, and he had absolutely no "tells." His eldest brother had been mopping the floor with all of them at poker since they were kids.

Grady got up reluctantly. "I'll grab the cards and chips."

Dante rubbed his hands together. "I'm the groom. It has to be my lucky night."

"We'll see," Evan said noncommittally, arrogantly. "But don't count on it. Lucky at cards, unlucky in love," Evan quoted the old saying drily. "I believe I'm the only one who can claim that truth anymore."

A few weeks ago, Jared could have argued with Evan. Nobody had been more unlucky in love than him. Now, thinking about Mara, he kept his silence. He'd happily let Evan take his money if he could just have the woman he wanted.

Evan kicked everybody's ass and left with a rather large IOU from every single one of his brothers several hours later.

He took his less-than-sober siblings home without ever cracking a smile for the pounding he'd given his younger brothers.

"I'm ruined," Mara told the four women sitting in Dante's living room as she downed the last of her second strawberry daiquiri. The bachelorette party was small, just her, Kristin, Randi, Sarah, and Emily. She wasn't much of a drinker, so after consuming two drinks that tasted like Randi had gone pretty heavy on the rum, Mara had become very talky.

Okay. Yeah. She'd let her relationship with Jared slip, and after that, she'd blurted out most of the story—minus the mind-blowing sex part. Some things were just too private and much too intimate to share, even if she *was* a little tipsy.

Picking up another satin bag, she started stuffing in the adorable wedding favors that Sarah had picked out: miniature bottles of cognac, gourmet coffee, tea diffusers, and a crystal from Beatrice's store, Natural Elements. She picked up the tiny card, an inclusion that Sarah had insisted on so that everyone knew about her fiancé's generous nature. It explained that one of the party favors was a donation to a charity for abused women in the guest's name. It was a unique idea, and Sarah had related the information to all of them earlier that Dante had donated an enormous sum of money to give a donation from every wedding guest attending. It was a charity being managed by Jason Sutherland, Hope's husband. Apparently, it was a major joint project for the Harrisons, the Hudsons, Max and Mia Hamilton, and the Colters of Colorado, all billionaires and obviously compassionate families. How many of the ultrawealthy actually gave up that much time to charity? Sarah had told her that Hope's husband, Jason, personally managed the funds for the charity, and the other billionaires donated a lot of time to fund-raising. Didn't people that wealthy usually just write a check and forget about it? It sounded like a wonderful cause, and Mara was glad that money had been donated for her by Dante.

Obviously not all of them just wrote a check and forgot about the cause.

Sarah had explained that even Evan was heavily involved with the project, and Grady had happily jumped on board quite some time ago. When Dante learned about it, he came up with the idea for a wedding favor of donating for every guest. It was thoughtful and sweet. As a physician who had seen her share of abused women, Sarah adored Dante even more for donating and coming up with the unique idea . . . if it was even possible for Sarah to dote on her fiancé more than she already did.

Closing the ties on the black bag, which was personalized with gold lettering, Mara added it to the growing pile of finished favor bags and reached for the next.

"He's *the one*, isn't he," Kristin said reverently from her seat beside Mara on the couch.

Yes. Yes. Yes.

The single word echoed in Mara's heart as she replied, "How do you know? How does any woman know?" Mara knew because she'd never felt this way before, and gut instinct had been gnawing at her insides since she'd met Jared. Something had been different about him, the connection she'd felt for him almost . . . magical. There was no doubt in her mind that she was in love with him. Deeply. Insanely. Passionately.

Sarah stopped stuffing her bag to look at Mara. "You just know, Mara. I think sometimes we fight it because we're afraid to really feel that strongly. But we sense it. If he's the man you're meant to be with, nothing is too embarrassing to talk about. He loves you exactly as you are and doesn't see your imperfections. He'll be willing to risk everything for you, and you'll feel the same way."

Mara knew about how Dante had saved Sarah's life. It was a small town, and the incident had been huge news. Although Jared hadn't done something like that, he *had* risked baring himself to her. He trusted her, and that knowledge made her heart melt into a puddle at her feet. "It's scary when you feel this way," she muttered. It was also exhilarating, thrilling, and breathtaking.

"It really is," Emily agreed readily from her seat in one of the recliners. "But the scary part eventually goes away and all that's left is the happiness. It's not like everything is always perfect. Grady and I disagree. We're both stubborn. But even when we do, we still love each other." She paused before asking, "Are you in love with Jared?"

Mara caught Emily's gaze and finally nodded. "I am. I don't know how it happened or why the two of us seem to fit together. We're so different."

"Different because he's so rich?" Kristin questioned.

"No. It's more than that. I don't care about the money. I care about . . . Jared." She wouldn't reveal any of Jared's secrets, even if she was a little intoxicated. "Jared is urbane, sophisticated. He's brilliant at business, and one of the most eligible bachelors in the world. I'm a small-town woman who isn't the least bit elegant. I had to drop out of college because my mother was sick, and I've only traveled out of the state a few times. I'm not worldly, and my life is fairly ordinary. *I'm* ordinary."

"That's just superficial differences. They don't matter. I think beneath all of Jared's bluster, he's a good man," Sarah mused. "I think Dante knew he was interested in somebody in town. I even think he knew it was you."

Mara's head snapped up. "He did? How? Even I didn't know."

Sarah smiled at her. "Cop instinct, I guess. He was on to the fact that Jared wasn't seeing anybody."

"He hasn't for a while now. Been with anybody, I mean," she added hastily. "He said he's seen with a lot of women, but some of them are just friends. I believe him."

"I believe that," Emily chirped. "The tabloids and media can be brutal. So much speculation without the facts. I think it would be great if you and Jared ended up together. I think he needs you."

I don't deserve you, Mara, but I need you.

She sighed as she remembered Jared's words. The big question was . . . did he love her? Was he starting to fall as hard as she was falling? "I guess we'll just have to see what happens." Her heart was now open to Jared, his to cherish or break. She was rolling the dice on him, and she hoped her instincts were right. If not, she'd be shattered.

"God, he's hot," Kristin commented enthusiastically.

"He is. That's why I don't understand why he's interested in me. I'm probably the plainest, most boring woman in town."

"That's not true," Sarah replied hotly. "You're pretty and sweet. Dante once said that sweet women are a Sinclair's downfall."

Randi snorted. "I guess I never have to worry about being any Sinclair man's downfall then."

Mara glanced at the petite brunette. She didn't believe Randi for a second. She might act like she was tough, but she was willing to bet the woman had a warm heart. She'd never been anything but kind to her, and Randi volunteered a lot of her time at the Youth Center when she wasn't teaching at the local school.

"Grady loves me, and I'm plain, tall, *and* curvy," Emily added firmly. "It's like he's blind to every fault I have."

"Jared is, too," Mara admitted in a perplexed voice. "He looks at me like I'm a supermodel. It's like he thinks I'm perfect." She rolled her eyes just at the thought of her ever being without fault, physically or emotionally.

"He *is* the one," Kristin affirmed with a smile.

"Definitely," Sarah seconded.

"He's in love with you," Emily confirmed with a nod.

Mara's heart beat faster and her palms grew sweaty at the thought. There was nothing she wanted more than for the women's predictions to be true.

The conversation turned directions after a few moments of silence, the ladies talking about the wedding as they stuffed favor bags. It was a simple task, but Mara had never felt more comfortable, so a part of something that bonded her together with other females, a group of women she could easily call friends. There wasn't a bit of cattiness in any of them, and they were genuinely warm and caring.

Cutting off any negative thoughts about Jared, she just enjoyed the memory of how blissful it had been when they'd woken up together that morning. Jared had held her close the entire night, his powerful arms still wrapped around her when they woke.

For now, those feelings, that sense of closeness would have to be enough.

CHAPTER 15

"Hey, beautiful . . . your website is up."

Mara gaped at Jared, who was standing right outside the door she'd opened to his knock, her first cup of coffee still in her hand. Jared was *never* this cheerful in the morning, and this was very unusual behavior for him before nine a.m. He generally woke up, drank his coffee, and grumbled as he went downstairs to his gym. By the looks of his damp hair and mischievous grin, he'd already gone through his morning routine, which included a shower after he hit the gym, and it was only eight o'clock.

He's up early.

Holding the door open for him, she watched him saunter into the living room, and he smelled deliciously of coffee, fresh air, and sandalwood as he brushed past her.

God, he smells good.

Dressed in jeans and his normal button-down shirt, he looked good enough to eat for breakfast, and Mara had to clench her fist around her mug to keep from reaching for him and making him her first meal of the day. "It's up?" The sight and scent of Jared distracted her so much that it had taken her a while to process what he'd said.

Moving to the kitchen and helping himself to a cup of coffee, he turned to her with a naughty grin and propped his hip casually against the cupboard. "It's been up since the second I saw you."

Her eyes went immediately to his groin, and then back up to his face. Unfortunately, she couldn't see anything because his shirttail was covering his crotch. She nodded. "Our website, you mean? It's live?"

He smirked. "That's up, too."

Too? Wicked man!

She tried not to smile, but her lips turned up as she watched him take a sip of his coffee. Jared Sinclair was way too hot not to appreciate when he was being perverted, and his flirty words made her heart flutter inside her chest.

He looks so damn perfect, and I'm a mess.

Mara had barely gotten out of bed. She ran a hand through her wild hair, fairly doubtful that her cotton, pink pajamas were really turning him on right now.

"You look beautiful," Jared drawled slowly, as though he could read her mind. "You look warm, luscious, and cuddly, like you just crawled out of bed."

"I did," she told him unhappily, still trying to finger comb her hair. "I never thought you'd be here this early, and I'm behind schedule." She walked to the cupboard and took out some ibuprofen for her headache. "I think I had one too many strawberry daiquiris with the bridal party."

"So the girls were playing last night?" Jared asked with amusement in his voice.

Mara shrugged. "Talking mostly and putting together the bags for wedding favors. And drinking." She swallowed the pills with a sip of her coffee, trying to forget just how much she'd said that she wished she could unsay now. Groaning inwardly, she wished she hadn't spilled her guts about Jared. Not that she thought the women would gossip, but just because the relationship was way too new to be so intense.

"How many did you drink?"

"Three? I think."

"Tell me you didn't drive home," Jared growled, crowding her against the cupboard.

"I didn't drive," she assured him quietly, knowing how sensitive he probably was after what had happened to his friend and girlfriend. "Dante just lives down the road. I walked. And please don't try to tell me you guys were angels at Grady's house." She looked up at him expectantly.

He lifted a brow. "We had a few. It was all very tame. Evan dropped us off. He wasn't drinking." Jared moved away from her and into the living room. "Do you want to see your website or not?"

She drained the rest of her coffee by taking several gulps, then set her empty mug down on the kitchen cupboard. "Yes," Mara squealed, then regretted it because it made her head hurt worse. Still, she was excited to see her completed site. Moving behind Jared, who now had his laptop open, she wrapped her arms around his waist and rested her head against his back. "Thank you."

Placing his coffee carefully on one of the low tables near the couch, Jared held the laptop with one hand and pecked the keys with another. Without stopping what he was doing, he muttered, "If you move those hands down another six inches, you won't be seeing this site until this afternoon." Setting the computer on the coffee table, he turned and wrapped his arms around her. Stroking a hand down her back, a lopsided smile on his lips, he said lightly, "Hmm . . . I was right . . . very cuddly."

Mara shivered as she felt the warmth of his palm through the light cotton of her pajama top. "I know, right? Very sexy lingerie." The top was flimsy, with spaghetti straps and lace, but it was far from seductive. The matching drawstring shorts hung almost to her knees. It was light, comfortable sleepwear for summer, but nothing to inspire a man to ravage her.

Jared tipped her chin and kissed her, a lingering, sensual kiss that nearly made Mara's toes curl.

"You look hot in anything you wear," he told her hoarsely, his mouth trailing over her temple. "Even hotter in just your soft, perfect bare skin."

Wrapping her arms around his neck, she pulled back and smiled at him playfully. "Uh-huh. Smooth talker."

Reaching up, he pulled her hand from his nape and moved it down to his cock. Mara's fingers flexed as they met his rock-hard erection.

"I'll never say anything I don't mean to you," Jared told her harshly.

Mara shook her head. "I'm sorry. Sometimes I just find it so hard to believe that you feel this way about me."

"Ditto," he answered in a gentler voice, pulling her hand away from his erection and wrapping it around his neck again. "I missed you last night. That's why I woke up early. I couldn't wait to see you, find out how your night went. I wanted to call you, but your lights were off and I didn't want to wake you up." He bussed her on the forehead tenderly and stepped back, fishing something from his back pocket. "I got this for you. I know yours was destroyed, and you're going to need it."

Mara gawked at the sleek, beautiful new iPhone. "For me?" she asked incredulously. She took it, cradling it in her hand. Her old cell phone had been a relic, and she hadn't planned on replacing it anytime soon. Every penny she had that wasn't needed for basic necessities was going back into the business.

"When I couldn't see you, I texted you," he said huskily.

Pushing the button to activate the phone, Mara clicked on the one text message showing as unanswered.

I miss you.

The message had been sent at two o'clock in the morning. Just three simple words that tugged at her heart.

Fumbling with the newer model phone that she wasn't used to, she didn't look up at Jared as she replied.

I missed you, too.

She heard the muted *ping* of his phone, and she waited breathlessly as he pulled it out of his pocket.

Lifting her head, she drew in a sharp breath as he tilted her chin and kissed her with a possessive voraciousness that held her in his thrall for a moment before she wrapped her arms around him and returned his embrace. Jared kissed her like a man possessed, his hunger undisguised as he plundered her mouth. His body shuddered, and he was breathing heavily as he pulled his lips from hers. "I don't want to miss you anymore. I think I've missed you my entire life. Be with me, Mara."

"I am with you," she whispered softly, soothingly near his ear. "I'm not going anywhere." The ferocity of his need for her fed her own cravings for him, and she wrapped her arms around him tighter, harder.

"I don't want anything to happen to you. I want you to live with me, be in my bed with me every night. I want your face to be the first one I see every morning when I wake up, and the last person I see or talk to before I sleep." He molded her body against his, the covetous hold enveloping her.

He's scared that something will happen to me.

Jared had only one other woman in his history that he'd cared about, and she'd died in a tragic accident. "I'll be here, Jared," she crooned, stroking the hair at the nape of his neck. She'd learned that life could end unexpectedly at any moment after her close call when her home burned to the ground. But she'd never leave Jared by choice. Not as long as he really cared about her.

Seeing him like this made her both elated and protective. This was the real Jared Sinclair, a big, gorgeous man with a tender heart. He'd opened his tortured, bottled-up emotions to her, and she was taking a leap of faith with him. She'd be just as open, just as willing to show him how she felt about him. She had the same fears, the same insecurities, but they weren't at the same painfully high level as his were. She'd had a mother who had loved her, and no painful past to overcome. Even with her lack of baggage, it wasn't easy to open her heart completely to a man that she cared about as much as she did about Jared. She wanted him so badly that it nearly terrified her. The emotion between them was so powerful, so intense that it was nearly painful.

"Stay," he grumbled greedily as Mara tried to pull away slightly to see his face. He dropped into the recliner and pulled her down onto his lap, keeping his arm locked around her waist as he reached for the laptop. "Here's your site."

Mara set her new phone down carefully on the small table beside their coffee and took the computer on her lap.

Incredible.

The site was amazing, colorful without being gaudy, and the name of her own business was sporting the logo she and Jared had designed together. It was classy and professional—everything she could have hoped for and more.

He reached around her waist and showed her how the site functioned, how to see her orders, traffic, and the various pages about her featured items.

When he was finished, Mara stared at the screen, lifting her hand to trace the logo on the website. "It's real. Mara's Kitchen is really happening." She and Jared had worked out most of the details except the actual business contract while she'd been laid up in his home, but this was so much more than she'd imagined. Jared had taken their ideas and made them come alive. Squinting at the screen, she clicked back hesitantly to her orders. "Oh, my God. Do I really have this many orders? How can that have happened so soon? The site just came up."

"I might have called in a few favors to advertise the launch of the site," Jared muttered sheepishly.

"You're already marketing?" She gaped at him, amazed at how efficiently and effortlessly he seemed to arrange things.

"I'm a billionaire with a hell of a lot of contacts, sweetheart. It doesn't exactly take a lot of effort on my part to get other businesses involved or to get the message out about an exciting new business."

"I have to get busy. I'll be dashing to fill these orders and get them out before Sarah's wedding. You called in what kind of favors?" She turned and looked at his face. He was smiling, one of those happy smiles that reached his eyes and turned her to mush.

"Okay. I called in quite a few favors. This is just the beginning. The orders will keep coming in."

"You're forcing friends or associates to order?"

Jared put his hands in the air in a sign of surrender. "I'm not forcing anyone to order. It's all about the products. I just asked for advertising and a few reviews from some food product reviewers. I sent them some of my personal stash for reviews. You owe me some more jam and taffy." He grinned at her.

"They all liked it?" she asked excitedly.

"They all loved it. Sweetheart, your skills are out of this world. I didn't expect anything less, and I asked them to be brutally honest. I didn't twist anybody's arm for a good review. I swear."

"Can I read some of them?"

Setting his head on her shoulder to see the screen, his fingers flew over the keyboard. "Here's one of them."

She read the words quickly but thoroughly, astonished that such a big food reviewer had actually tried her products. There wasn't one negative word, every bit of the review positive. At the bottom of it, her website link was displayed boldly. "No wonder I have orders already. Most of the country follows her advice and recommendations. Anybody who likes to cook or bake uses her recipes. I know I do."

"I know," Jared replied with a touch of arrogance. "You're going to outgrow this house and the equipment very quickly. And you're going to need some help."

"I have you." Not that she really expected Jared to don an apron and get to work, but she could do the cooking. He'd incredibly managed everything else with ease.

"Sweetheart, you want your products to succeed. I don't cook. You need help in the kitchen."

Mara lowered the computer to the floor. Her hands free, she swung her leg over and straddled his lap. "You're amazing." Eyes watering, she stroked a palm down his strong, freshly shaved jawline. "I think you'd look hot in an apron," she teased.

"Not happening," he rumbled. "But I'll do whatever else I can to make the launch fantastic."

"It's already incredible. I have to get moving and start getting the products ready." She started to scramble out of his lap, but a steely arm around her waist kept her planted exactly where she was.

"Not so fast. I expect a proper thank-you." His jade gaze drilled into her dark eyes.

"What do you consider proper?" She'd give this man anything he wanted. "Thank you for the phone, and everything you've done for the business. I'll reimburse you for it. I probably really do need a cell." If her business was going to start booming like this, she needed to be reachable at all times, and she could access the Internet with her phone.

"I don't want you to pay me back. It's a gift. I want you to kiss me," he demanded bossily.

"I'd do that anyway. The things you give me have nothing to do with how much I care about you." Her love for Jared was just there. But the thoughtful things he did just made her fall deeper and deeper in love with him.

"Show me." His tone was domineering, but his eyes were pleading.

Leaning down, her mouth so close to his that she could feel his warm breath on her face, she murmured seriously, "We have to solve your big problem before I get to work."

"Do I have a big problem?" Jared sounded puzzled.

Wiggling her hips, she pressed her core against his hard erection. "Very big."

"You're the only woman on earth who can fix that now," he replied, both challenge and desperation in his voice.

"Done," she whispered as she lowered her head and kissed him senseless.

She didn't get her orders started until noon, but it was time well spent. When she finally started cooking to fill orders, she did so with a whimsical smile on her face.

CHAPTER 16

Mara's Kitchen kept right on growing, and Jared was there every step of the way, clearing out other problems so she could focus on the products. She started working early and finished late at night. But she'd never been happier in her life.

The evening before Sarah's wedding, she and Jared sat at the living room table signing the contracts he'd finally produced. It had taken another threat of switching her business partnership to include Evan instead of Jared to get him to finally do the business paperwork. Mara had hated every moment of using that against him, but she'd hate herself even more for continuing to take advantage of Jared's kindness.

He'd hired a few teenagers temporarily for a summer job because her orders were getting overwhelming. She now had Nina to help her do some of the basics with the cooking prep, and Todd to do the continual cleaning of the kettles and equipment she needed several times every day. Jared had asked Emily to help him recruit the teens, both of them coming from families that Emily knew could really benefit from the extra money, since she ran the Youth Center and was aware of which families in the area were in need. Both of them worked hard at their assigned tasks, and it took a considerable amount of pressure off Mara to have their help every day. Jared worked on the marketing and business aspects of Mara's Kitchen, and he was doing an incredible job, judging by the explosive amount of orders she was getting on a daily basis. She knew that Jared was also starting to work on contracts for restaurants and businesses outside of Amesport to use her products on a regular basis.

"We need a hell of a lot bigger site for production, and a bunch of permanent employees," Jared grumbled as he signed his name grudgingly to the contracts that gave him equal interest in the company after Mara had signed.

Mara smiled at him, both of them sitting at the dining room table, papers spread out in front of them. "We can keep going like this for a while. We need to make money before we spend it."

"You need to invest money to make more money," Jared rumbled. "And you can't keep working these kinds of hours." He paused for a moment before he asked hesitantly, "Do you miss the doll shop?"

"No," she answered honestly. "I still regret the irreplaceable things I lost, stuff that belonged to my mom, but I've always loved making my consumable products more than I loved making dolls. I'll enjoy it as a hobby someday when I have more time, but making my products for the market has always been my favorite thing to do. Coming up with new things is challenging, new products that can be used for different recipes. Cooking has always been my first love." Mara sighed. "I wanted to hold on to my mother, but I've realized I didn't need the doll shop. She'll always be here." She put her right hand over her heart, her finger adorned by her mother's wedding ring. "I think she'd be proud of what I'm doing now. I may not be making dolls, but I'm still using traditions that have been passed down for generations, with my own twist. Honestly, I don't think she would have cared what I decided to do as long as I was happy doing it."

Jared leaned toward her and clasped the hand over her heart, bringing it to his lips to kiss her palm gently. "I think she would, too, baby," he said huskily.

"Do you think you'll ever go back to doing what you really love someday?" she asked him carefully. His former love of restoring old homes was a touchy subject.

"How did you know?" He released her hand gently, busying himself with arranging the papers they had signed.

"Evan. He told me you loved restoring old homes, that it was your first choice of careers. It's what you were going to do with Alan. I know you have some bad memories about that, but I want to see you be happy doing what you want to do." Would he ever be able to do it again? If she were in his place, she wasn't certain whether or not she could go back. Mara wasn't even positive that he should unless he could completely let go of the bitterness associated with what he loved. But the fact remained that it was his passion, something that gave him an immense amount of satisfaction. It broke her heart to think he might never pursue it again someday.

Jared released a heavy, masculine sigh and pinned her with an open gaze. "I don't know. I've never stopped studying the latest methods of restoration, or looking at old homes and imagining how they could be restored to their former glory, but I've never quite been able to gather the same enthusiasm I had when I first finished college."

Mara felt her eyes begin to water. Jared was an enigma to her some-times. He was over-the-top gorgeous, and completely confident in run-ning his commercial real estate company. He was a dirty-talking, arrogant, completely alpha male who seemed like he was in command of every-thing he touched. But there were times when he was vulnerable, exposing a gentle, wounded spirit that she was fairly certain was only visible to her. Now was one of those moments. "I just want you to be as happy as I am right now. It doesn't seem fair that I'm getting my dream and you aren't."

"I'm happier with you than I've been in my entire life, sweetheart. Don't cry for me." Leaning over, he snatched her out of her chair and into his lap. "I like helping you build something that you want. I'm enjoying what I'm doing right now."

"But later—"

"Later will take care of itself. Right now all I want is you," he growled. "You fill all of the lonely, unhappy places inside me, Mara. That's a damn miracle for me."

His words made the tears flow, and she hugged him to her, hoping the Fates would let her keep him forever. "I love you." The three little words popped out of her mouth unchecked. She'd been wanting to say them, needing to say them, but she'd been hesitant, unsure of whether he wanted to hear them or not. Now, she needed him to hear her, needed him to know he was loved. Between his loveless childhood and the big betrayal, Jared Sinclair needed somebody who loved him no matter what.

"What did you say?" he asked dubiously, as though he wasn't certain he'd heard her correctly.

"I said that I love you," she said firmly. "It doesn't have to mean anything to you, and I'm not saying it to trap you into anything. I just need to say the words and have you know how I feel. I promised myself and you that I'd be open. That's how I feel. I love you. It's just that simple. We don't need to act on it in any way. I just wanted to be able to tell you."

"Tell me again," he demanded, taking her face between his hands and forcing her to meet his gaze. "And it does mean something. It means everything to me."

"I love you, Jared Sinclair." Her voice was even louder, certain now that it was something he needed to hear.

He jerked her lips down to his, as though he was trying to capture the words with his mouth. Mara wrapped her arms around his neck and kissed him back, opening to him and shivering at the fierceness of his embrace. He devoured her as though he hadn't had a meal in days, penetrating her mouth desperately, but with a reverence that made her heart melt. The kiss was as worshipful as it was erotic, and the combination made her heart skitter as she tangled her tongue with his, needing the connection as desperately as he did.

Having said the words, she felt vulnerable, defenseless. But Jared's reassurance was in his nonverbal communication, wrapping her in his protection with every stroke of his tongue. His hands threaded through her hair, holding her mouth exactly where he wanted it and kissing her until she was breathless.

Finally, he released her mouth and buried his face in her hair, his powerful arms holding her tightly against him. "I need you, Mara. I need you so damn much that I can hardly breathe. Don't leave me. Please don't ever leave me."

Her heart wrenched with pain, his agonized voice shooting a burning ache through her soul. Everyone he'd ever cared about had left him and betrayed him. If he was feeling as raw as she was right now, he had to be in hell. "I won't. Not ever." And she meant it. He'd have to pry her off him to get rid of her now, unless he didn't want her around anymore. She wanted to be with him forever, help him heal all of his wounds. She wanted him to finally be happy.

"If you do leave, I'll find you," he growled.

Mara smiled against his chest at his sudden arrogance. He was a conundrum . . . again. But he was getting easier to unravel. Hot and cold. Demanding and kind. Dominant and vulnerable. She loved every single stubborn part of this man she was clinging to at the moment, because she was starting to understand every one of his reactions. His strength of character was incredible. Though he may have buried the sensitive part of himself for protection, it was still there. It showed in just about everything he did, even though he tried to hide it, tried to bury it forever.

"How hard would you look?" she asked him teasingly.

"I'd follow your beautiful ass to the ends of the earth," he vowed fiercely. "Now that I know that you love me, you're never getting rid of me."

Like she'd ever want to? Highly unlikely.

She shivered at his declaration. When Jared was possessive and dominant, he gripped and jerked an answering carnal response from her that she couldn't deny.

The jarring ring of Jared's cell phone interrupted her thoughts, and she glanced up at the clock. "The family dinner," she reminded Jared reluctantly. "It's probably Emily. We're late."

"You think I give a shit right now?" His lips skimmed over the vulnerable skin of her neck.

"Yes," Mara answered with a feigned calm she wasn't feeling at the moment. "Hope and Jason are there. You haven't seen them yet." Hope and Jason Sutherland had flown in this evening for the wedding tomorrow. Mara knew Jared hadn't seen Hope in a while. "Answer the phone and tell them we're coming."

Jared let go of Mara with an irritated sigh. "I wish we were coming at home right now," he grumbled unhappily, pulling the phone out of his pocket once Mara had slid off his lap.

She tried to stifle her laughter as Jared reluctantly answered the phone.

The evening dinner at Grady's home was casual, almost everybody in jeans . . . except for Evan, of course. He was dressed in his usual pristine suit and tie. The moment she saw Evan at the gathering, Mara swore she was going to buy the man a pair of jeans.

Emily had barbecued for the get-together, and Sarah had opted to keep the guests to just the Sinclair siblings and their significant others. Evan was leaving right after the wedding reception; Dante and Sarah were sneaking away for a week to honeymoon since Dante would be starting his new job as a detective for the Amesport Police Department right after they returned. Since Hope was pregnant and suffering severe morning sickness, Jason was taking her with him back to New York so he could finish his commitments there as soon as possible. Mara could tell by the way Jason looked at Hope that he wasn't letting his pregnant wife out of his sight. All the family was ecstatic over Hope's announcement that she and Jason were planning on making Amesport their permanent home in a few months. Her husband had to wrap up some things in New York and they'd be free to move their home base to Amesport permanently.

Mara didn't miss the satisfied light in Jared's eyes as Hope stood in the family room after dinner and made her official announcement.

Sitting next to him on the couch, she leaned in closer and whispered, "That's been your plan all along, wasn't it? You built a house for every one of your siblings here on the Peninsula to bring your family back together again." Mara knew it was true as certainly as she knew she loved Jared. He hadn't come here and built homes for all of his siblings after the accident just because he was bored, or because he'd wanted to escape from the pain of losing his friend and girlfriend. Jared had yearned to have his siblings back in the same area, together after years of being scattered across the country, and in Evan's case, across the world. Mara's heart skittered, aching for a man so lonely that he had come to where Grady had already made his permanent home and had meticulously used his architectural skills to carefully construct what he hoped would become more than just a vacation home for each of his siblings. For years, the plan hadn't worked, all of his siblings single and busy with their own lives. Now, he was going to have Hope, Grady, and Dante all in the same location, something Mara was pretty certain had been Jared's secret longing all along.

"I didn't admit it at the time, but I think that *was* what I really wanted," he answered in a husky whisper near her ear. "It's hard to believe it's actually happening. There's only Evan now."

Mara's heart skipped a beat. Did that mean Jared was planning on staying in Amesport forever? That his home on the Peninsula would be his permanent residence? Obviously he'd have to travel at times. He had projects all over the world. But was he planning on spending the majority of his time here in Maine?

"I'm not certain the little Amesport airport can accommodate that many private jets," she said with a levity she wasn't feeling, trying to calm her agitated nerves.

Jared grinned at her. "Then we'll make it bigger. That's one good thing about having a lot of billionaires in one town. There will be plenty of money around to help with improvements."

Mara could think of plenty of benefits, the most important one being that Jared would be in Amesport often. She opened her mouth to answer him, but her attention was taken away from Jared as Hope sat down on her husband's lap in a recliner and spoke more quietly. "Since we're all here right now, there's something else I need to tell you. I hid some things from all of you, and I'm sorry."

Mara saw Jason's face change instantly, his expression immediately concerned, his eyes growing dim as he ran a hand up and down Hope's back. "Sweetheart, maybe now isn't the best time . . ." Jason started to speak gravely.

"It is," Hope interrupted. "We're never all together, and I want them to know the truth. We're going to be close again, living in the same place. I need this for closure, Jason. I don't want to go on living a lie with my family. I love them. It's time."

Mara watched the interplay between Hope and Jason as they looked at each other, so much communicated without words, before Jason finally nodded his handsome blond head reluctantly. It was a signal that he was standing beside Hope no matter what.

The beautiful, auburn-haired Hope opened her mouth to speak, but her voice was weak and tremulous. "I lied. I've been lying to all of you for years until recently."

"Why?" Grady asked, sounding confused as Emily slipped her hand into Grady's from their place on a love seat.

"How?" Dante questioned gruffly as Sarah wrapped an arm around her fiancé's shoulders from her place in his lap in another chair.

Mara reached for and clasped Jared's hand, sensing that whatever Hope was going to say would impact the Sinclair siblings emotionally.

Tears sprang to Hope's eyes, and she tried to continue. "I-I hid things," she said in a voice heavy with sorrow.

Evan's voice boomed from his position in another recliner across the room from Hope. "She went to school for photography, a fact that none of us really knew. We all thought she was getting a useless degree, but in fact she graduated as a very talented photographer and started making her living traveling around the globe on risky assignments as an extreme weather photographer. She never shared what she was doing or where she was going because she knew we'd stop her." Evan turned his ice-blue eyes toward his sister as she gaped at him. "And damn right we would have if we had known. She would have had protection around the clock." Evan's voice was matter-of-fact, but his eyes never left Hope. "While she was in India chasing a cyclone, she was kidnapped, tortured, and . . ." Evan coughed into a fisted hand before he got out the last words. "She was repeatedly beaten, assaulted, and raped."

For the first time, Mara heard a note of anguish and remorse in Evan's usually ice-cold voice as he spoke the last sentence. His face was still neutral, but he hadn't been able to hide how he felt about what had happened to Hope. Mara squeezed Jared's hand as she saw the disbelieving, tortured look on his face.

"How did you know?" Hope asked Evan flatly, lowering her eyes to her lap.

"I didn't know until after you were involved with Sutherland, or I would have done something to prevent your dangerous activities. I only sent investigators on your trail when you disappeared in Colorado. I got the sense that everything wasn't quite what it seemed," Evan replied, his voice stern and angry.

"I was found the same day," Hope argued.

"I didn't give a shit," Evan snapped. "You're my baby sister, and I wanted to know what the hell I was missing."

"What the fuck happened after you were kidnapped?" Jared growled.

"Who the hell did it?" Dante asked angrily.

"We'll kill the bastard," Grady interjected furiously.

"He's dead," Hope explained quietly. "He was a political radical and crazy. Our Special Forces were already tracking him in a top-secret mission because they knew he was hiding in India. They saved my life, and they killed him when they stormed the remote building he was using for cover. He was holding me there." Hope took a deep breath before adding, "I'm sorry I lied to you all. After the way we were brought up, I just wanted to be free. You're all overprotective, and I love that about all of you, but I needed to live my own life."

Hope answered all of her brothers' rapid-fire questions, trying to smooth over all of the hurt feelings. The women all backed up Hope's decision, pointing out to their men that they *were* all overprotective, and that Hope had a right to her own life. Even if meant that she had to lie to them to get her independence.

"I admire your work, Hope," Mara told her during a rare period of silence. Hope had mentioned her professional name of H. L. Sinclair while everyone had been arguing. "I've never seen any of your extreme weather pictures, but I have actually seen some of your nature shots. I wanted some prints to put on my wall a while ago, and I came across some of your photos. They're extraordinary." She looked around her, noticing every set of eyes in the room was on *her*. "Hope is incredibly talented. Have any of you actually ever *seen* her photographs?"

"She's a photography genius. Hope is probably one of the most respected photographers in the world for her extreme weather photography. She has a gift, and she's amazingly skilled," Jason said supportively. "Luckily, her focus is now on her landscapes and nature photographs. She has nothing to prove to anyone anymore." Jason and

Hope exchanged a look of understanding, something that nobody probably understood except them.

Everyone grumbled that they hadn't . . . except Evan. "I've seen them all," Evan mentioned nonchalantly. "I agree she's incredibly talented. I have a number of her works on my walls now," Evan admitted. "I have to admit that I'm relieved that she's decided to change her focus. If she hadn't, I'd have agents all over her."

"They'd have to get in line after mine," Grady said sullenly.

"Mine would be there, too," Jared added.

"I'd hire some," Dante agreed in a surly voice.

"You'd all be too late," Jason told them defensively. "I'd already planned her protection had she not chosen to get out of the field on her own. And I would have been with her every moment no matter where she was."

Hope leaned over and kissed her husband tenderly before focusing her attention on Evan. "You really have some of my photos on your walls?" Hope asked hesitantly, hopefully, her eyes expressing her surprise.

Evan nodded sharply. "I'm proud of you, Hope."

Mara knew Evan's simple comment encompassed more than just her work as a photographer. Mara's heart squeezed thinking about what Hope had endured in the hands of her kidnapper, although she hadn't shared the gruesome details. She hurt for the physical and emotional pain that Hope had been through. "You're incredibly brave," Mara told Hope earnestly. "I'm just sorry for what happened to you."

Hope gave Mara a small smile. "Thank you. I got through it, and I'm happier now than I could have ever dreamed I'd be." She stopped to give her husband, Jason, an adoring look, her hand going to her still-flat abdomen protectively.

"We should have been there for you. You could have told us," Grady rumbled.

"Please understand that I needed time, Grady. I love you all, but I had to have time to heal," Hope answered softly.

"If this incident was top secret and it was hidden from the public eye, how the hell did Evan find out?" Dante questioned, looking directly at his eldest brother.

Evan stared back at Dante, his eyes neutral. "There aren't many areas where I don't have contacts." He shrugged mysteriously.

Jared let go of Mara's hand and stood, making his way slowly to his sister. "We weren't there for you then, but we are now. Hug me, dammit," he insisted gruffly.

Tears streaming down her face, Mara bit her lip as Jason let go of his wife, a tearful Hope rising to fling herself into Jared's arms. "I'm so sorry. I love you all so much," Hope sobbed as she clung to her youngest brother.

Everyone else except Evan rose, including the women, and passed Hope around for heartfelt hugs of forgiveness and love.

Although Evan watched every moment of the reunion, he never moved to hug his sister, or to join in the family rebonding.

He remained alone.

CHAPTER 17

"You have an incredible family," Mara told Jared an hour or two after Hope's revelation had shaken up the entire clan of Sinclairs. Although Evan tried not to appear affected by any of it, Mara knew better. While the rest of the family had been able to talk things out, hug each other in forgiveness and support, Evan had been brooding by himself. There was no healing for Evan, and her heart ached for him.

"I've missed them," Jared admitted in a low, thoughtful voice as he watched the whole bunch of Sinclairs around him laughing and teasing each other about everything from childhood exploits to their sports team preferences. "I just wished I had known about Hope."

"Nobody did. Evan didn't even know until it was over. I'm glad she showed everybody her work. You should be proud of her. She's talented," Mara told him thoughtfully.

Hope had brought up her portfolio online after every Sinclair had insisted on seeing it. They'd all spent some time marveling at her talent, and Mara could see that Hope was relieved and pleased that her family could finally acknowledge her career. Although Hope was now done shooting extreme weather and chasing natural disasters around the world, she was still building her name in nature photography. And in Mara's opinion, she was damn good at it.

"Jared? Somebody is here for you. She says she's an old acquaintance of yours." Emily hovered near where they were seated on the couch, her face appearing uncertain.

The doorbell had rung a few minutes ago, and Emily had hopped up, Grady right behind her protectively, to see who was visiting. Since the family was all here, and the Peninsula was private, he'd acted concerned. Obviously, they hadn't been expecting any more guests.

The room grew quiet, all eyes on Jared. "Who is it?" he asked, appearing confused.

It's a she? He isn't seeing anyone else right now. He told me he isn't.

Mara's heart started to race, her fear that it was an old flame that he'd taken to his bed who had tracked him down making a cold chill move slowly down her spine.

He wouldn't lie to me. He wouldn't. Even if it is an old flame, he isn't sleeping with her now.

Emily stepped aside, and a haggard-looking woman stepped up. "It's me. I'm sorry to intrude, but I had to see you." The older female was nervous, wringing her hands as she stood in front of Jared.

Mara turned her head in time to see a flash of intense pain cross over Jared's expression. She very much doubted that the relationship was sexual. The woman was old enough to be his mother, but judging from Jared's reaction, he obviously knew her.

"Mrs. Olsen?" Jared's voice cracked as he acknowledged her.

For the first time, Evan rose and strode over to the couch. "Ah . . . it seems to be the night for family skeletons to come out of the closet. But not this particular secret, and not tonight. You, madam, may leave immediately or I'll call the police and have you thrown out." The eldest Sinclair brother's voice was chillier than Antarctica.

"The police are already here," Dante growled as he rose and stood next to Evan. "What the hell is going on?"

"Who is she?" Mara asked breathlessly, sensing the tension in Jared's body.

"Selena's mother," Jared ground out painfully.

Mara vaulted to her feet, unable to contain her fury that this woman had actually sought Jared out after all he'd been through, after everything he'd done to protect her feelings in the past. She gritted her teeth as she spoke. "I'm sorry you lost your daughter, but Jared has been through enough over the years. Enough! Now leave." She wasn't letting this woman anywhere near Jared, and she stepped between them, essentially blocking Jared's vision so he didn't have to look at the woman who had slapped him down and blamed him for her daughter's death.

"I'm not here to hurt him again," the woman said nervously, anxiously.

"Then why are you here?" Mara demanded to know.

"I was hoping I could have a word alone with Jared," Mrs. Olsen said quietly, fidgeting uncomfortably.

"Not until hell freezes over," Mara spat out at her vehemently. She wasn't leaving this woman alone with Jared so she could spew more venom at him. It might have been understandable when Selena's death was so new, so heart wrenching. But several years later, she wasn't getting her claws into Jared again.

"We're all family here. Say what you have to say now or leave," Evan demanded icily. "But be warned that if I don't like what you're saying, your ass will be outside in seconds."

"I can't say I know exactly what's happening, but I'll be helping him remove you," Dante agreed.

"Selena kept journals," Mrs. Olsen blurted out suddenly. "After she died, I couldn't bring myself to read any of them, and I wasn't sure I should. About a month ago, I found them packed away. I decided that I wanted to know her thoughts during the year before she died. She'd grown distant, and I wanted to know why." She stopped and took a deep breath. "I know she was in love with Alan, and she was sleeping with him even though she was in a relationship with you, Jared. I want to know what really happened the night she died." Tears flowed down the woman's haggard, worn-out expression. "I don't think I can let it go until I do know, now that I've read those journals."

Jared stood and brought Mara up against his side. "There's no point in rehashing it now," Jared insisted. "Selena and Alan are gone, Mrs. Olsen. As much as I wish that wasn't true, we can't bring them back. I told you how sorry I was, and I don't expect you to ever stop hating me. But let it go."

"I just need to know, Jared," the woman pleaded.

Jared kept his mouth clamped shut, shaking his head regretfully.

He can't do it even now. He can't get the words out or hurt her mother.

Mara clasped his hand in support. Obviously, he still wasn't going to tell the truth, even though Selena's mother knew the worst of it.

So Evan spoke for him. "My brother didn't know about the two of them, or that they were sleeping together. Jared was working, trying to get the business going that he generously offered to partner with Alan. On the night of the party, Jared was there, and he was sober just like he had promised to be. When your daughter and Alan disappeared, he went looking for them and caught them having sex in one of the bedrooms where the party was being held. Feeling heartbroken and betrayed, which he was, he left. An ordinary reaction from a man who'd just had his heart figuratively dug out of his chest with a spoon, madam." Jared pinned the woman with his intense, blue-eyed stare. "Nobody knows what happened after that except the three people involved, and they're all dead. I understand you were devastated when your daughter died, and so was Jared. He took the blame at an extremely high price to his own mental health. He never said a disparaging word about your daughter to you or anyone, never told anyone that she had cheated. He wanted you to have your happy memories without besmirching your daughter's reputation." Evan's voice had been eerily calm, as though he'd been talking about a minor business deal. He crossed his arms in front of him, his gaze never leaving the distraught woman in front of him.

"Evan. Stop." Jared put a hand on his oldest brother's shoulder. "This won't change anything."

Shaking off Jared's hold, Evan said, "I hope for your sake that it *does* change things for you, Jared."

"I'm so sorry," Mrs. Olsen wailed. "I understand why you left. It was a natural reaction. You were good to Selena, and I'm so sorry she hurt you."

"I should have stayed," Jared grunted uncomfortably. "I should have taken both of them home myself even though I was hurt."

"I don't think Selena would have gone with you once you knew the truth. She wanted you to help her pay the rest of her way through school, and once you knew about her and Alan, she would have known it was over. You did what any person would do. The two people you cared about the most betrayed you," Mrs. Olsen sobbed out. "I loved my daughter, and I wish I could have her back, but she was using you, and *I'm sorry* for that. I really did think she loved you. For what it's worth, Alan did try to stop the affair, and he wanted to tell you the truth. It was all in her journal. He did love Selena, apparently." She swiped tears from her face as she looked up at Jared. "You didn't do anything wrong, Jared. I'm so sorry. I don't expect *you* to forgive *me*, but I suspected something like this had happened when I read Selena's journal. I had to seek you out. I needed to know the truth so I could lay everything to rest. I loved Selena more than anything, but I don't like the things she did."

"I do forgive you," Jared said huskily. "Selena was a beautiful woman, and she wasn't evil, Mrs. Olsen. She just fell in love with some-body else and wanted to finish school. She knew you didn't have the money. I did. I don't hate her, and I wish she wasn't gone. She had some wonderful parts of her that the whole world will miss."

Mara's heart squeezed with love for this incredible man beside her. Even after all he'd been through, after all he was finding out about a woman he had loved, he still mourned her death.

Mrs. Olsen sniffled. "That's very kind of you to say after how I treated you at her funeral, after I blamed you."

Jared shrugged. "I understood. You were mourning a daughter. I can't imagine anything more painful than that. I just wanted you to remember the good things about Selena."

"I try to remember the good things," she told Jared quietly.

Jared nodded. "You should. I know I will. Selena, Alan, and I had a lot of good memories. We were all young and made our mistakes."

"But what she did to you—"

"Doesn't matter anymore," Jared finished for her. "We were still college age, Mrs. Olsen. Selena was a smart, headstrong girl, and Alan fell for her like a ton of bricks. Selena was still in college, not quite grown up yet. Focus on the good things she did. We all make stupid errors when we're young." He put a hand on her shoulder sympathetically.

"You were a good boy, Jared. And it looks like you've grown into a fine man, too." The older woman looked up at him. "Are you happy?" She looked at Mara. "Is this your wife?"

"I am happy now. And this is Mara, the woman who changed my life," Jared said in a graveled voice.

"I'm sorry about your daughter, Mrs. Olsen," Mara said gravely, holding her hand out to the woman who had caused Jared so much pain. Although she hated the anguish this woman had put Jared through, she hadn't known the truth. Now that she did, Mara admired the elder lady's gumption for seeking Jared out to find out what had really occurred the night her daughter died, and trying to right some of the wrongs. Many parents wouldn't want to know. Obviously, this woman did, and Mara was grateful to her for finally giving Jared the closure he so desperately needed, at the expense of her own pain. It was almost like the relationship between them had come full circle. Jared had suffered in silence for all these years, blaming himself. Mrs. Olsen had suffered thinking she'd blamed Jared unfairly, and then started blaming herself. Finally, they could both find peace, or so Mara fervently hoped.

Mrs. Olsen took Mara's outstretched hand, shaking it and then patting it gently. "Make him happy then, Mara."

"I plan on it," she answered reassuringly.

Jared stepped forward once Mara had let her hand drop to her side and scooped the older woman into a hug. Mara watched as Mrs. Olsen closed her eyes and hugged him back. Tears sprang to her eyes as she watched Jared actually embrace his tormenter, forgiving so easily because the woman had lost her daughter. Jared's ability for compassion and empathy humbled her.

Wrapping an arm around the woman's shoulders, Jared walked her out to her car. Trusting that the woman wouldn't harm Jared emotionally now, Mara stayed behind to give them a few minutes of privacy. The minute they'd exited through the doorway, the room exploded with questions.

"What the hell was that all about?"

"What happened to Jared?"

"Who the hell was she?"

Evan motioned for all of them to sit, and he calmly answered their questions. Mara smiled at him, knowing he was answering the difficult inquiries so that Jared wouldn't have to do it. Just like Evan had spilled the stories about Hope, so she didn't have to go through the pain of doing it herself.

Evan explained the entire incident, not going into any of the details about Jared's subsequent bender. All he told the other Sinclairs was that he'd visited Jared and he was taking the deaths of his friends hard and blaming himself.

"I wish I had known," Dante grumbled. "How did we ever get so separated? Hope and Jared both went through hell, and none of the rest of us knew except Evan. Why? I knew Jared was different, that he'd changed. But he wouldn't talk about it. Maybe if we'd stayed closer, he would have."

"I knew because I know everything," Evan answered arrogantly. "Jared wasn't ready to talk back then. No amount of discussion would have convinced him that what happened wasn't his fault. He needed time."

It *might* have helped Jared if he'd had support, but Mara noticed that Evan didn't go there. She assumed it was because the incident was over, and he didn't want his brothers taking on any guilt for what Jared had gone through alone, just like he didn't want them to have excessive remorse over what had happened to Hope.

Grady glared at Evan. "Why didn't you tell us about Hope and Jared?"

Evan shrugged. "Neither of them were my stories to tell. I knew you'd all know the truth someday, and there wasn't much you could do after those things had already happened."

"How did you think we were going to find out?" Dante asked.

"We're Sinclairs," Evan drawled. "We might be separated by distance, but we're bound by blood and our histories."

"And because you all love each other," Sarah added fiercely. "You've always been there when you needed each other. Maybe it wasn't the time for Jared and Hope to share, but we all know now. And you're all supportive."

"I'm so glad you're all together again," Emily said with a sigh before looking at Mara expectantly. "Does this mean you and Jared are getting married and staying in Amesport?" Her voice was hopeful.

"No," Mara replied hastily, not wanting Emily to have any expectations. "I mean, we're just . . . um . . . dating."

Sarah snorted. "He said you're the woman who has changed his life. That doesn't sound like a 'just dating' scenario to me."

"Leave the poor woman alone," Evan said imperiously. "Taking Jared on for life would be a big decision for any woman. Sinclairs aren't easy to deal with, and Jared's no exception. He's a pain in the ass."

Dante chuckled. "Don't say that too loud. I'm getting hitched tomorrow."

"I have no doubt that Sarah heard me, and that she's well aware that you're a pain in the ass, too," Evan answered, deadpan.

Sarah giggled. "He can be occasionally." She exchanged a sultry look with her fiancé.

"It's a damn good thing that I'm perfect," Grady commented in a cocky voice.

Emily trilled with delighted laughter. "Only in your dreams, big guy. But I have to admit you're pretty close."

Mara's heart swelled as she watched the whole Sinclair clan rib each other good-naturedly. It was remarkable that after a night of so many shared secrets, so much drama and pain, all of them could come together again so seamlessly. They were all survivors, and so resilient that Mara admired every one of them.

She now saw being a part of Sarah's wedding taking place tomorrow as an honor instead of a chore or a favor. This was a special family, born of wealth and privilege, but all with good hearts.

Hopefully, meeting with Selena's mother would be a turning point for Jared. Every day he had become more and more open, but she could tell he was still struggling, still hesitant. Tonight might have finally brought him absolution, his way back to living a normal life again. She wanted that for him so desperately that her heart ached.

"Anybody up for dessert now?" Emily asked loudly. "Mara made a chocolate turtle cheesecake. I can make coffee and we can dish out dessert."

"I'll dish it up," Dante offered hastily, springing out of his seat.

"I'll help," Jason insisted, springing to his feet.

"Oh, no you don't," Hope said as got to her feet with a delighted laugh. "It will be gone before it's on the plates. Chocolate addict," she accused, following her husband toward the kitchen.

Sarah and Emily came over and each of the women grabbed one of Mara's hands. "Come on. We'd better hurry before your dessert is gone. Poor Jared doesn't even have a shot because he stepped outside. Dante and Grady are playing dirty," Emily said jokingly.

A giggle escaped Mara's mouth as the two women pulled her to her feet. "Evan?" Mara looked over at the eldest brother. "Would you like some?"

"No thank you," he answered haughtily. "I try to avoid carb- and sugar-laden products that have no nutritional value whatsoever." .

"No junk food?" Mara gasped. "You're missing out on something good."

"I'm accustomed to that," Evan mumbled under his breath.

Mara heard him, or she thought she did. Maybe she hadn't understood him correctly. "Did you say something?"

"No," Evan answered cantankerously.

She looked at him quizzically, trying to figure out the oldest Sinclair brother. If she took him at face value, he *was* actually a jerk, and she had no doubt that arrogance and testiness were genuinely parts of his personality. But there was something else, something she couldn't quite put a finger on. During certain moments, Evan was so much more than he seemed, most of those instances revolving around protecting or shielding his family. Did anyone else see how dedicated he was to his siblings? Or was she the only one who could see something else beneath his finely sculpted image of snobbery and control?

Her heart went out to Evan, sitting by himself there in the family room, his face devoid of emotion. He seemed so separate, so . . . lonely. Honestly, she didn't think he was happy that way, either. So why was he continuing to live that way?

"Mara, are you coming? Grady's got the pie!" Emily's laughing voice floated out to her from the kitchen.

Shaking off her desolation from watching Evan Sinclair sitting isolated in the family room, she smiled as she walked to the kitchen. Once there, she realized pandemonium was breaking out, everyone fighting to take possession of the pie.

"What are they doing?" Jared moved behind her and wrapped his arms around her waist as he came back inside.

"Fighting over the chocolate turtle cheesecake I brought," she answered, amused.

"Maybe I should be in on that." He tightened his arms around her waist and kissed her on the temple.

"No need." She turned and wrapped her arms around his neck. Leaning closer, she whispered in his ear, "Don't tell anybody, but I made one all for you. It's at home in the refrigerator."

His deep green gaze captured hers, his eyes filled with humor. "No wonder I fucking worship you."

"For my pie?" she teased.

"Because you actually made one especially for me, and a million other reasons." He lowered his forehead against hers. "Pie later. I think I'd rather have you for dessert. Let's go home, unless you want to fight for dessert."

Sweet Jesus. All she really wanted was to lick on him for an after-dinner treat. He looked so damn handsome he took her breath away. "I'm sure you'll share."

"Everything I have, baby," he answered, his words almost like a vow.

"I want to lick your entire body for my dessert," she whispered in his ear, nipping his earlobe lightly.

"Holy fuck. We're out of here," Jared declared, lifting her up and carrying her toward the door.

"Aren't we going to say good-bye?"

"Later," Jared bellowed to his family, his eyes never leaving hers.

His back to his family, Jared never noticed that all of his siblings stopped fighting for a moment to smile after their retreating figures with hope in all of their eyes.

CHAPTER 18

"So did you really build all these homes on the Amesport Peninsula just because you hoped all your family would come back here someday?" Mara was salivating to touch Jared, and she distracted herself with the question as he drove the short distance back to his house.

"I think I did," Jared answered in a low, thoughtful voice. "After Evan sobered me up and went back to his business, I needed to feel like I was doing something useful. I told each of my siblings that I was building them a house after I went and visited Grady and saw this peninsula. It was like some kind of compulsion. None of them objected, so with their input on what they wanted, I did it. I wanted to make everything just right, maybe because I really did want them to stay."

"Did you stay with Grady all that time?"

"No. I took up almost permanent residence at the Lighthouse Inn. They have a good breakfast," he answered, his voice light.

Mara knew the adorable bed-and-breakfast that had been in Amesport for years. "Somehow, I can't see you staying there."

"Why? I liked it."

The place was nice, but rustic. "It's lovely, but you're a bit too pretty for a place that rustic." She knew she'd be in trouble for saying it, but she couldn't resist.

"You're in trouble, woman," he growled ominously.

"Good. I want to be in trouble." She unbuckled her seat belt as they pulled into Jared's long driveway. Rising onto her knees, she leaned over the console of the vehicle and started to unbutton his shirt, delving beneath the hem with her other hand to make contact with his warm skin.

"I'm driving here," Jared said with very little conviction.

"I'm not," she answered mischievously, popping the top button on his jeans and lowering the zipper. "You're hard."

"It's a chronic condition whenever you're around," he grunted. "Hell, it's constant even when you're not around because I'm fucking thinking about you."

"I love you, Jared. Right now, I can't wait any longer to touch you." Mara's heart was overflowing with emotion for this man, and that organ was taking control. The entire evening had been so intense, and she'd wanted to touch him, comfort him somehow.

"Fuck! You're killing me."

"You'll live," she purred, liberating his enormous cock and stroking over the shaft. The feel of him delighted her. He was like steel covered by silk, and stroking him was divine. "I have to touch you or I'll die of longing."

"Do you know what you do to me, Mara? Do you have any idea how good that feels, and how incredible it is to me that you're that eager for me? That's why it makes me crazy when you beg for me to make you come. No woman has ever wanted *me* that damn badly," he said with a groan.

Scorching liquid heat flooded between her thighs, and her heart raced like she'd just run a marathon. Jared should be loved like this, needed to be loved like this. The women he'd been with mystified her.

How could any woman *not* want Jared desperately? "I don't just want you. I need you." Her mouth closed over his cock with a hungry moan.

A deep, reverberating sound left Jared's throat as he braked the vehicle in front of his house and slammed the car into gear and cut the engine. He wound his hands into her hair and fisted the locks desperately. "Not. Like. This."

Disappointed when Jared used his grasp on her scalp to lift her head from his cock and open his car door, Mara reluctantly straightened up and licked her lips, still drunk from the taste of him as her gaze met Jared's. Her pulse began to race as she observed the dangerous, feral look in his eyes. "I'm sorry. I thought you might like—"

"Don't ever fucking apologize for touching me," Jared demanded, ripping his gaze from hers and coming around the car in nothing more than a few heartbeats, snatching her from the seat. She wrapped her legs around his hips instinctively as he grasped her around the waist. "I need you to touch me. This body belongs to you, baby. Understand?"

Mara's breath hitched as she nodded, her eyes locked with his, his words making her shiver with need. *He belongs to me.* "Then why did you stop me?"

"Because I'd have been a goner after just a few more sucks of that gorgeous mouth, or a few more flicks of that hot little tongue. Fuck knows it makes me crazy, but it isn't what I need right now, and I don't think it's what you need, either."

She lowered her feet to the ground after he'd taken a few steps. The motion lights had come on at the front of the house automatically when they'd pulled into the drive, and Mara bit her lips as she nearly drooled at his muscular chest, bared because she'd opened the buttons. The tails of the light green shirt dangled at the sides of his hips, and his jeans hung low and sexy with the zipper open and his cock standing about as erect and rigid as possible. "God, you're beautiful, Jared," she said in a soft, breathy voice. "What do you need right now?" Mara was aching to give him anything he wanted, anything he needed.

Jared yanked at the hem of her shirt and she lifted her arms as he made short work of removing it and then the flimsy bra she was wearing. Dropping on his knees despite the cement on the driveway, he unfastened her jeans and yanked them down with her panties until she could step out of them.

He stood, crowding her nude body against the bumper of his SUV. "I need us to lose ourselves in each other. I need to feel you clinging to me, touching me like you'll never let go. I need to touch you, fuck you until the only thing you can think about is me. I want to hear my name on your lips with every breath you take while I make you come." He slapped his hands on the hood of the vehicle, putting a palm on each side of her body, his eyes burning with an intensity that was nearly blinding. Lowering his head, he moved his lips along her temple and down her neck. "You smell so fucking good. I want to breathe you in until the scent of you permeates every cell in my body so I'll never inhale again without savoring your essence."

Mara was panting just from listening to the erotic, romantic words he was saying in a husky, *fuck-me* voice. "Jared. Please. I need you." She moved her hands to his shoulders and lowered the shirt to his upper arms. He shrugged it off impatiently, and she stroked her hands over his chest, letting them glide to his back and then into his hair. She couldn't get enough of him, couldn't get close enough to him to satisfy her. "Fuck me, Jared. Fuck me now."

His mouth crashed down on hers as his muscular arms wrapped around her waist. One of his hands threaded through her hair, and he held her prisoner, tilting her head so he could take complete control of the demanding embrace. Lifting her bare legs around his waist, Mara moaned and writhed against his burgeoning cock, desperate to feel him inside her.

He conquered her with his mouth, spearing between her lips again and again, entangling her tongue with his until she was breathless. Panting, she begged him again, "Please."

"What do you need, sweetheart?"

"You. Just you. Make it hard, make it rough. I need you to make me yours." Mara wanted to sob with the need for him to claim her with a possessiveness that would satisfy her unbearable craving for him.

Lowering her legs from around his waist, he stepped back and turned her body, pressing her hands onto the hood of the car. "Like this?" he asked roughly, demanding an answer as his hand stroked down her back and over the cheeks of her ass.

Oh, God, yes.

"Yes. Please."

Jared delved between her thighs, spreading her flesh and running his fingers through her moist heat.

Mara threw her head back as he probed her pussy with expert fingers, her ass in the air, her hands on the car hood keeping her in a bent-over position. Jared brushed against her clit just enough to make her moan.

Her body jolted as he slapped her ass. Hard.

Whack.

The carnality of his erotic punishment nearly made her climax right then and there. He had her in a vulnerable position. Standing at her side, he was able to tease her pussy with one hand and smack her ass with the other at the same time. The pleasure-pain sensation nearly drove her insane, and she screamed his name as he slapped her ass again.

Whack!

"That's for calling me pretty," he told her dominantly, huskily.

If this was what she got, she'd call him pretty ten times a day. "Make me come, Jared." The spiral of tension in her belly was almost unbearable.

He moved behind her and grasped her hips. "I'm going to go deep this way, Mara," he told her in a strangled groan.

"Good. Go deep," she panted, more than ready to feel him inside her. "And don't be careful. Claim me. Please." More than anything, she wanted Jared to lose control. He'd never hurt her, and she wanted him just as raw as she was at this moment.

He slammed into her, and he wasn't gentle. Mara could feel his control had snapped, and instinct and elemental desire had taken hold.

"You feel so fucking amazing. It's like we were made just for each other." He pulled back and stroked into her again.

She wanted to tell him that she felt the same way, but all she could do was moan, words escaping her as her need tore at her. His hips began to move faster, and Mara thrust back to meet every frantic thrust, her climax clawing at her.

So close. So damn close.

"Jared. Jared. Jared." She started chanting his name with every breath she took, unable to stop herself. Nothing else mattered. Nothing else existed except him.

"Come for me, baby," he commanded, taking one hand off her hip and wrapping it around her waist, stroking down to her pussy.

Mara ignited as Jared took the tiny bundle of nerves between his thumb and index finger, putting pressure on it while he stroked. She came screaming his name, her sheath tightening against his cock.

He threaded a large lock of her hair through his fingers and tugged her head back, nipping at her neck with a love bite that sent her reeling, tumbling end over end. The only thing keeping her grounded was Jared's tight, possessive hold.

Pumping into her several more times, he spilled his warm release inside her with a feral groan of satisfaction. Lowering his body over hers, he turned her head with her hair, capturing her lips in a raw meeting of mouths that left her chest heaving as he rested against her back, his breath ragged and uneven as he buried his face in her hair. "Christ. Did I hurt you?" he asked in a low, anguished voice.

Mara let out a strangled laugh. "No. I'm starting to think I need it a little rough. Did that orgasm seem like I was in pain?" she teased.

Jared straightened and turned her body, lifting her ass onto the hood of the car and wrapping his arms around her protectively. "I just don't ever want to hurt you."

"You won't," she assured him, hugging him until their bodies were skin to skin and wrapping her legs around his waist to bring him closer.

"It was a nice way to initiate your new car," Jared said with laughter in his voice. "I'll never look at this vehicle again without getting a boner."

Puzzled by his words, Mara asked, "What new car?"

"The one your beautiful ass is sitting on." He pulled back and grinned at her.

Oh, God, what did he do?

Turning her head, she finally noticed that the vehicle they'd been using as makeshift furniture was not Jared's SUV, but parked right next to it. This particular shiny new vehicle was very similar, but as she looked closer, she realized that the color was a deep metallic red. She hopped off it with a squeal of distress, Jared catching her as she moved. Mara lowered her feet to the ground and gawked at the car parked right next to Jared's. "You bought another Mercedes SUV?"

"A work vehicle for you. Mara, you can't keep driving your old truck. Everything on it needed to be fixed. The business is growing. You need a new vehicle."

She looked at Jared as he tucked himself back into his jeans and zipped them, leaving his shirt open. Her mouth went dry as she eyed the beautiful vehicle. "I can't keep this. It's too expensive. I know I need a newer car, but this is too much." She looked around her. "What happened to my truck?"

"Todd said he'd take it. He's mechanical and can fix everything on it with the money he's earning. Then his family will have a vehicle. He's seventeen. He wants wheels."

"You just gave it to him?" she asked indignantly, reaching for her clothing. She pulled her bra and T-shirt back on, then tugged on her panties and jeans awkwardly, well aware that Jared was watching her.

"You'll have to sign it off to him. But he wanted to get to work on it. He's really excited."

"Dammit. You knew I'd never take back a vehicle that was promised to Todd." She folded her arms in front of her and glared at Jared. She loved him with every fiber of her being, but his actions were way too high-handed, even for Jared.

"Why in the hell would you want to take it back? If you don't like this one, I'll get you something else." He looked at her like he was really confused.

Mara tapped her foot against the concrete, trying to keep her temper. "Because it was my truck, and I can't take a gift this expensive. Jared, you've already helped me out enormously, and I don't know what I would have done without you. But this is too much." Honestly, she really didn't know what she would have done had Jared not come into her life. He'd been her rock, the person who had saved her from homelessness. And for him, the things he was doing for her weren't big things. "Why didn't you ask me first?"

He shrugged. "Why? I handle the business part of Mara's Kitchen, and a new vehicle for you was in the contract. I guess I should have checked with you about giving your truck to Todd, but I didn't think you'd mind since you have a new SUV."

Oh, God. She hadn't really read every line of the contract. She trusted Jared, and she'd only checked to make sure he wasn't screwing himself. And all things considered, she wouldn't have minded giving her truck to Todd at all. His family had so little, and if the vehicle would help him, she would have gladly turned it over to him if she got other transportation. "I should have been consulted. We're partners, and it was my personal property."

"You're right. I should have. But you've been working yourself into the ground. I thought it was something I could take care of for you."

Mara's heart dropped to the ground at Jared's contrite expression. He'd been trying to help, and it made her feel like a bitch. "We really are from two different worlds," she mumbled irritably, unable to make Jared feel worse than he did by being upset with him. "If it concerns my personal property, I'd appreciate it if you'd ask next time." Dammit. She was so easy. But Jared had been through so much today that she didn't want to argue. She wanted to talk to him about how things had gone with Mrs. Olsen, and find out if he felt better, if it had helped resolve anything for him. All she really wanted right now was to touch him and for him to hold her while they talked about it.

"Okay," he agreed gruffly. "But if I had to, I would have had someone do you a favor and steal that damn truck. It was dangerous. And you needed a new vehicle, dammit."

Okay . . . maybe he wasn't *all* that remorseful. Mara had a hard time biting back a smile. Jared was incorrigible and so honest that he could get himself in trouble very easily. The problem was, she could see his concern for her. He wasn't doing this for any other reason. "You're lucky you gave me that fabulous orgasm. I'm too sated to argue with you."

"So that's how I can get whatever I want? Make you come?" A slow grin formed on his lips and spread to his eyes as he looked at her hungrily.

She couldn't help herself. She teased him back. "It certainly wouldn't hurt, I'm sure."

"If you want something from me, all you have to do is smile at me like you are right now. I'll give you anything you want," he told her bluntly, genuinely.

"You know it's almost impossible to get angry with you for very long." Mara moved forward and stroked his sexy, stubbled jaw. "What if I want you to stop buying things for me?" She beamed at him to make her point.

"Everything except that," he grumbled, leaning down to kiss her tenderly. "If you're in need of something, I want to be the one to provide it."

"Thank you for the vehicle. It's beautiful. But since when is a car part of a business contract?"

His grin grew broader. "Since I asked the attorney to put it in there and hoped you wouldn't notice."

She lifted her eyebrow at him. "So you were actually hoping I wouldn't read the fine print?"

"Yep," he admitted shamelessly.

Sweet Jesus. Jared was breathtakingly gorgeous even when he was being an arrogant ass. "You win. This time."

"Is it really so hard? Letting me get you what you need? I want to know you're safe." His tone was hesitant and confused.

"Yes." She sighed, knowing Jared had gone through the trauma of losing people he loved, and she *did* understand that he wanted anyone he cared about to be safe. "Every woman in your life has used you because of your money. I want you to trust that I'm *not* after your money."

"I already do know that. You've had to do things yourself your whole life, Mara. Let me do some things for you. I can't cook, so I can't make you incredible meals just because I want to, and I can't make sure you have an extra pie just because I know you like it. Let me do what I *can* do. Please."

She could hardly compare the two things, but she got his point. For him, getting her what she needed was his way of showing he cared. Throwing those gifts back in his face hurt him as much as it would hurt her if he refused to eat things that she made especially for him. "I appreciate them, Jared. I'm just not sure how to accept them. In my world, men don't give women they're dating a new vehicle that costs more than some people's houses."

Jared shrugged. "In my world, women don't waste their time making their man homemade baked goods. I'm willing to bet you spend more time cooking for me than I spent buying this vehicle."

Mara caved, understanding what he was trying to say. If the two of them were going to be together for however long it lasted, she was going to have to accept Jared as he was or not at all.

Fact: He was a billionaire.

Fact: For him, the money he spent on her was nothing.

Fact: He wanted to do things for her, and this was his way of showing that he cared. It was no different than when she did things for him.

"Okay," she conceded. "I'll get used to it. Just no more giving away my personal property without asking me first."

"Agreed. You're right about that. I thought I was helping, but when you put it that way, I understand why you're upset," he answered agreeably. "So I can get you whatever I want now?" he asked hopefully.

God, she loved this man. "I don't need anything else right now except you, Jared. Let me get used to this before you spring anything else on me, okay? I need to work into this slowly." She held out her hand. "Can I have the keys? I want to look at my gift."

He dug into the pocket of his jeans and held out the keys. "It's nothing flashy. I didn't think you'd like that. It's practical."

Mara smiled at him, thinking the expensive luxury vehicle was anything but practical. It was a Mercedes, for God's sake.

Remember Jared's status. For him it probably is practical.

She snatched the keys and ran a reverent hand over the shiny surface of the car. "I can't believe I screwed on a new Mercedes," she muttered.

"We didn't exactly fuck on it," Jared commented, sounding disappointed that they hadn't.

She fumbled with all of the fancy buttons until the car unlocked. Nearly gasping at the plush leather interior, she inhaled, still unable to believe that the new vehicle was really hers. "Want to take a ride?" she asked Jared, her heart hammering at the thought of actually driving a car this expensive.

Jared hopped into the passenger seat like an eager teenager as she slid into the driver's seat.

"I love the smell of leather," Mara mused, inhaling deeply.

"Does that mean you like it?" Jared asked anxiously. "Because if you don't, I can get you—"

Mara pressed her hand over his mouth and met his deep green stare. "Don't go there. I love it. But not nearly as much as I love you." Her heart swelled as she replaced her hand with her lips, savoring the sensual feel of his mouth under hers.

"Are you sure you really want to go for a ride?" Jared asked when she pulled back reluctantly to start the vehicle.

"A short one," she agreed, her body aching for Jared's again. "First the new car, and later I'll ride you."

"Would that be before or after I get my chocolate turtle cheese-cake?" he asked in a sexy, husky baritone as he nibbled at her neck, his big palm running erotically up the inside of her thigh.

Mara's core flooded with heat, and she squeaked, "Before *and* after. Definitely." She could barely think as she put the purring vehicle in gear and started turning it around. It was going to be a very short ride.

"I love the way you think," he said with a chuckle as his hand finally landed between her thighs.

"I'm driving here," Mara parroted his earlier words desperately.

Jared simply laughed harder.

CHAPTER 19

Dante and Sarah had wanted an informal wedding at the Amesport Youth Center, the very place where Dante had saved Sarah's life, and the building with the biggest ballroom in town. With Grady's wife, Emily, running the Youth Center, Grady Sinclair had been a huge donor for the refurbishing of the entire building, and what had once served as a recreation hall was now an enormous, beautiful ballroom. It was the venue for both the wedding and the reception.

It was a Sunday, and the Youth Center was closed. Guests had poured in early for the noon wedding, all of them eager to see their new felony detective for the Amesport Police Department get hitched to one of their own local physicians.

Dante's three handsome and very eligible cousins had arrived, and as Mara peeked out of the area behind the stage and saw all of the Amesport Sinclair brothers and Jason Sutherland speaking with the Sinclair cousins, Micah, Julian, and Xander, her breath caught and refused to move smoothly in and out of her lungs. "Sweet Jesus," she murmured.

"What is it?" Randi asked quietly from behind her.

"The Sinclair men and Jason Sutherland," Mara replied, moving aside so Randi could look. Although her eyes had automatically

gravitated to Jared, the eight men together were breathtakingly beautiful. Dante, Jared, Grady and Evan were in black tuxedos, and Jason,
Micah, Julian, and Xander were in custom-tailored suits.

"Holy hotness," Randi whispered loudly. "They make this event
look like a hot male model convention instead of a wedding."

"How can eight men, seven of them Sinclairs, be that perfect?"
Emily asked as she shoved her way in to look.

"Excellent gene pool," Sarah whispered, not bothering to look since
she'd met the cousins earlier. "It's almost impossible that at least one of
them isn't a hottie. But the Sinclairs defy conventional wisdom." She
sighed as she adjusted the small wreath of red roses on her head, a trail
of fine lace hanging down in the back. Sarah hadn't wanted a typical
bridal veil, telling all of the women with a laugh that she didn't want
her face covered. She'd wanted to see Dante in a tux as clearly as possible for as long as possible.

Sarah was a beautiful bride, and Mara couldn't wait until Dante got
an eyeful of his wife-to-be. Her makeup perfect and her beautiful blonde
hair swept up on top of her head in an elegant style, Sarah looked sophisticated and beautiful in her strapless white gown, the skirt covered entirely
in pearls and lace. "You look amazing," Mara told Sarah reverently.

"Thanks. I feel so nervous. There are so many people here."

Sarah was a genius, but she had shared that she'd always been
socially awkward and not particularly good with crowds.

"You won't notice any of them once you see Dante," Emily said
soothingly. "Weddings go by in a blur. You'll be married before you
know it."

Sarah moved to smooth down wrinkles in her skirt that were non-
existent. "I wish we would have eloped. Dante and I talked about it,
but I think he wanted a reason to have his family here."

"I think they all miss each other," Mara contemplated, turning
away from her peeping spot to finger the string of pearls around her
neck, a bridesmaid gift from Sarah. Thinking about Jared's admission

that he'd built all of the houses on the Peninsula in the hope that his family would all be together again sometime in the future made her eyes tear up.

Don't cry. Your makeup will run and you'll look like a raccoon.

Mara had wanted to look as nice as possible for Sarah's wedding pictures, and she'd let Randi do her makeup much heavier than she would have done herself.

"Stop ogling my male relatives. It's nauseating." Hope spoke from the other side of the small room. She was sitting in a chair waiting until the ceremony was about to begin before taking her place, nibbling saltine crackers because her morning sickness hadn't quite ceased for the day yet.

Mara thought Hope looked a little better than she had an hour or so ago, when she'd been positively green. "Are you okay, Hope? Jason is still out there talking to your brothers. I can go get him for you."

"Don't you dare!" Hope shot her a warning glance. "I love him dearly, but if he hauls me back to bed one more time because he thinks I'm sick, I'm going to kill him." She nibbled a little more on a cracker and put a hand to her belly. "It's subsiding now. If I thought Jason would take me to bed for any other reason, I'd have you getting him for me immediately. He acts like I'm as fragile as blown glass because I'm pregnant."

Mara smiled at Hope's disgruntled expression. "He's an amazing guy."

"Yep. Now *he's* completely drool-worthy. I still can't believe he's mine." She paused before asking quietly, "So will I be coming back to Amesport for Jared's wedding soon?"

"Jared?"

"You and Jared," Hope clarified. "Are you guys going to bring me back here again before I move permanently? I really wouldn't mind. I don't think my morning sickness will last that much longer." Hope's voice was hopeful as she spoke about the possibility of coming to Jared's wedding.

Mara's heart skittered. "No. It's not like that. Jared and I are just . . ."

What the hell *were* they doing? "Seeing each other," she concluded. "Jared said he doesn't really believe in love."

Hope snorted, nearly choking on her cracker. Sarah, Kristin, Randi, and Emily chortled along with her. "Uh-huh. He so completely looked like he wasn't in love when he hightailed it out of Grady's house last night carrying you like he was afraid you wouldn't go with him if he didn't."

"He hasn't had the best of luck with women."

"His college girlfriend?" Hope asked curiously. "Evan answered more of our questions after you two left last night. Jared did have it rough, but I don't think he's really given up on love. It's not that easy, although he'd like to think it is. To tell you the truth, he was always the most sensitive of all of my brothers. I wish I would have known. I hate that he was hurting and none of us knew except Evan. I love my oldest brother, but he isn't the most compassionate man in a situation like that."

"I think it helped that Selena's mother finally took the blame off Jared's shoulders. And I think Evan helped a lot in his own way." Mara wasn't going to reveal any information about how low Jared had sunk, and she didn't think Evan would reveal those secrets, either.

"I'm worried about Evan," Hope confessed. "He just seems so . . . alone."

Mara thought Evan was probably the loneliest man alive, even though he was surrounded by people most of the time. "He doesn't date?"

Hope's face scrunched up in a look of concentration. "Honestly, I can't remember him even dating one woman in his past. And he's never been seen with anyone for as long as I can remember, unlike Jared. Evan goes everywhere alone."

"Maybe there are just some men who are happier alone," Kristin said soberly from her seat beside Hope, her ankle propped on a chair.

Randi nodded. "I'm happier alone. I know that for a fact."

Mara watched as Sarah, Hope, and Emily shook their heads slowly. Hope finally spoke. "I don't think he's happy being alone. I think he lives his life that way for some reason."

"I think you're right," Mara whispered under her breath, hoping that Evan Sinclair found the right woman to break the heavy layers of ice that surrounded him. It was going to take an extraordinary female to accomplish that task.

"He'll find somebody someday," Hope declared optimistically.

Mara hoped that Evan's sister was right as the wedding planner entered the room to hurry them all out to take their places to walk up the aisle.

⌒⟶

The wedding was beautiful, and Mara knew her mascara was smudged after the ceremony. Just watching Dante and Sarah face each other, the look of love so clearly on both of their faces as they spoke their vows, made Mara start to weep.

She'd felt Jared's eyes on her several times during the ceremony, no doubt checking out the plunging neckline on the beautiful black tea-length dress each of the bridesmaids had worn for the ceremony. It wasn't like he hadn't seen her before she'd left the house, and even though he'd made it very clear how beautiful he thought she looked, he hadn't been crazy about the daring neckline.

Mara smiled at herself in the bathroom mirror as she gently wiped the dark smudges from under her eyes. Jared had been perfectly fine with her wearing the dress for *him*, but he had told her he'd be distracted during the whole ceremony and reception, declaring himself her personal wardrobe watcher to make sure her breasts didn't pop out of her dress.

Tossing the damp tissue into the trash, she tugged on the scraps of material that covered her cleavage. She hadn't popped out. Not once. Granted, the top portion *was* a little bit narrow. Running short on time, she'd concentrated on making certain the waist fit properly and hadn't bothered with the neckline. Kristin was slightly smaller busted than she was, but not *that* much.

She smoothed on a little more lipstick and put the container back in the tiny black clutch purse she was carrying. At some point during the ceremony, she must have been chewing on her bottom lip, because most of the color was gone.

Probably while I was drooling over Jared in a tux.

It had been hard not to look at Jared when he'd been standing directly across from her in black formal wear as casually as he did wearing a pair of jeans, not looking the least bit uncomfortable.

He's a billionaire.

No doubt he dressed that way often. But damn, he could rock a tuxedo . . . or anything else he chose to wear. She guessed that's the way it was when he'd been brought up wearing fine clothes, attending social occasions of the very wealthy.

Taking one last look at herself, Mara sighed. She'd pretty much given up wondering *if* Jared wanted her, but she hadn't quite stopped wondering *why.* She wasn't ugly, but she wasn't a bombshell, either.

Enjoy it. Who cares why? He's not faking his interest or his desire. Let him keep making you feel like a goddess. It feels good. You've been lost and lonely since your mom died. Jared makes you feel loved, even if he hasn't said the words.

Jared Sinclair had changed her life in ways she never could have imagined. Her loneliness was gone, and being a part of Sarah's wedding and the Sinclair family was amazing. She missed having family, somebody she could talk to when everything in the world seemed bleak.

You have Jared now.

Mara knew how much Jared had altered her life, and she tried not to contemplate where she would have been right now had he not appeared to help her, to be her confidant and her lover.

She *felt* different.

She *was* different.

And feeling this way *was* damn fabulous.

She refused to sabotage herself with negative emotions. So what if

Jared didn't believe in love? He cared about her. What did it matter what he called those emotions? People said the words all the time and didn't mean them. Jared's actions, the way he treated her was the most important thing.

I want to stop needing to hear the words.

Turning away from the mirror, she decided she was just going to be grateful to have Jared in her life and stop questioning the way he felt about her. She wasn't sure where everything was going between them, but she had a fantastic start to her business. Her life was changing in positive ways. And she had a man who was supportive of her dreams, and who wanted her desperately. Mara wanted to enjoy her good fortune instead of analyzing it to death.

After leaving the restroom, she looked around the crowded ballroom, her eyes automatically seeking out Jared. She saw him almost immediately even though the big room was crowded, his back to her, sitting at a table with his brothers and Jason Sutherland while they waited for the sumptuous buffet to open.

Dodging bodies to make her way across the room, she was stopped when a hand curled around her upper arm, ceasing her forward progress.

"Your aura is almost fixed, honey." Dressed smartly in a purple dress and matching shoes, Beatrice smiled at Mara.

"Is it?" Mara smiled at the elderly woman fondly.

"Yes. That man of yours is looking good, too . . . in more ways than one. I'm liking his aura now. Something positive happened to him," she said sharply. "He's nearly healed."

Mara wanted to tell Beatrice that Jared was never sick, but she knew it wasn't true. His entire emotional being had been injured, and he'd been stuck. "I'm glad. But he isn't exactly my man, Beatrice."

"He will be," the older woman answered slyly. "I'm glad you're not lonely anymore. A sweet girl like you shouldn't be so alone."

Oh, God. I hope Jared will be mine forever someday. I might keep telling myself not to expect it, but I can't help wanting it to happen.

She hugged Beatrice tightly, smiling even broader because she'd referred to her as a sweet girl. She was hardly a girl, and she wasn't all that sweet, but she knew it was the older woman's term of affection. "I'm glad, too," she whispered quietly.

Beatrice patted her shoulder. "I'm off to find Elsie. If she drinks too much champagne, she gets wild."

"Oh, I won't keep you then," Mara answered, biting into her fresh lipstick to keep from having images of an eighty-something-year-old woman dancing on tables from too much champagne.

Beatrice wiggled her fingers in good-bye as she turned to go find her friend.

Mara giggled when Beatrice was out of hearing range, and continued on her trek across the crowded room toward Jared. She'd known Elsie and Beatrice most of her life, and she adored both of the quirky women.

Finally, she halted, unable to get past a bulky older man to reach Jared. She hesitated as she heard her name mentioned, unsure if she should intrude on a conversation about her.

"I have to tell Mara," Jared said irritably. "I just don't know how. She cares about me now. We have a business together. How do I tell her that I bought her house, that I was planning on getting her evicted from that home as quickly as possible?"

Mara's heart clenched. Jared was the buyer for her house? Jared had purchased her home and was going to have her thrown out on the streets?

"You need to just tell her. She'll find out eventually. There's a fire investigation happening now, but she's going to know once you start building it up again for investment property," Jason told him calmly. "I assume that's why you bought it. It's prime real estate in a coastal town with an old home sitting on it. You got a good price, right?"

"Yes," Jared said angrily.

Oh, my God. He just wanted my home. He felt sorry for me because I was going to be displaced, but his primary motive from the beginning was to get that house. It belonged to a Sinclair at one time. That's why he was interested in the property history, his family history. Bastard! And I helped him find out everything he wanted to know.

No wonder he'd helped her, wanted to help her start a business. He'd felt guilty. Remorse was a weakness for him. He'd proven that over and over by never forgiving himself for Selena's and Alan's deaths.

He pities me.

"He never really cared about *me*," she whispered, horrified that she'd let him help her just to nullify his guilt.

She cares about me now. His voice, those words kept echoing in her mind. She'd told him she loved him, and now he was worried about how to break things off without hurting her. His desire had been real; he couldn't fake that. But he really didn't love her. He felt sorry for her.

Mara started to hyperventilate just as the man in front of her stepped aside and her eyes met the icy stare of Evan Sinclair.

"Mara," Evan drawled, probably to stop the men from talking.

She shook her head, wanting to be in denial about Jared's betrayal, but she couldn't.

Don't make a scene. This is Sarah's wedding. It's her day.

Struggling to breathe, tears starting to trickle unchecked down her face, Mara did the only thing she could do. Her heart feeling like it was being torn from her chest, she bit back a sob and fled.

CHAPTER 20

Away from prying eyes, Mara had bawled her eyes out in the home that she'd lived in all her life. Seated on the soot-covered floor in the kitchen, the only room still partially standing, she'd let go of her sorrow about everything: her loneliness, hopelessness, the pain of missing her mother, and most of all the betrayal of a man she loved.

Her arms wrapped around her upper body, she rocked on the floor, wondering where she could go from here. She'd thought she might find comfort in the old kitchen where she'd spent so much time with her mom, but all she felt was shame and failure as she sat in the burned-out remains of what had once been her home.

"I'm not so sure all will be better in the morning anymore, Mom," she whispered huskily, as though her parent were listening. "And I don't think you'd be very proud of me for being such an idiot. I guess maybe I thought that I loved him enough for both of us, but I was wrong. So wrong. He told me he didn't believe in love, and he doesn't. I just didn't want to listen."

"He loves you," a low baritone spoke above Mara, startling her. That last thing she'd expected was for anybody to answer her heartbroken ramblings.

Mara swiped the tears from her face as she glanced up to see Evan Sinclair standing over her, big and intimidating. Strangely, she wasn't the least bit surprised to see him there. Was there anything the man couldn't find out? Her location had probably been easy. "What are you doing here?"

He grimaced and then lowered his bulky body down beside her. "This is my favorite tux," he grumbled, sounding unhappy that he was soiling it.

"You can leave. There's no point in you being here. The house isn't safe, and the fire is still under investigation." She was too distraught to care that she was in a restricted and potentially dangerous area, but she didn't want Evan to get hurt.

They weren't quite touching, but their shoulders were close as they both leaned back against what used to be the kitchen cupboard.

"You're here," Evan answered, as though that explained everything. "Jared loves you. I think you need to know that. He's looking for you. I doubt it will be long before he thinks of coming here."

"Why did you come here?"

"This is where it all began. I think it's human nature to return to the place where you were happy once when you're troubled," Evan said gravely.

Mara turned her head and gaped at him, surprised that he was so insightful. "Jared and I are done. I don't know what will happen to the business now, but I can't live with him anymore. It's pretty obvious that everything he's done was out of pity and guilt."

"Then you can use my house," Evan offered stoically. "And my offer still stands to help with your business. Same terms. Although I doubt it will be necessary."

"You feel sorry for me, too," Mara replied, feeling pathetic.

"I don't do business deals because I feel sorry for someone, Mara. I do it to make money. Your business is extremely viable, and the growth potential is enormous."

"Jared and I signed contracts." *An agreement I insisted on making.*

Now, she wished she would have lagged a little more. It was going to be a lot harder to end a business arrangement that was completely in writing.

"You did more than that," Evan mentioned irritably. "Maybe my brother didn't always believe in love, but he has since you came into his life. He bought the house because he was already head over heels for you. Maybe he didn't realize it then, but he knows it now."

"Why would he do that if he cared about me?" Mara asked, puzzled by his observation. She felt compelled to listen to him because, like it or not, Evan Sinclair *was* rarely wrong.

"The same reason that he almost ran in to his own death the night of the fire. To protect you. If I hadn't caught him in time, he would have run into that damn inferno after you. He didn't know you weren't inside, and like the hothead he is, he plowed ahead into the fire to rescue you when you were already safe. I caught him just in time."

"Jared went after me into the fire?"

"Yes."

"He could have died," Mara said shakily.

"There is no *could* . . . he *would* have died. The house collapsed completely the second I pulled him out," Evan corrected angrily. "How in the hell can you doubt his affection for you? He literally walked through fire to try to save you, and he didn't give a damn if he died doing it."

"I didn't know," Mara replied, dazed by Evan's revelation. "Then why did he buy the house in the first place?"

"Not for the reasons you think," Evan said enigmatically. "You'll have to ask him."

"Not for profit or because it once belonged to a Sinclair and he wanted the property back in the family again?"

Evan balked. "Like any of the Sinclairs need the money? We have literally hundreds of properties that are or have at one time been owned by a Sinclair, historical properties. Why would he be so obsessed about owning that particular property? Think, Mara. Your reasoning is irrational."

"It's emotional," she confessed. "I love him, but he's never told me that he loves me."

Evan rose gracefully to his feet for a man his size and held his hand out to her. "After he risked his life for you, don't you think you owe him a chance to explain and an opportunity for him to let you know he returns your affections?" He lifted a lofty eyebrow at her.

Mara was still reeling with the knowledge that Jared had almost died because he thought she was still in her home when he arrived during the fire. "He would have died for me. He would have died on the off chance that I was still in the house. He didn't even check." She put her trembling hand in Evan's and let him pull her to her feet.

"Emotion does strange things to people," Evan replied drily.

"You came into the fire," Mara reminded him.

Evan shrugged. "I *knew* you were in there, and I was fairly certain that I had enough time to get you out."

Mara examined Evan's detached demeanor. "But it was still a risk."

"A calculated risk," he countered aloofly. "It happens in business all the time."

Mara took a calculated risk of her own and wrapped her arms around Evan's neck and hugged him. "You still saved me. Thank you."

She laid her head on his chest and hugged him tightly, waiting, breathing a sigh of relief as his arms came around her awkwardly, returning the embrace.

"No need for all this," Evan said in an uncomfortable, husky voice.

"There's every need," Mara argued. Evan Sinclair needed somebody to care about him, show him some kind of affection. And although he was an easy man to dislike, Mara felt just the opposite. She adored his manipulative ways because they were proof of how much he cared, even though he couldn't show it.

"I swear to God, I'm going to kill you," Jared's furious voice bellowed from behind them.

Mara let go of Evan slowly and turned to face Jared, the pure wrath on his face jolting her into motion.

"I told you to claim her before someone else did," Evan cajoled, calmly wiping soot from his tux as he turned and started walking away.

"Goddammit, get your ass back here. I'm going to kick it until you can't walk," Jared vowed through gritted teeth.

Mara flung herself at Jared as he lunged toward his brother. "Don't, Jared. Please don't. You'll regret it. He was trying to help me." Wrapping her arms around his neck, she lifted her legs around his waist so he had to bear her weight. He'd either drop her or stop going after his brother. *Calculated risk.*

He halted and propped his hands under her ass to hold her up. "I'll find him."

"No, you won't," Mara told him soothingly, running a hand over his jaw. "What you saw was completely innocent. I need you to believe me."

The tension in his body started to relax. "I've always believed in you," Jared growled.

"Then take me home," she begged. "Please."

He hesitated for a fraction of a second, his expression still raw and enraged. Mara hugged him tighter and put her head on his shoulder, trusting him completely to make the right choice. The last thing she wanted was to put a void between Jared and Evan. She had no idea why Evan had chosen to tweak a tiger by its tail in provoking Jared that way, but after he saved her life and cared about her as a person in his own peculiar way, she didn't want Evan to get hurt. And she knew that once Jared threw a punch, it would wound Evan greatly, and not just physically. It would kill Jared to have taken a shot at his brother in anger. It just couldn't happen.

"Fine. You're going home with me, and then you can explain why my brother had his hands on you and you were in his arms. Again," he demanded in a graveled voice.

"I'll explain."

Without another word, Jared carried her out of the house and into his car. As he put her gently in the seat, he said fiercely, "You. Belong. With. Me."

His touch and the ferociousness of his words soothed her soul. She didn't know what the truth was about why Jared had bought her house, but she already knew it wasn't for nefarious reasons. She trusted him, and she vowed right then and there she'd never doubt him again. He'd given him his faith by not going after his brother, and he'd been willing to die for her. If he never wanted to give her the real reason behind his purchase of her house, she didn't care. She loved him, and she finally knew with absolute certainty that he loved her back.

Jared was silent as he led her into his house instead of the guest house, taking her by the hand as though he was afraid she'd disappear.

"Explain," he said irritably. "What the hell did Evan mean by his comment? Are you two attracted to each other? Is he really what you want? Does he want you?"

Mara busied herself making coffee. "Sit," she requested as she watched him pace.

He sat at the kitchen table, his glare never leaving her.

"Evan knew I was upset by what I'd heard about you buying my home." She lifted her hand as he started to speak, signaling him to let her explain. "He found me first. I guess all I wanted was to go home, but that's not my home anymore. All he tried to do was make me understand that I wasn't giving you a chance to explain, and I should. He was right. He also told me that you foolishly ran into my burning house to try to save me." She slammed a cup into the coffeemaker with more force than she needed to. "You could have died, Jared."

"I didn't," he grumbled. "And I wasn't about to let you die in that fire."

"But you could have. You would have if Evan hadn't stopped you." The reality of that statement hit her straight in the gut. "I hugged him. I wanted to thank him for saving me, and I wanted him to know that somebody cares. Evan is troubled. I don't think he's happy. I wanted to see if he'd hug me back."

"He did. The bastard."

"Reluctantly," Mara mused, sliding a cup of coffee in front of Jared. "He's not used to affection, Jared. No, I don't have any secret longing for your older brother. I love you. I love you so much that I was temporarily insane when I thought you might have betrayed me. I'm sorry." She put another cup in the machine and waited for her coffee to finish.

"You don't need to be sorry. I should have told you a long time ago. I was afraid you'd hate me," he admitted despondently.

"Don't be upset with Evan. I don't know why he was encouraging you to be angry, but he isn't interested in me that way. He's been more like a brother or a friend to me. I think you already know Evan was yanking your chain. He'd never betray you that way. None of your brothers would." Pulling the cup from the coffeemaker, she added creamer. "I hope you can believe that, because it's the truth."

"I believe you." He didn't look at her as he took a sip of his coffee. "I think Evan was trying to get me to do something I should have done a long time ago."

"What?" She sat down at the table beside him.

"Claim you as mine."

"I don't think Evan would push you to do something you don't want—"

"I want to. I've always wanted you, and Evan knows it. I love the bastard, but he's manipulative as hell."

Mara smiled at Jared's disgruntled look. "I think he means well."

"He's conniving," he grunted. "Likes things to work out the way he wants them to be, or the way he thinks they should be." He heaved a loud, masculine sigh. "I should have told you about the purchase of your house."

Mara's heart hammered as she asked hesitantly, "Did you offer me help because you felt sorry for me because I wasn't going to have a home?"

He finally met her eyes, his deep jade glance piercing her. "No. I wanted to fuck you. It was more than that, but that was my primary goal in the beginning when I offered to help you. I won't lie to you. I wanted you the first time I saw you. My dick knew how I felt about you immediately. It took my brain a while to catch up."

Mara's breath hitched as his penetrating gaze impaled her, holding her eyes captive. "Tell me why you bought the house in the first place."

"Because I knew the house was a death trap, Mara. I'm an architect, and I know old houses. I couldn't inspect everything, so I bought the damn house and looked at what had—or should I say hadn't—been done to it over the years. The fire was my fucking greatest fear come to life. I wanted you out of there before it happened. I was too damn late, and it nearly killed me when that house caught fire." He paused for a moment before continuing in a forlorn tone, "I knew you'd be upset that the house had been purchased, but at least you'd be alive," he said huskily. "I also knew you'd probably hate me, but I couldn't leave Amesport knowing you were living in a house that was dangerous. I couldn't do it."

Mara's heart felt like a large fist was wrapping around it and holding it in a crushing grip. "So you were trying to save me?" Sweet Jesus. He'd been trying to save her life even back then. "What were you going to do with the house?"

"I had no fucking idea. I don't need another place in Amesport. It would have had to go through costly renovation or come down." He was silent for a moment before he added, "I'm sorry I didn't tell you. Once I fell completely in love with you, I didn't want you to hate me. Once you said you loved me, I was terrified that you wouldn't love me anymore."

She felt like her heart was completely exploding, the pressure unbearable. "I'll always love you, Jared," she choked out. Getting up, she pushed their coffee to the center of the table and straddled him on the chair. "You love me?" Even now, Mara longed to finally hear the words.

He grasped both sides of her head so she'd look directly at him. "Jesus, woman, if you haven't figured that out by now, I don't know how else to show you how much I love you. When you left the reception today, I was more afraid of losing you than I've ever been scared of anything. I need you, Mara. I love you so damn much that I can't fucking breathe."

"I'm not going anywhere. I was scared, too. Loving a man this much is frightening," she whispered as she lowered her mouth to his.

Snaking his arm behind her head, he took control of the embrace immediately, ravaging her mouth with such ferocity and desperation that Mara could do nothing except wrap her arms around his neck and hold on. He conquered. Controlled. Adored. Loved.

Wrenching his mouth away from hers, he growled, "I love you, dammit. I love you."

"Show me," she panted.

He stood, taking her body with him, and Mara lowered her feet to the ground. He stripped her quickly, lowering the zipper on her dress and letting it drop to the floor.

"Christ!" he cursed in a low, predatory voice. "If I would have known this was beneath this dress, I would have fucked you before we ever left home."

"You like?" she teased, glad that Jared appreciated her sexy lingerie, black thong panties with a matching garter belt and stockings. She tore at his clothing, divesting him of his jacket, shirt, and the accessories of the tuxedo. Once he was bare from the waist up, she stroked her palms lovingly over his chest, savoring the rippling muscles as she moved her hand lower.

"No," he growled as Mara reached for the zipper of his pants.

Tossing their coffee cups into the sink with a loud clatter, he lifted her onto the kitchen table, his hands immediately reaching for her bare breasts. "These have haunted me all day. All I could think about was getting you out of this damn dress so no other man could see what was mine." His mouth closed over her nipple, biting gently before laving it with his tongue.

Mara clutched his hair, urging him for more. He gave it to her, his mouth alternating from breast to breast, teasing them both until they were so sensitive it was almost unbearable.

Finally, Jared straightened, his hungry gaze fixed on her. Mara felt wanton and beautiful, her sexy, lingerie-clad body sprawled out on the kitchen table, Jared's hungry eyes devouring her. "You're so fucking beautiful," he said fiercely, his fingers stroking lightly over the silk panties. "And you're so wet for me."

"No teasing," she begged. "I need you today."

"You have me forever," Jared pledged gruffly. "I hope you're not too attached to these panties." One hard tug pulled them from her body, a loud ripping noise audible as the material gave way to Jared's considerable strength.

His fingers stroked through her welcoming heat, sliding against her clit.

"Jared. Please," she pleaded, writhing on the table.

He unzipped his pants and liberated his cock, using the head to tease her clit. "You're mine, Mara. Say it," he commanded.

"Yes. Yes. I love you, and I'm yours," she whimpered.

"I love you," he groaned, plunging deeply inside her, his hands gripping her hips as he slid her ass to the edge of the table.

"Oh, God. You feel so good." Mara thrust her hips forward, savoring the feel of him inside her. She wrapped her legs around his waist, needing him even closer.

"I'm claiming you. No more bullshit about me not making you mine," he said gutturally as he slammed into her again.

"You're mine, too," Mara asserted with a loud moan.

"Always, baby." He started moving inside her faster, harder.

The spiral in her belly started to unfurl, tension spreading to every part of body. "Yes. Fuck me, Jared. Hard."

He pumped into her with an intensity that took her breath away. Panting for air, she moaned as her sheath started to spasm, clamping down on his cock. She splintered as Jared pounded in and out of her unceasingly, no mercy, his fingers searching and finding her clit. He stroked over the tiny bundle of nerves as she shattered screaming his name. "Jared!"

He pulled her up and wrapped his arms around her protectively, lovingly. "I love you, sweetheart. Never forget. Never forget," he insisted, the muscles in his neck straining as he let out a tortured groan.

Wrapping her arms around him, she dug her nails into his back as she milked him of his orgasm, her body trembling against his.

"Mark me, Mara," he growled carnally, spearing his hand into her hair and burying his face in her locks.

Primitive instinct surrounded them, and she finally stopped clutching at his back and leaned against him, spent.

They stayed that way for moments or hours. Mara felt like time was standing still as they clung to each other, both of them gasping for breath.

"I love you," she told him breathlessly, her voice muffled against his chest.

"I love you, too, baby. But I'll never be able to look at this table without getting hard," he rumbled, his voice sounding amused.

Mara laughed, hugging him harder against her body. "Are we going back to the guest house? I have no clothes here."

"No. No more guest house. We can work there, but I want you in my bed where you belong."

Her heart soared with joy. "Yes. Please."

"Fuck it. I'll bring your stuff here later. You aren't going to need any clothes for a while."

Lifting her off the table, her legs still around his waist, Jared carried her up the stairs and to his bed.

Mara sighed against his shoulder, knowing the emptiness and loneliness she'd felt since her mom had gotten sick were finally gone forever.

"You're going to marry me. Soon," Jared demanded as he dropped her gently on his bed.

Her pulse raced as she looked up at him. "I think we've had this discussion before. You didn't ask." She was teasing him just like she'd done the first time he'd gone to the market and demanded she spend the day with him, but once again she saw a quick flash of vulnerability in his intense green eyes before it disappeared. She had to wonder all over again if he demanded because he was afraid she'd say no. "I guarantee I'm a sure thing if you ask," she told him softly.

"Well, will you?" He parroted exactly what he'd said at the market that day, a grin starting to spread across his face as he relaxed and teased her back.

She beamed at him. "I'd love to, Jared. Thank you." She repeated the same words she'd said to him at the market.

His grin grew even broader as he climbed onto the bed and crawled toward her, stalking her. She squealed as he pounced, trapping her body beneath his powerful form.

"Now that I know you'll say yes, I'll ask you for real. Will you marry me, Mara? I swear I'll spend the rest of my life trying to make you happy." He was still smiling, but his eyes were predatory and filled with adoration. And love.

"Yes, of course I'll marry you. I love you." Mara's heart was pounding as she gazed back at him, knowing her heart was in her eyes, too. "You've already made me happier than I ever dreamed I could be." She reached up and smoothed back an errant lock of hair from his forehead lovingly. "You love me, and that alone gives me more joy than anything else in the world."

She could feel his heated breath on her face as he started to lower his head. "Then prepare yourself to become completely elated, sweetheart, because I know damn well I'll love you more and more every damn day, every time I touch you or see you smile at me."

She smiled at him tremulously. "Lay it on me. I think I can take it." She could more than take it; she'd be wallowing in it.

"I'm planning to start working on it right now," he said huskily as his mouth covered hers with a tender passion that rocked her to the depths of her soul.

Mara was more than elated. She was completely ecstatic as Jared proceeded to show her how much he loved her, and she gave herself up to him completely, giving all the love he gave to her right back to him.

They both had a lot of catching up to do when it came to truly being loved, but Mara wasn't worried as they spent the rest of the day and night together doing nothing but trying to make up for lost time. They had a lifetime now, and it would be filled with nothing but love.

EPILOGUE

Six Months Later

Mara sighed as she watched her husband hammering nails into a board in the new interior of what used to be her old home, ogling him openly as she watched the powerful muscles in his arms and back flex. He was sweating even though it was winter, shirtless because of the manual labor he was doing at the moment.

Unaware of her presence, he kept working, and Mara kept watching, still wanting to pinch herself to make her believe that the life she was living now was actually real and not a very lovely dream.

A whimsical smile passed over her face when the glitter of the enormous diamond wedding ring on her hand winked at her as she lifted her hand to pull the warm knit cap from her head. She'd just come from her new site, situated right outside of town, an enormous warehouse and shop that produced and sold the products for Mara's Kitchen. The small business she and Jared had started had grown into a monster in a very short amount of time, and her products were now in demand all across the country, her consumer list growing larger every day.

She had more employees than she could count, and a huge storefront that was managed by a lovely woman who she worked with on a daily basis. Jared was already searching out more sites for the business because it was growing so fast, and the demand was already getting too high for just one large site. The products were currently being produced in a special kitchen with commercial equipment in the enormous warehouse that was separate from the shop. Even though she had plenty of employees, Mara still supervised the production kitchen and the shop every day, never wanting her product to lose its original taste or appeal because it was being produced in mass with commercial equipment.

The presence of a large, new business had brought incredible economic growth to Amesport, employing many people who needed jobs. For Mara, that was one of her greatest accomplishments.

As she eyed her husband hungrily, she knew Jared was her greatest asset and always would be, no matter how large her business grew in the future. She could live without the business; she couldn't live without *him*.

Just like he'd promised, he *did* seem to love her more and more every single day. So much so that they'd both had a hard time parting in the morning since he'd started work on rebuilding the house, doing some of the manual labor himself.

Jared had needed to make a few short business trips for his commercial real estate business since they'd gotten married, and separation for even a few days had been excruciatingly painful for both of them. Maybe it was the newness of their love, or maybe it was just because they were addicted to each other and couldn't bear to be apart. Now that she had so much competent staff, if he needed to go away, she tried to arrange to travel with him.

```
I love you even more today. I miss you.
```

That text appeared on her cell phone every day without fail while she was working at Mara's Kitchen, and her heart never ceased to skitter every time she saw it, and she quickly texted back.

```
I love you. I miss you, too.
```

Today, his text had been different, throwing her off balance.

```
I love you even more today. I need you.
```

He'd never texted that he needed her, and the slight difference had put her senses on high alert. She handed everything over to her manager and left Mara's Kitchen early, suddenly needing to see Jared, to assure herself that everything was okay.

Now that she was here, she could see that her husband looked fine in more ways than one, and she wondered if she'd just panicked for nothing.

She removed her jacket and gloves, dropping them onto a newly built countertop by a beautiful, large window. Jared had done a complete teardown on the old, burned-down structure and had started over again. He was building a replica of the old house, trying to duplicate everything to resemble the same model and period of the previous residence. The majority of the house was up, and there was heating and wiring installed, but many of the details on the inside still needed to be completed. Eventually, Jared wanted to make the old home a museum, displaying antique items to tell the history of Amesport. She'd cried like a baby on the day he'd shown her the plaque he planned on designing, dedicating the museum in memory of her mother and her gran because her family had spent so much time on this small plot of land.

Mara kept her eyes glued to his muscular back as she moved toward him anxiously, needing to touch him.

I need you.

It wasn't like Jared didn't tell her that all the time, but he'd never changed his text. They'd been married for five months, having an even hastier wedding than Sarah and Dante had put together. Evan had come back for their wedding, as had Hope and Jason. A few months later, Jason had brought Hope back to live in Amesport permanently, and she and Hope had become extremely close. Actually, she'd become good friends with Sarah, Emily, and Randi, too, all of the women—including her now-healed best friend, Kristin—getting together as often as possible.

I have family again. Lots of family and friends.

It didn't matter that none of them were blood related. Mara had quickly discovered that once you became a Sinclair by marriage, or were taken under their wing, you were family to them. And oh, it felt good to have brothers and sisters, something she'd never had before, people she knew she could count on to support her through anything.

Mara carefully slipped her arms around Jared, hugging him from behind after he'd put down his hammer. "Hello, handsome," she purred against his back.

"Hey, sweetheart. You're early." He turned instantly and wrapped his arms around her. "I'm sweaty and I probably smell," he warned her huskily.

"I happen to love you hot and sweaty." Visions of the many times he'd been hot and perspiring with exertion from making her come until she screamed floated through her mind. She inhaled his musky scent, the erotic images becoming more vivid. She had plenty of those memories due to Jared's insatiable desire to make her come. Not that she was complaining.

"I love you that way, too. Wanna work up a sweat with me?" he asked hopefully as he moved his hands down the back of her sweater.

She pulled back and looked into his eyes. "Are you okay?" She could see that he was fine, but the sense that something was troubling him still lingered.

He hesitated a moment before replying, "Yeah. I'm good. Why?"

I need you.

She shook her head slowly, realizing she'd overreacted. "Your text was different today. I thought you needed me, so I left early."

Jared pulled back for a minute to dig into his pocket for his cell phone. He stared at it for minute before he replied, "I guess I typed what I was feeling at the moment. It is different." He frowned as he looked up at her with an intense expression. "I can't believe you even noticed." He put the phone back into his pocket.

She tried to explain. "It wasn't just the words. After I read them, it was like I sensed . . . something."

Jared released a masculine sigh. "I was thinking about an idea I'd been considering right before I texted you."

"What?"

"Since I've been working on this house, I realize how much I miss doing this. I know I'm only doing a replica, and I'm not doing all the work myself, but I miss working to restore history. I got a crazy idea to stop my commercial real estate business and start up a new venture."

Mara's heart skipped a beat. Did he want to go back to his original passion? "You want to start restoring old homes again?"

He shrugged. "It was just a thought, and not very realistic. How can I relinquish control of a business that makes billions now to go into a new one that's not going to make a ton of money?"

"Very easily," Mara said fiercely, wrapping her arms around his neck. "We have billions, Jared. You don't need to make even more money. Are you ready to go back to restoring old homes again?" She wanted this for him desperately, but only if it would make him happy.

He grinned at her. "You're willing to watch me let go of a corporate life to restore old homes?"

She smiled up at him. "Gladly. You look hot when you're sweaty and shirtless. And I think your butt is delicious in jeans." He'd played the corporate game for years, trying to be more like his brother Evan. It was time for Jared to just be himself. "Is it really what you want?"

"Yeah. It is. I guess I finally realized that what I want to do and Selena and Alan's deaths aren't really connected. They were only linked in my head by guilt."

Mara stroked over his whiskered jaw tenderly. "Then do it. I want you to be happy." She was jubilant, knowing that Jared was finally free. After years of tormenting himself, he could finally move on.

He pulled her tightly against him and buried his face in her hair. "I'm already happy because I have you, sweetheart. Going back to restoring old houses like I'd like to do would just be a very small amount of icing on an already very sweet cake."

"Then bring on the frosting," she murmured right before she pulled his head down and kissed him tenderly. "A cake can never be too sweet."

"You're amazing," he said huskily. "I think I really did need to talk to you."

Mara thought he did, too. Otherwise, he would have talked himself out of it, claiming he was too invested in commercial real estate to pursue his original dream. The last thing they needed was more money. Jared was already one of the richest men in the world.

She was startled when Jared's cell phone rang, and he scowled as he pulled it back out of his pocket again. "It's Jason." He answered it immediately.

Mara listened intently as Jared spoke, his voice sounding nervous.

"Okay, we'll be there soon. I don't care if there's nothing we can really do. I want to be there. This is my first nephew, and I want to be around when he's born," Jared grumbled into the phone.

Mara smiled. Obviously Hope was in labor, and it might be a very long wait at the hospital since it was her first child, but Mara wouldn't miss being there for any reason. She knew Hope was excited and nervous. If Hope had to wait around for her labor to start in earnest, Mara wanted to be there for her.

Jared hung up the phone. "Hope's in labor. Jason said it could be a while, since the contractions are pretty far apart. I should be able to grab a shower."

"I'll make us all something to eat while you clean up," Mara agreed as she moved to put her jacket back on. "I'm so excited. I can't wait to see my new niece."

"Nephew," Jared rumbled. "It's the first Sinclair of the next generation. It will be a boy. In case you haven't noticed, boys seem to run in the Sinclair family."

Mara laughed. "You know Jason and Hope didn't want to know the sex of the baby beforehand. You're basing your information on the fact that there are historically more boys than girls in your family?" Nobody would know the new infant's sex until he or she was actually born.

His shirt and jacket now on, Jared grinned. "Not really just that."

"You just hope it's a boy," Mara accused him with a laugh as he pulled her toward the door, her heart light at the thought of welcoming a new baby into the family. "It could just as well turn out to be a niece. Would you really care?"

"Nope. I don't really care whether it's a niece or nephew. I'd be just as excited to have either one."

Mara stopped at the door to stare at her husband. "Then why do you keep saying it's going to be your nephew?"

"Because Beatrice told me. She said her spirit guides are speaking very loudly to her."

Mara burst out laughing. "Yeah. And she told me Evan would be married within the next six months to a woman who would be his perfect match, just a few days ago. She met Evan at the wedding."

"She predicted Sarah and Dante. And she predicted us." Jared pulled out his keys as he opened the door, dangling his key chain that still sported the Apache tear stone that Beatrice had given him. "Call me crazy, but I'm starting to wonder if there isn't something kind of interesting about her predictions."

Mara did have to admit he was right. Beatrice did seem to have a few rather eerie and unlikely predictions that had come true lately.

"We'll see if I end up with a nephew or a niece," Jared teased as he pulled her out the door and locked it behind him.

They sprinted to their vehicles because of the frigid temperatures, Mara following Jared back to the Peninsula so he could shower and she could put food together before they went to the hospital to await the arrival of Jared's first nephew . . . or niece.

It *was* a very long night, but they had plenty of company with all of the Sinclair family gathered there in the waiting room. In fact, Hope didn't deliver her healthy baby boy until the next morning.

Mara walked out of the hospital the next day yawning, her head resting on Jared's strong biceps after they'd finally had a chance to welcome the new baby to the family.

"It was a boy," Jared said smugly.

"Coincidence?" Mara asked sleepily.

Jared shrugged and pulled her closer to him to shield her body from the cold wind as they walked toward their vehicle. "I guess we'll see if Evan ends up married soon. That would definitely make me a believer in Beatrice's predictions." Jared's voice sounded slightly amused.

Mara nodded and huddled closer to Jared's warmth. That particular prediction of Beatrice's *was* a long shot. But she silently hoped that it did come true, no matter how unlikely it might be.

Somehow, she'd ended up married to Jared, and to her that occurrence had been nothing short of a miracle. She yawned as Jared unlocked the door of the vehicle and opened the passenger-side door for her.

"Tired?" he asked in a concerned voice.

"Definitely." Now that the excitement of the new arrival was over and both Hope and the baby were healthy, her exhaustion had hit her like a rock.

"Let's go home so you can get some sleep." Jared settled her into her seat and belted her in before he jogged around to the driver's side.

She smiled as her husband got into the car, shooting him an adoring look before she closed her eyes peacefully and started drifting off to sleep. Home wasn't a place or a building for her anymore; it was a state of mind. As long as Jared was with her, she'd always be home.

THE END

ABOUT THE AUTHOR

Photo © 2013 Carrie Herzog

J.S. "Jan" Scott is a *New York Times* and *USA Today* bestselling romance author. She's an avid reader of all types of books and literature, but romance has always been her genre of choice. Writing what she loves to read, Jan writes both contemporary and paranormal romances. They are almost always steamy, they generally feature an alpha male, and have a happily ever after, because she just can't seem to write them any other way!

Jan loves to connect with readers.

You can visit her at:

Website: http://www.authorjsscott.com

Facebook: http://www.facebook.com/authorjsscott

You can also tweet @AuthorJSScott.

For updates on new releases, sales, and giveaways, please sign up for Jan's newsletter by going to http://eepurl.com/KhsSD.